SABBATH

SABBATH

NICK MAMATAS

A TOM DOHERTY ASSOCIATES BOOK
NEW YORK

This is a work of fiction. All of the characters, organizations, and events portrayed in this novel are either products of the author's imagination or are used fictitiously.

SABBATH

Based upon the comic book series *Sabbath: All Your Sins Reborn* created by Matthew Tomao

Concept by Matthew Tomao and Nick Mamatas

Designed by Mary A. Wirth

Title page image: © iStockphoto/stockcam

A Tor Book
Published by Tom Doherty Associates
120 Broadway
New York, NY 10271

www.tor-forge.com

Tor® is a registered trademark of Macmillan Publishing Group, LLC.

The Library of Congress Cataloging-in-Publication Data is available upon request.

ISBN 978-1-250-17011-8 (hardcover)
ISBN 978-1-250-17010-1 (ebook)

Our books may be purchased in bulk for promotional, educational, or business use. Please contact your local bookseller or the Macmillan Corporate and Premium Sales Department at 1-800-221-7945, extension 5442, or by email at MacmillanSpecialMarkets@macmillan.com.

First Edition: November 2019

Printed in the United States of America

0 9 8 7 6 5 4 3 2 1

For my son Oliver,
and specifically for his 529 college savings account.

SABBATH

1

Proclaim ye this among the Gentiles; Prepare war, wake up the mighty men, let all the men of war draw near; let them come up.

—Joel 3:9

Hell, thought Duke Richard II. *This is Hell.*

That's what it was. All of it. The invasion of the Vikings, who were more beasts than men. More brutal even than the Great Heathen Army of Duke Richard II's grandfather's time. The conduct of the war, which had led Richard here, his whore sister and quaking idiot brother-in-law—Æthelred the Unready!—begging Richard to travel to this godforsaken hole. The horrid marriage he arranged between them in the first place, which is what brought him to this peat bog of an island, far from his beloved Normandy. The dull mud-brown glare of his sister's eye as he indulged her husband, who had just a lovely idea to save them all from the ravishment and pillaging of the Danes. Pay them not to invade! Pay pillagers in pillage! And then Æthelred died, leaving his third son, Edmund II, to rule and fight the war. And oh, did Edmund II, called Ironside by his friends and Ironhead by Richard, have a *lovely idea* to save England.

The lovely idea—send his dearest ally, Richard, to the

ass-end of England to recruit the land's most talented warrior, who was himself a talent of piss filling his armor like it was a barrel latrine. *Sans* retinue, *sans* horse, as every available body and beast was needed to enforce the shield wall. Send Richard to Hell, this place, Assandun.

And speaking of Hell . . . Hexen Sabbath, who flaunted hell in his very name. He would be easy to find. Richard II just had to find the tavern with the cheapest ale and the loosest whores.

Truth be told, Richard's own plan was to nail the door to the tavern shut if he could, then chuck a torch into the thatching and kill everyone in it. Then he'd throw in with the Danes, who were surely in need of an intelligent polyglot fellow like himself, given that they were hell-spawn pagans who wouldn't understand God's word even were it whipped letter by letter onto their backs by Richard's own hand.

But the Danes would probably kill him as soon as parley with him, especially now that he was alone, on foot, his clothing stained rags, his beard unkempt.

Hexen Sabbath might not believe him either, truth be told. The damned knight, the son of a witch and a pervert, might run the duke through as soon as look at him. If it came to that, Richard just hoped that the last thing he'd smell would be his own lifeblood pouring from his guts, and not Sabbath's foul breath or his own bowels giving way.

He stumbled and took a knee into a mud puddle. In the distance, a pair of peasant children pointed and laughed. Richard had half a mind to run them through and leave their bodies for their parents to discover later, but something about the skeletal pair touched his heart. What would their lives be like under pagan rule, divorced from the Word of God and the protection of God's chosen king? These poor imbeciles just needed to understand that the nobility truly cared for them, and were ready to sacrifice all for their lives.

"Hallo, children," said Duke Richard II, unsheathing his sword and waving it jauntily at the poor rag-dressed kids. "It is I, the Duke of Normandy, brother to your queen Emma. I am on a mission from the king to save—"

"Papa says we're all going to die today!" shouted one of the children—a girl, from her voice.

"What does your father know?" Richard spat.

"He's just come from the Royal Standard tavern!" said the boy. "Your own knights have retreated there to whore and drink. They've given up the battle!"

"Well, it was only one knight," said the girl. "But only because most of the others have already abandoned the field."

"Or are decorating it with their innards," said the boy. He cackled madly, his face like a half-sliced gourd. He had probably been brought to the front to scavenge arrows and driven mad by the scene.

Better just to address the girl, Richard thought. She looked as if she might still be sane. "The tavern, you say . . . Is it there?" Richard pointed.

"Yes, right up Shite Hill, and down the other side," said the girl.

"Shite Hill . . . ," Richard said to himself. "I suppose they named it that to differentiate it from all the other mounds of shite around here." Then to the children, "Thank you! God bless! The Lord will reward you for your service to King and Crown!"

"Yeah?" said the girl. "Reward us with what?"

"A quick death, I hope . . . ," muttered Richard.

Were he in a better mood, Duke Richard might have called the Royal Standard unassuming, or perhaps even quaint. There is something about having knowledge of the sure and imminent death of not only oneself but of one's whole world that allows one to gaze upon the universe as it truly is, and not as one wishes it to be. The Standard was, in fact, a lopsided hovel he wouldn't stable a donkey in. Perhaps the name was a prophecy. England would fall, the kingdom reduced to nothing more than a place to rot one's guts with hops and loins with whores. With some regret, Richard noted that the walls and thatched roof were so filthy that even were he to take a torch to it, the dirt would extinguish the flame before it did any damage.

"Ah, it is this for which we are all eager to lay down our lives; this is what the dark-haired Danes struggle so mercilessly for," he muttered. He should simply offer to parley with Cnut himself, invite the Danish warlord over to the Royal Standard for the drink, and let the fleas and vermin do an assassin's work. Then Duke Richard II would be the hero of the day, not that execrable . . .

"Hexen Sabbath!"

The patrons of the crowded, squalid pub turned to stare at him. There was no steward to speak of, or even proper chairs. Just ragged, bleary-eyed people, some with still-open wounds, hunched on barrels and loose bales of hay, with planks for tabletops. Except in the very rear of the establishment, where in the shadows far from the candlelight, a certain jovial squealing emanated.

"You, Sabbath!" Richard said as he strode across the tiny, crowded room. "You're needed at the battlefront—now." Sabbath didn't even care to look up from the bosom his face was pressed against. He was barely visible beneath the tangle of limbs and yards of fabric from the rawboned women who were crawling all over him, fondling him. The knight's mail and armor lay nearby in a heap. Richard was aghast.

"Pardon me," said one of the women. All three turned to glare at the duke. "You're interrupting something."

"I know," said Richard.

Sabbath smiled and said cheerfully, "Ho, Dick! How goes the war?"

Duke Richard II, his tunic and leggings and cape still splattered with mud and filth, held his arms out wide and said, "Please, Sir Hexen, I beseech thee. Accompany me to the lines. You could turn the tide of the battle." This was not a moment for sarcasm or japery; Richard knew that much. For all the travail it had meant, his mission was crucial, sacred. "As you wear the most Holy Cross round your neck, come and repel the pagan horde from our motherland, in the name of the King, and Christ!"

Sabbath touched the rounded cross hanging over his tunic. "I suppose I could win the war for you. Or I could stay here and catch up on my consumption . . . and fornication!" He casually fondled the woman nearest him. "Right, girls?" They cheered. "Right, everyone?!" The whole tavern roared in approval.

"Do any of you care who rules you?" Richard demanded, turning on his heel to sneer at the patrons. "Would you live in pagan darkness, under the rule of the foreign Danes?"

"Where's your accent from, bright-eyed Norman?" shouted a man behind a plank between two barrels that served as a makeshift bar top. Perhaps he was the steward, though he was as drunk as everyone else. "Unless Danes are teetotalers, I couldn't give a fig who sends out a man twice a year to rob me, and thrice a year to relieve my custom of their little wealth."

"Oh, Dick, you do have a knack for speaking with the commoners," said Sabbath, rising. "They're not educated in the ways of statecraft like you and I. You cannot simply demand their obedience, especially not in those rags."

"Sir Hexen, simply demanding obedience is literally what our kingdom is based on! God rules over king, king over noble, noble over knight! It is what you were trained to uphold since the day we took you from your blasted parents," said Richard.

"I'm just saying you need a gentle touch," Sabbath explained as he demonstrated by palming the bottom of one of the women. She flashed a near-toothless smile. "And your appeals to the Lord, well . . . as I was telling Margaret here, it was the blessed Augustine of Hippo who said, *Da mihi castitatem et continentiam, deus meus sed noli modo.*"

Richard grimaced. "'Give me chastity and continence, my God . . . but not yet.' But, Sabbath, the moment has arrived. You are to accompany me to the field of battle, now, even if I must bring you to heel myself and lead you there like a dog."

Sabbath turned his back on Richard and fetched his large stein from the table. He lazily spun back around on one heel and sipped his ale carefully, peering at Richard from over the rim. "Oh?" he said finally. "I think we'd all like to see that."

Richard could tolerate not another moment. He took a step back and moved to draw his sword, but before it was unsheathed, a great wave of beer slammed against his face. He struck out, blind, his blade finding only air. Sabbath swung his stein hard against Richard's wrist. The sword clattered to the floor. Sabbath's foot caught Richard's ankle, and the duke fell flat onto the hard-packed dirt. In the course of three blinks, Sabbath had his right foot planted on Richard's groin and was holding out his stein for a refill from a pitcher handled by one of his lady friends.

"You are a fucking worm," said Sabbath. "If you're an exemplar of our mettle, perhaps you do need me after all. Unfortunately, I have a problem. My armor."

"What of it?" Richard's voice was an octave higher than usual. Sabbath settled the weight of his boot on the duke's groin. "It's right there!"

"My squire is dead. My page is . . . indisposed," said Sabbath. He nodded to the opposite corner of the room, where a young man had fallen asleep in a puddle of . . . something. "You know we mustn't let a commoner handle a knight's armor. I am nothing if not a stickler for the rules."

"Put it on yourself," Richard squeaked.

"I could do that . . . ," said Sabbath. "Save for the codpiece. You must do that for me. Your noble blood makes this most delicate task suitable for your fine fingers."

"You wear a codpiece into battle? Like a pagan Roman? But why?"

Sabbath ground his heel. "You know why . . . now." He took his foot off Richard's crotch and planted it on the sword. "Fetch . . . Your Grace." Richard got to his knees, but before he could pick himself up, Sabbath added, "Crawl to it. Like a dog."

"Your Grace!" added the woman with the pitcher.

"Your Grace," Sabbath repeated.

Richard made his way on his hands and knees to the pile of mail, and found the codpiece. "I'll do it," he said. "For England, I do this! For all of you, I do this!"

"Hip hip hooray," said the steward unenthusiastically.

Sabbath loomed over Richard, his legs thick and bowed, his hands raising the hem of his tunic. "Give it a little tickle while you're down there."

"You disgust me. Is there no sin you'll not commit?"

Sabbath shrugged. "Not as of yet," he said.

Richard fastened the codpiece and tightened the straps. "Your parents named you well. It's a wonder you were ever baptized, *Hexen Sabbath*," Richard said through clenched teeth.

"The village priest was very fond of my mother," said Sabbath. He winked. "Right, off to kill some Danes!" He reached for his mail and his broadsword.

The shield wall had already broken by the time Hexen Sabbath arrived, on foot and alone, at the scene of the battle. Duke Richard had merely pointed Sabbath toward the direction of the battle, then took the knight's place at the table with the women. Cnut's raven banners, symbols of the all-seeing Odin, overwhelmed the battlefield. The English were in a rout, screaming and choking on blood as Viking axes ate into their backs. If there was anything that separated Sabbath from his fellows, it wasn't his good sword arm, though it was excellent, nor his strong back, though he could put a horse across his shoulders like a sack of wheat; it was something inside him.

His mother, a witch, told him when he was a young boy that he would die on a Sunday. And today was Friday. Knowing this, Hexen Sabbath feared for nothing, worried for nothing, thought for nothing. Men who feared death fought differently. Some hid behind their shields, jabbing with their blades and hoping that their archers launched a fusillade that vanquished the enemy for them. Or they went mad and ran screaming toward their foes, limbs exposed, breath hot, overcommitted. The first type succumbed to the fear of death; the second hoped to defeat fear by embodying it.

One Dane came running toward him now, his face red and eyes wild. Sabbath simply drew his sword, sidestepped, and stuck it in the man's ribs. He then pulled it out and with a great swing tore apart the shield of another. That Viking hefted his axe high with both hands, leaving his torso exposed. Sabbath slashed open the man's belly, letting intestines fall free like bloody scarves.

Men grunted or yelled when they threw javelins, a peculiar breathless exhalation that Sabbath's sharp senses could hear under the clash of sword and axe. Sabbath moved to the left when he heard that sound and kept swinging, not looking to see where the projectiles landed. A tall Viking deflected the blade with his shield and ran the head of his axe along the shield's rim, parrying Sabbath's sword and pushing the knight back onto his heels.

"Hey, you're pretty good!" Sabbath said. The Viking crouched behind his shield and jabbed with it, seeking an opening for his axe. Sabbath smiled. The enemy was fearful, despite his skill.

The Viking swung his shield, rolling the axe around its edge, at Sabbath's head. Sabbath's sword battered uselessly against the shield, and the axe blade nearly nipped him. Sabbath scuttled back and readied his sword with a two-handed grip.

"Fine," he said. He rolled his hands around the hilt of the sword and stabbed the Viking through his lead foot, staking him to the ground. The Viking howled, and Sabbath punched the man's teeth down his throat, then freed the sword, slashing the Viking open from groin to gullet.

"It's Sir Hexen!" cried an Englishman. "Form a wedge behind him. Push the Danes back to the River Crouch!"

"Yes!" called Sabbath over his shoulder. He heard another distant grunt. "Just beware—" A knight hit the ground hard, a sapling sprouting from his chest. "—javelins."

Another clever Viking met Sabbath's blade with an

underhand swing of his axe, hooking the sword. Sabbath caught a glimpse of gritted teeth, then smiled again and let go of the hilt. The sword went sailing into the face of another Dane, and the one who'd snagged the sword fell onto his back. Sabbath rushed over him, jumped on his skull, reclaimed his sword from the head of the other, and swatted an incoming javelin out of the air.

"Spearmen!" a banner-wielder called out, waving a raven flag. A trio of men holding long lances at their hips converged on Sabbath, jabbing and thrusting, looking to surround him.

"Well," said Sabbath, "any coward could use numbers"—he deflected a spearhead—"and strategy"—barely dodged another—"if they're weak." He winced as a point found his thigh. The men stayed at the end of their spears. These men were confident, assured that close cooperation would see them through. Sabbath didn't have the reach to use his foot trick again. He planted himself, struck a simpleton's expression on his face, lowered his sword, and let himself be surrounded.

"Oh Lord, oh Lord," he cried, whipping up a few tears and sniffling loudly. "Sweet Christ Jesus, accept my soul in Heaven tonight!" He dropped his sword. The spearman behind him moved. Sabbath threw himself to the ground. The spearpoint thrust right where Sabbath had been standing and found the sternum of the Viking opposite him. Sabbath rolled onto his back, upsetting the third spearman. Then he was up, with a borrowed spear, and pierced the neck of the Viking who was still struggling to pull his weapon from the chest of his countryman. The third spearman got up and tackled Sabbath, but couldn't hold him down. Sabbath scrambled and took the mount. He pulled the helmet from the spearman's head and turned it in his hands, holding it high, ready to bash in the enemy's face.

"Die, pagan!"

"Wuh-we're Christian too," said the spearman. His tears, the snot running down his nose, were real. He was a child, a fair one whose face burned with blood.

"Your king, your banners . . ."

"We Danes have been Christian for generations . . . the banner . . . we do not worship the old gods anymore. . . ."

Sabbath peered down at the bloody face he was about to ruin in the name of the Lord. He saw that his enemy was a youth, unbearded and sniveling. He had perhaps never made war before, never killed a man, never even lain with a woman. Sabbath put the helmet down beside the youth and clambered to his feet.

He clutched at the cross medallion around his neck and wiped a tear from his eye. "I'm sorry," he said, but the youth at his feet didn't hear him. "I'm sorry!" he bellowed, louder. "The world is fallen; men like us should not be butchering one another like animals!" He cast his gaze about the battle. His presence had for a moment served to rally his people, but dozens of Danes had also regrouped behind their shields and recommenced their march.

"Danes! Come collect this youth and take him back behind your lines! He does not belong here, in this field of blood! In the name of Christ, come and save your man!"

The Danes answered with a storm of javelins.

2

> Above it stood the seraphims: each one had six wings; with twain he covered his face, and with twain he covered his feet, and with twain he did fly.
>
> —Isaiah 6:2

The eyes of Hexen Sabbath burned as though the sun had swallowed him. His mother, the prophecy, the curse of his name, the reality of death, of Hell, weighed him down like bones of molten lead. He was drowning in light and fire.

And then Sabbath was borne aloft into cool darkness, into frigid black, and then into an icy white.

He could speak.

"Wh-what . . . day . . . is it?"

"Sunday," said a thousand voices at once.

Sabbath was dropped into a puddle of water. His throat burning, he lapped at it desperately, like an animal.

"That might kill you," said a thousand voices converging into a single baritone.

"I'm already dead," said Sabbath between gulps. "I did not know Hell had water."

Sabbath looked up. "Are you Satan, then?"

"No."

"I wasn't supposed to die," said Sabbath. "It was written in the stars that I would never die except on the Sabbath."

"Prideful."

Sabbath snorted, collected water in his palm, drank it.

"You aren't dead. I'd hope that much would be clear."

Sabbath stood and took a swaggering step toward the man whom he had been addressing. "Your dress and manner are strange to me," he said. He peered up. "You are very tall. Very tall."

The man smiled. He straightened his necktie. "I've taken on the seeming of a twenty-first-century man. You were a giant in your time, Hexen Sabbath, but ten hundred years later, you're a poorly shaved bear cub."

"Prideful," said Sabbath.

"No," said the man. "I state that which is true, always."

"Then tell me truthfully, who are you . . . and where are we, if not Hell?"

"I am called Abathar, and I am an Angel of the Lord," the man said. "And you, Sir Hexen Sabbath, are a man who cannot die, save on a Sunday, and indeed tonight you live! I have plucked you from the battle in which you have taken part, and transported you here, to a part of the world unknown to you, exactly ten centuries hence. The city is called New York."

"Ten centuries . . . it is two thousand and sixteen? New York? As in York, so recently ruled by the Vikings? Has their strength persisted for so long? Have you brought me into a nest of my enemies, my murderers? My sword!" Sabbath reached for his scabbard, but it was missing, as were his belt, his mail, and his tunic. He was naked save for the weighty cross around his neck.

"Abathar, I appear to be naked," he said expectantly.

"You have been born a second time, after a fashion," said Abathar. "Like Christ, you journeyed to Hades on Friday and ascended to Earth on a Sunday. To answer your other question, the Vikings are no longer your concern. Names persist in strange ways, as someone with a name as strange as yours should understand. This is a city far across the sea—empires have fallen, new ones have risen. But some things remain the same, Hexen Sabbath. This world is a fallen one, beset by sins. The seven deadly sins."

Sabbath said, "Ah, I've come to the right place." He poked Abathar in the chest. "And I'm dressed for it."

"You have indeed," said Abathar. "For in seven days, this world will end."

"Well, then, I'd better get started!" said Sabbath.

"Every seven hundred and seventy-seven years," said Abathar, "the seven deadly sins assume human form. In times past, they walked among mortals for seven years, causing mischief, seeking to bring this world to a premature end. In this era, seven beings can end the world in a matter of weeks. They have been planting their seeds for some time. There is but one week remaining to stop them."

"End the world in a week? You don't say!" Sabbath looked around at the alley he stood in. The walls on either side were filthy brick, and despite the architecture and smells and noises being largely alien, Sabbath knew rubbish when he saw it. He proceeded to a dumpster, opened the lid, and started poking around, looking for clothing. "What did they get up to in the year 1239, then?"

"They broke the Church, pitting Pope against Holy Roman Emperor. They drove the wildmen of the East into Rus and created a great plague. The presence of the sins made flesh on this earth corrupt. The world nearly died then. It is seven days from dying now. You, Hexen Sabbath, are uniquely immune from their influences because, to be perfectly honest about it, you are an absolutely loathsome and degenerate sinner. You can sink no further. The sins cannot influence and corrupt you as they would any other champion. The Lord has tasked me with the weighing of souls, and I've rarely seen one so densely wicked as yours."

Sabbath pulled forth a plastic garbage bag and tore it open with his hands. "What *is* this?"

"Sabbath, you are to find and kill the seven deadly sins, so that the world may be set to rights. Or God's love will be as unto an eternal fire. You have a chance, one you do not deserve, to sit in the presence of your Father and bask in his glory. The sins must die by your hand. Collect their heads and present them unto me in seven days, and earn your heavenly reward."

"Will I be provided pants, O Angel of the Lord?" Sabbath asked with a gesture toward his naked form.

"I sense that you are not taking this seriously," said Abathar.

"Would you, in my situation?" asked Sabbath. "I fought for my liege and my Lord for my entire life, sir, and I've never heard so outlandish a tale. Why did you pluck me from my time to bring me a thousand years hence? Why not have a man of this era do your work for you? There are sinners aplenty in every era. Why not deliver me unto the year 1239 or, for that matter—" He paused to do a little mental math. "—the year 2793? This is a hellish trick, to give me hope and then smash it, I tell you."

"You, Hexen Sabbath, have a tainted soul. You've indulged in lust, gluttony, sloth, wrath, envy, greed, and pride to the point where your soul is damned. You believe yourself to be in Hell because you know it is your deserved fate. And yet, you fought valiantly for the Lord. You sought to spare a young man, your enemy, and died for him. Your very soul hangs in the balance, as does the fate of Earth."

Sabbath smiled as he walked back to face Abathar. "Abathar, Angel of the Lord. Could you not be a devil seeking to tempt me? Could you not be the final dream of a feverish warrior whose lifeblood has spilled out from his heart, leaving behind only regrets?"

"No."

"Prove it."

Abathar shrugged. His humanity fell to the floor of the alley like a coat shrugged off his shoulders. Eyes and wings and ageless light filled Sabbath's senses. The universe as he knew it *was* Abathar . . . and something else. An energy at the core of time and space, uncreated but omnipresent, stitched into the fabric of the cosmos. It burned and soothed him at once, like red-hot wire dragged over his skin, followed by a healing salve. His whole life was compressed into the most minute of instances, a grain of sand resting atop a pebble called the world.

When Hexen Sabbath awoke, he clung to Abathar, who

was a man again, and pulled himself up by gripping the angel's trousers and suit jacket.

"Was that . . . ?"

"God's love for you, Sabbath," Abathar answered.

"It . . . hurt," Sabbath said.

"Of course it hurt," said Abathar.

"He is angry with me."

"No," said Abathar. "He loves you, as he loves all men. Recall your childhood, Sir Knight, when you would displease your mother and feel ashamed. It would burn in your stomach like a hot coal. It was *your* understanding of your shame that knotted your guts. That is Hell. And when you pleased her and she would smile upon you, and you would feel light, as if the sweetest breeze has filled your lungs. It was *your* understanding of your good words and deeds that made your heart sing. That is Heaven. God's love for you is a fire that purifies, or incinerates. But it is always love, and it is always fire. Choose wisely."

"But where do I begin?" Sabbath asked. "I don't have even a rag to wear. You cannot leave me entirely bereft."

"We have not," said Abathar, who put a strange emphasis on the word *we*. "The English these people speak would be foreign to you, and your tongue to them. We have fixed that. And—" He took a hold of Sabbath's arm and pressed his palm to the flesh of his wrist. "—there!"

A complex mark had been left behind, shapes and lines crisscrossing, a bit like a tree torn from its roots. "What is it?" Sabbath asked.

"It's a map of the city streets, and its subway," Abathar said, and Sabbath understood without experience what *sub-*

way meant now. He could see himself swiping a MetroCard, waiting on the platform, hanging on to a strap in a crowded tube of screeching steel.

"But this is a tattoo. Couldn't you have just given me a map?"

"Look closely. Put your mind to the task. The sins you strive against will reveal themselves on your map," said Abathar.

"Thank you . . . but . . . a knowledge of the contemporary tongue, and a guide? No weapons, no food, no clothes? Is this it?" Sabbath said. "And why do you want the heads?"

"No, that is not quite it." Abathar did not vanish in a puff of smoke or ascend to Heaven on a pillar of holy light. He was simply not standing in the alleyway with Sabbath anymore. Sabbath's last question echoed off the filthy walls of the alleyway.

Sabbath peered at the map on his left forearm and did what the angel had bidden him to do. He noticed something else—a countdown clock. It was a Sunday night, 10:34 P.M. It occurred to Sabbath now that *he could die*. He knew, somehow, that the people of this far-off era, the twenty-first century, believed that the new day started at midnight. But Sabbath's mother, the prophetess and witch, always reckoned that the new day started with the cock's crow. Dawn. If only Abathar would appear again to answer the question. . . .

And there it was, the fiery turning of his guts. Would God want Sabbath to depend on angelic help, or the guarantee of a witch that he could not die? The fact was, as far as such a miracle could be called a fact, that Sabbath had already felt his lifeblood leave his body once. The sensations of dying, of one's limbs turning to driftwood, one's heart shriveling even as one's mind begs it to keep pumping, was not one he was ready to repeat.

But he couldn't stay in the alley till dawn. When the washerwomen and servants awoke and came to the windows to empty their pots, they would see him and raise the alarm. He could potentially wait till midnight, and then as the city slept, steal some clothing, food, a weapon.

Sabbath approached the mouth of the alleyway. Information flooded his mind. Well, no need to worry about chamber pots in this century, and in this Manhattan, there was no sleep. Motor vehicles amazed him even as the basics of internal combustion, oil, electricity, and even traffic laws were somehow gifted unto him as if the Holy Spirit bade him to think in tongues. He didn't actually learn the skill of driving, or knowledge of Spanish or Fujianese, though he heard men shouting both from their motor vehicles as they passed on the street before the alleyway.

Sabbath had English. He knew enough to stay out of the street as cars rolled by and to flush a toilet and that money was everything. That the people of this city were more varied even than the port precincts of London. That the aristocracy had been eliminated, and replaced by social climbers adept at handling money and even the signs and portents of money yet to come. That God was, for most people, an afterthought.

That war was fought very differently now.

The modern world, this tiny peek through the keyhole

of history's grandest castle, was so enthralling that Sabbath forgot his nakedness, and he was not ashamed as he stepped onto the sidewalk and craned his neck to peer at the buildings of SoHo.

Something slammed against him. "Look where you're goin', tourist!" growled a large man whose breath stank of beer. He was with a coterie, and they were dressed oddly, and not just oddly to a man from another era. Leather and PVC, face paint smeared across the eyes like a peacock's spray of feathers, straps and harnesses.

"Hey, nice dick!" said one of the girls, who wore a scandalous top made of mail, and an even more scandalous bottom that was little more than a rag. Even Sabbath's favorite tavern wenches would have blushed to wear such things. Sabbath would have blushed to see the costume, but most of his blood had already rushed elsewhere.

"What party did you just leave?" said another man, a Moor with prodigious pants and an oversized winter coat that suggested he was experiencing a radically different type of weather than the woman next to him. "Bruises aren't clothing, man!"

Another fellow, this one much wider than tall, said, "Dude, you just . . . dude!" His garb, black leather festooned with useless-seeming chains and tiny spikes, was especially attractive to Sabbath.

"A big one," said the woman. And then she laughed a bit like a nervous donkey. *Heehheeheeheeh.*

"Are you—" Sabbath searched for the word, and it came to him after a moment of struggle. *Idiots,* no. *Defectives,* also wrong. *Failures,* not quite . . . "—club-hoppers?"

"Are you . . . a crazy homeless person?" asked the tall one.

"I'm a stranger in a strange land," said Sabbath as he put his hands on the tall man's gleaming red vest, "but I know some few things of this place. I believe that one can beat a man as soundly as one likes and be lauded for it, so long as one is well muscled and handsome . . . and I am well muscled and handsome."

The fat one put his hand on Sabbath's shoulder. Sabbath pushed him to the ground with a palm to his chest and immediately clamped his grip back on the tall one's outfit.

"So, this vest. The Moor's leggings—"

"The *Moor*?" said the man with the too-large pants. The heavy one got to his feet. The woman glared. Something in Sabbath's mind started shuffling, rearranging. . . .

"The *African*'s leggings?" he asked. "I am going to take your clothes. If you wish to contend for them, I will beat your bones to paste. All three of you if I must." He nodded toward the woman of the party. "Never a lady, of course." His gaze lingered on her chest. "But the rest of you, one item each." To prove his point, Sabbath gathered the material in his hands in a bunch and with nary a grunt lifted the tall man off his feet.

"Jesus Christ, fine!" said the man, choking, "Just let me down."

Sabbath dropped him, then smacked him across the face. "Vanity! Keep the name of the Lord from your mouth!"

"Just don't take our wallets and our phones," said the man sliding off his leggings.

"Fucking creep," said the heavy one as he pulled his

arms from his jacket. The woman had an object in her hand—a smartphone—and was recording the whole scene as Sabbath dressed.

"You said you wouldn't hit a lady," the girl reminded Sabbath.

"I won't." But he plucked her by the wrist and twisted till she yelped and dropped the phone. He kicked it into traffic. "Now, go, all of you!" They scuttled away, threading into the crowd.

The crowd. Sabbath had never seen anything like it, not in court, not in the streets of busy London, not in a muster. Even the battle in which he had fallen involved some scores of men, and in that battle, the fates of two kingdoms were decided. Along a single block, he had passed by as many men as he had slain in his life. The idea haunted him. If he had been snatched up from time like an autumn leaf plucked from a river, could his enemies have followed him here? If so, perhaps they'd never find him, as New York was less a city than it was a patchwork of stone islands. The complexion of the town shifted every few blocks, from the huge windows of SoHo displaying sculptures and paintings and assemblages of what looked like garbage Sabbath could not comprehend at all—something in the store of knowledge Abathar had gifted him prodded Sabbath to never mind, as nobody understood this art—to a rough residential district full of trucks and trade.

And now he found himself in a precinct populated by people he couldn't understand at all. Dark-haired with epicanthic folds; he'd never seen men like these, and only knew there were men such as these at all thanks to a knight he once knew. Sir Leofric had journeyed to Byzantium as a free lance, and returned with stories of far Asia and the multitudes there. Travel that would have taken three years in Sabbath's time could be accomplished in fewer than three days. Men could fly! They could send great arrows over the horizon to unleash a fire that could destroy cities, and poison the earth till the Great Day of Judgment. He was being told too much. Sabbath shook as he waited on the corner; he threw his arms around a lamppost for support. He needed Abathar.

Sabbath needed God.

He gasped when he saw the church. It was out of place among the fire escapes and foreign scripts of the surrounding buildings. He quieted his mind as if before a battle; even had Sabbath cared about the finer points of theology, the gibbering about schisms and reformations reverberating in his skull would serve him no good now. It was a church, there was a cross upon it, and it felt old, like something from his time.

The doors of the Holy Trinity Ukrainian Orthodox Church were open, but the building seemed empty, or at least ill used. Candles blazed in the small narthex and sent light flickering across the dark-robed icons and murals in the nave beyond. Paintings he could understand! The smells of wax and incense hung heavily in the still air. Sabbath could understand that as well. There was no statuary, no Latin inscriptions, but it would do.

Sabbath trembled as he knelt, remembering the experience of Abathar revealing his true form and giving Sabbath a glimpse of God as well. In truth, it terrified him. Sabbath had always pushed religion to the back of his mind; bishops were politicians as corrupt as the nobility, and he'd seen many more catastrophes than miracles in his life—men torn to pieces, dead children in the arms of diseased mothers, fires and hail and locusts damning towns to the slow misery of starvation.

Sabbath had learned about God as a child, from the village priest. He had taken a special interest in his mother, a simple woman who knew something of herbs and the stars. He had come to her one evening after a day of solemn prayer, and told her that she could be forgiven for her many heresies via the acquisition of an indulgence. "And by that, I mean you may indulge me," he said, making himself comfortable on the pile of straw that made for her bed, and young Hexen's. And now, centuries later, Sabbath had a chance for heavenly reward, and not despite his sins and blasphemy, but *thanks* to them. Perhaps the priest had been on to something. He smiled at that. Maybe it wouldn't be so bad. . . . He just needed a little help.

"Lord God," he whispered, his hands folded before him. "Abathar, Angel of the Lord, please attend me—"

A scream echoed throughout the church. Sabbath jumped to his feet and ran back through the narthex and onto the street. There were two people screaming, one a woman struggling to free herself from the grip of a large man, and the man himself was also screaming. His face had been dyed red; he was clawing at his eyes with one hand and trying to control the woman with the other. Sabbath's own eyes and nose started to burn as he rushed forward and brought down his strong right arm on the man's wrist. The woman tumbled to the ground, and the can she was holding in one hand sprayed another burst of the noxious mist.

"Two of you!" the woman screeched. "You fuckers!"

Sabbath was used to fighting blind with sweat in his eyes and a tight helm covering his face. He planted the crown of his head on the man's sternum and nudged him off balance, then started pounding on his ribs and liver. Sabbath felt a pang of disappointment when the man fell so easily. The woman kept screaming and cursing like a man. Then Sabbath understood—the fellow curled up in a ball at his feet was no warrior, just a man who had gotten into an argument with a whore. He frisked the man, found his wallet, and sought the coins inside. His mind prodded him—*the green paper notes are worth much more*—but Sabbath couldn't bring himself to believe that.

"Hey, girl, here you are," Sabbath said, letting a handful of nickels and pennies fall from his palm. She wasn't quite prime material, this one, but Sabbath would roll with her. Red hair in curls fell past her shoulders, and her nose and eyes were sharp. Just the kind of face he'd like to make break into a smile and satisfied sigh under him. And her clothing: a jacket with wide shoulders like a man's, but her bottoms—he'd never seen so short a skirt. It looked as though she could stand up, spread her legs, and piss a puddle between her feet without adjustment had she wanted. Her knees, her *thighs.* Had Sabbath been in a church just moments earlier? Oh Lord . . .

"What are you fucking looking at?" she said, picking herself up. He smiled dumbly at her, blinking the cinder-hot mist from his eyes. She caught a glimpse at the man curled up on the sidewalk and twisted up her lips. "Oh, sorry. Thanks. I could have handled him—" She waved her can and coughed up a bit. "—but thanks. We should go." She looked Sabbath up and down. "What's up with you?"

"Up . . . with me?" Sabbath asked.

"You're dressed like you lost a bet."

"Well . . ." Sabbath could feel that he was not impressing this woman, despite his valor moments prior.

"God, I need to wash my life . . . I, uh, I mean my face . . . I mean . . ." She blinked hard. "Thank you. My name's Jennifer Zelenova," she said. "What were you doing in my church?" She tentatively offered a hand to shake, but then withdrew it and hugged herself instead.

"Your church?" Sabbath asked. "You're not a—"

"Not a what?" Jennifer asked. Her eyes were tearing, only partially from the pepper spray.

"Not a whor . . . are you all right?" The man groaned. Sabbath kicked him in the ear, putting him down again.

"We both need a milk bath," she said. "I have some in my gallery, three blocks from here." She reached out and touched the cross around his neck with a forefinger. "Nice. Canterbury cross. Is it part of the costume, or are you a believer?"

"It's not a costume," Sabbath said. "I . . ." He winced. Lying was a sin. Sinning came so easily, but perhaps he should try to do better. "I . . . appropriated the clothing from some youths who were in costume."

"'Appropriated,'" Jennifer repeated. She had a toothy smile and a lip that curled slightly. "Did you just mug some club kids, go to church to beg forgiveness, and then come outside and stop a second mugging you randomly witnessed?"

Sabbath shrugged. "That is somewhat what happened, I suppose . . . but I needed the clothes. You see, I was nak—"

"Whatever," Jennifer said. "It's actually pretty cool. You don't give a fuck about anything. My eyes are killing me. Follow!"

Twenty minutes later, after washing out the pepper spray with the quart of milk and dish soap from the small kitchenette in the rear of the gallery, both Sabbath and Jennifer could see properly. He'd had some time to contemplate what he should do. She was interested in the cross; perhaps she had some coin and would buy it, then Sabbath could procure a weapon and some food. Jennifer was all right, he decided. She didn't even blink when he said that he was called Hexen Sabbath. She had even snorted and muttered, "Typical."

"What do you think of Above Below Arts?" she said now, gesturing toward her space. It was a narrow hallway not even the size of the alley Sabbath had been brought to from the eleventh century—white walls, white canvases, hardwood floors. Warm and brightly lit, though. Sabbath knew about lightbulbs, thanks to the knowledge imparted unto him by Abathar, but was still impressed. "Get it, we're above TriBeCa; above the triangle below Canal. I opened the place a year ago, the day I broke free from my cubicle life. I'm all about personal freedom."

"Ah," Sabbath said. "So, this place is for the display of

art." He was mostly interested in electricity, and how the small dorm fridge stayed cold despite not containing ice.

"Yes," snapped Jennifer, rolling her eyes.

"Well, where is it?" Sabbath said.

"On the walls!" Jennifer said. "The forthcoming exhibit is called *Ylem.* It's what physicists call the stuff that was around before the Big Bang?"

"The Big Bang is . . ." Knowledge flooded Sabbath's mind, but Jennifer was faster, and more annoyed.

"How the universe began! Are you okay? . . . Did you get a head injury in that tussle?"

"I'm just . . . from far away," said Sabbath. "But I don't understand. . . ." He took in the room with a turn of his head. "There are seven canvases on the walls, all white. Nothing has been painted on them at all!"

"It's a blank-canvas exhibit," Jennifer said plainly.

"Yes, but will the painter come in and finish them?"

"The works are complete," Jennifer said. "It's a group show, not just one painter."

"But how could someone even tell one canvas from another?!" Sabbath demanded.

"They're by *different artists,*" Jennifer said, waspish. Then her mood dissolved, and she added quietly, "They're also slightly different sizes." She leaned back in an uncomfortable-looking chair and sighed. "Maybe you're right. I even have to launch the show next Sunday, the worst day of the week, because of all the local competition from better . . . well, better-known galleries in the neighborhood. I was even going to church to light a candle and pray to Saint John of Damascus; we haven't sold a single work yet. I hadn't even been to church since my grandmother died. I'm broke as a joke, and the landlord has plans to triple the rent and make this place a frozen yogurt salon." She made a twitching gesture with her fingers to somehow encircle the word *salon.* Sabbath had never seen anyone do such a thing before. He swallowed a snort. "There's literally already a frozen yogurt *refectory* at the other end of the block!" Those fingers again.

"I also have money woes," said Sabbath. "All I own are the clothes on my back—"

"Which you stole," Jennifer interjected.

"And this," he finished, touching the cross.

"Does it have sentimental value?" Jennifer asked, walking across the gallery in two long strides to him.

"No . . . ," Sabbath found himself saying. A day ago, a thousand years ago, it was nothing but a symbol of his rank, a way of making sure he wasn't confused for any other whoremonger or throat-slitter. Today, the cross also meant very little to him. He no longer had faith in the Lord; the Lord was a fact as plain as his standing in this strange room in a future he could scarcely imagine. If anything, the Lord had placed some faith in Hexen Sabbath, the thought of which made Sabbath's knees quaver.

"We could sell it," she said. She turned the cross in her hands, scrutinizing it. "It's an interesting piece. Almost exactly like an eleventh-century Anglo-Saxon Canterbury cross, but clearly it's contemporary. It looks like it was made yesterday, albeit from period materials is my guess. Where did you get it?"

"England," Sabbath said, relieved to speak nothing but the truth for once. Jennifer smiled at him, placed her palm on his chest. His PVC shirt had given her a glimpse of his physique, and she was examining his pectoral muscles as closely as she had his cross.

"Let me give it to you," Sabbath said, pulling it over his head by its string and sliding it onto her neck. Generous, yes, but it also put him in the perfect position to place his broad hands between her shoulder blades and the small of her back, and pull her close.

"This is probably just the adrenaline," Jennifer said. "We'll regret this in the morning. I always wanted to have a weird one-night stand with a stranger, but . . . what's your *real* name?"

"Hexen Sabbath," said Sabbath.

Jennifer smirked. "Okay, that's pretty kinky."

He cupped the back of her neck and moved in. She eagerly reciprocated, tongue already sneaking out between her lips. Sabbath was learning to enjoy the modern world. How many more times, how many more women, could he lay before he saved the world and all his sins were forgiven . . . or before he failed and the world ended? He knew to fear what the seven deadly sins had planned, but even if he could not stop them, Sabbath realized that he would have plenty of company in Hell. She reached out to dim the lights in the gallery.

Sabbath was amazed. Jennifer had been so wanton. She presented herself on all fours, moaned for him to be rough, demanded that his handprints be left marking her ass, grabbed that same hand and sucked his fingers greedily, as though wanting to be filled from both ends, then licked him clean after they both came. She kept herself warm in his arms afterwards—it was nothing but a pile of their clothes between them and the hard floor—for only a moment, then got up and poured them both glasses of red wine from large plastic cups. She gulped down a quarter of a bottle.

"You're fucked up, Hexen Sabbath," she said. "Were you in a car accident?"

"War," said Sabbath.

"Iraq?"

"England. Against the Danes." Sabbath regretted the words as soon as he said them, but he liked this Jennifer, and couldn't bring himself to lie to her. Sin *with* her in bed to their mutual joy and pleasure, yes, but not lie to her. To tell her the truth would draw her into the fatal drama of which he was a part, would risk her life, and the possibility of her love, it would . . .

Jennifer smiled widely, his cross jostling between her breasts as she swallowed her laughter. She failed at it, gulped, and guffawed like a horse. "Haw!"

"It's true," Sabbath said. "Look at my wounds." He stood up, planted his feet apart and twisted his torso. His body was an atlas of battle lines, a history of war. Scars and divots, the ghosts of crude stitches decorated his flesh, bones that never knit together properly lurked under his muscles. In the low lights of the art space, Sabbath looked like Michelangelo's *David,* after a madman had taken a chisel to the marble. "These are not the scars left by guns and bullets, but by sword and spear, mace and arrow."

"C'mon," said Jennifer.

"I'm from a thousand years in the past," said Sabbath. "I was brought here by an angel of the Lord."

She reached across the floor for her purse, brought out the mace. "I can't believe I fucked you. I can't believe I let you finger my ass."

"That is why the cross looked new to you. It is from the eleventh century, brought here round my neck—"

"You're obviously some kind of crazy, violent homeless person!" She got to her feet, her jaw clenched. "You admitted to me that you attacked people on the street!"

"Hwæt!" Sabbath said.

"I went to college too—art history major and a minor in English! I've read *Beowulf,*" said Jennifer. "Everyone knows *hwæt.*"

But Sabbath kept speaking in his native tongue, pleading with her. When she leveled the can of Mace at him, he grabbed her arm to jerk it away. She struggled, then stopped.

"Your tattoo . . . ," she said.

The subway map Abathar had seared on his flesh. Just another bit of proof that Sabbath was a modern man, except for seven dots of various colors, which glowed brighter than any ink. And two of them were moving, traversing the city.

"Hold this!" Jennifer pushed the Mace at Sabbath, then jabbed at one of the moving dots with her fingernail. "What is this? Nanotech LED . . ." She tried to dig at the skin, making Sabbath wince, but the dot traversed atop the length of the nail. She peered up at the ceiling, looking for a source of the light.

"What is it?" Jennifer demanded, her eyes wide, her tone still angry, but tremulous now. "What does it mean?"

"These are the personifications of the seven deadly sins, branded on my skin by the angel Abathar, who weighs the souls of men and found mine wanting." Sabbath said, "They have gathered here and will destroy this world in one week's time, and I have been tasked to stop them. Thanks to my past . . . debauchery, they have no influence over me."

"Angels? That's insane! And how are seven people going to destroy the entire world?" asked Jennifer. "Really, they may just need to wait around. Lots of countries have nuclear weapons these days, and they can't all be trusted. Maybe even we can't be trusted, uh, I mean the U.S. . . ."

Nuclear weapons. Sabbath had grown used to sudden revelations about this new world in which he found himself, but this phrase did something more profound to him. He saw great cities being blasted away, felt the marrow in his bones boiling, felt the planet under his feet cracking open—even the air was on fire.

"Hexen . . ."

The sins had, in times past, attempted to wipe out humanity when the species was weak and scattered across tribe and nation. This time, the sins had no real need to spend years cultivating plagues and engendering war. The billions of people on this earth had handed the keys of power to a handful of madmen, and these madmen had commissioned weapons that would not just wipe out humanity but destroy the planet itself. No resurrection of the dead to greet the risen Lord, no Day of Judgment, no world without end, not even a new Adam and Eve to begin again . . .

"Hexen!"

Hexen snapped out of his reverie. "Yes," he said. "Nuclear weapons. That is how the sins seek to destroy this world. I have been brought here to stop them. To kill them and take their heads. You're right."

Jennifer shuddered, met Sabbath's gaze. Then she looked down at the tattoo, clamped her palm over it. The tiny lights representing the seven sins weren't traveling over her flesh, but were visible *within* it, bright pinpoints pushing up from Sabbath's arm. She gasped, then peered up at Sabbath.

"Fuck," she said. "How can I help you?"

"Can you . . . procure a sword for me?"

"Actually, I think I can," she said. "Good thing you hooked up with me. I trade in art, so I know people in auction houses, even some archaeologists. And, you know, private collectors. Extremely private, if you get my drift." Sabbath just looked at her blankly. "Organized crime. Portable art and historical items are a great way to launder money, even when provenance is shaky."

"Ah." The gift of Abathar whispered the broad strokes of the facts of international criminal syndicates in Sabbath's ear, but he still didn't understand what Jennifer was getting at.

"But I'm broke, and I bet you don't have any money either."

Sabbath shrugged.

Jennifer glanced down at her chest. "But we could sell this to someone who will turn around and sell it again to a private collector. I'll take a picture and send out some texts. There are some antiquities catalogs online you can peruse while I do that."

Jennifer snatched her phone up from the receptionist's desk by the rear wall of the gallery and handed Sabbath a tablet. She gave him a brief demonstration of its capabilities, and got to work thumbing the screen of her phone, taking photos of the medallion against her still-nude chest—"A bit of skin always helps," she explained—and occasionally looking at her desktop computer.

Sabbath scanned the images of swords and other weapons. Most of them were after his time, more decorative than martial. But after some browsing, he found a Carolingian that seemed to fit the bill. Long and heavy, with relatively few pits along the edges, the lobed guard he preferred, a blunt rather than spiked pommel, and a hilt wrapped in shark leather.

"I found one," he said. "I could wield it well."

"So that's your plan?" Jennifer asked him. She was sitting in her office chair, back straight, legs crossed, one hand on the computer mouse. If not for her nudity and the ancient cross medallion, she could have been posing for a stock photo of a young professional. "You're gonna go kill seven people."

"And save—" Sabbath paused until the correct number came to him. "—seven point six billion." He didn't believe there could be that many people; he could scarcely understand such a figure at all. He had seen a beach at Grimsby once, and heard from a priest accompanying his troop that there were more grains of sand upon it than there were men, living or dead, in the world. He couldn't even imagine a beach long enough to hold nearly eight billion grains of sand.

"I mean the police. If these people are here in Manhattan, and planning to launch a nuclear missile or start World War III somehow, they're not going to be your average schmuck walking down the block. If you slice off the head of a VIP, every cop in town will come looking for you. So will the FBI, maybe even the military! I mean, what are you even going to do with the heads!"

"In addition to a new blade, I'll need some sort of . . . sack. As if for potatoes," Sabbath said.

"You can't carry a sack of potatoes around Manhattan at all hours of the day either," Jennifer said. "I'll lend you my duffel bag. I use it . . . for laundry," she explained, suddenly disgusted at the idea. "Why do you need their hea—?" A bell chimed in her computer; then she smiled, her question forgotten. "We got a bite. Twenty grand. How much is the sword you want, Hexen?"

He looked down at the tablet. "Twenty-two thousand."

Jennifer pursed her lips. "Fine." She typed some more, and after a long moment, raised an eyebrow and smiled. "Okay, they'll do twenty-two."

"Excellent," said Sabbath. "It was exactly what we need."

"I was hoping for a commission," she said. "A little extra cash could come in handy . . . I mean if I have to bail you out of prison or something. But lacking proper provenance for this piece, it's all we can get for a 'possible eleventh-century Canterbury cross.' Basically, they'll sell it again, and it'll just be a way for someone to explain to their bank where their cocaine money came from. Praise God, eh?"

"I was brought here for a reason," Sabbath said. One of them was his outrageous propensity for sin, including his eagerness to sleep with strangers, though such a sin seemed common enough now, even among women who went to church and lit candles. "I will not be caught, nor will I be stopped. This I swear."

"Well, I guess if you are stopped, I won't have to worry about bills, anyway," Jennifer said. "They're sending a car down for the cross. I'd better put on some clothes." She took the tablet from Sabbath and looked at his selection. "Huh, a coincidence. Same auction house holds the sword. We can just swap and sign the papers."

Sabbath nodded.

"They're sending down an UberBLACK now, with a handler and the papers."

"I see," said Sabbath, who did not.

"You should probably," Jennifer said as she pulled a T-shirt over her curly hair, "hide behind the desk or something. I'll meet them outside. This whole place smells like a sex club."

Sabbath grunted at that and hurried over to the desk.

It was strange, he thought, as he curled in the desk's foot well. Here he was, in an unimaginable future, tasked by an angel to kill seven devilish creatures in as many days, and there was still both time and opportunity for sex. There wasn't even a need to make some false promise to a silly peasant girl or exchange gold for cunny or pay a visit to the one jolly good woman in town whose name was passed between men. This Jennifer—what a name!—had come in exceptionally handy. She might even have been sent by the

Lord, except for the fact that she opened her legs so easily, and blasphemed so readily with her moans. And now she was procuring a weapon, for free. He'd had to surrender his cross, but it was of no matter. It had looked good on her bosom, and that blade would surely feel even better in his hand.

It was time to kill again. And it was nearly midnight, nearly Monday. Hexen Sabbath inhaled deeply and smiled.

3

The slothful man saith, There is a lion in the way; a lion is in the streets.

—Proverbs 26:13

The city was confusing enough, even with his map, that Sabbath had turned himself around entirely after leaving Jennifer's. He found his way back to the church where he'd met her, nearly colliding with other pedestrians as he walked while peering down at his forearm, and then re-oriented himself, headed south, finally feeling a bit more comfortable walking the streets. The Bowery reminded Sabbath of home. Oh, like the rest of Manhattan, the boulevard was an assault on the senses—exposed flesh that would send an eleventh-century harlot screaming into a nunnery, motorized wagons that sounded like a whole troop of men, the stench of bodily fluids Sabbath only otherwise sniffed in open battle, and lights everywhere. Night itself had been vanquished. But the Bowery was familiar, for at the foot of every edifice clung the desperate and the starving. They were like lepers at the gate, or the most ragged of the camp followers that had once trailed Sabbath into war, to pick rags and coins from corpses when they could. The wealthy—and on the Bowery, they were as obvious as the duke with their clean clothes, their unmarked skin, and their dizzying talk—strode past the suffering poor as though there was no price to be paid before the Lord for such arrogance.

Indeed, Sabbath thought. *There probably is not. Not in this world.* Sabbath had certainly never given alms to the men of rag and bone who groveled in his shadow, not unless some attractive woman was watching. He served Christ in his own way. And here he was, in this world of sordid delights.

And speaking of sordid delights . . . what was the word for the food he smelled now? Oh yes, *pizza.* If a deadly sin were to be vanquished this evening, Sabbath would need a full belly. It wasn't a retreat, just a tactical withdrawal, to Ray's Pizza Bagel Café on the well-omened Place of Saint Mark.

It was a large pizzeria, and packed despite the late hour, thanks to the amazing electrical bulbs that Sabbath could not help but stare at. And the people! In his own time, Hexen Sabbath had been a giant among men. Here, in the twenty-first century, he was chagrined to find himself shorter than many of the men around him, even if most of them were flabby, with bellies that preceded them into a room like a fleshy little page. He could use some food, Sabbath thought, and the pizza looked and smelled delicious.

The workers were efficient enough, and New Yorkers not a people given to gossip while at the market, so after four minutes Sabbath was at the front of the line.

"Hail, Ray!" he said. "I would have two of your shield-sized pizzas."

"I ain't Ray," the man at the cash register said. "You want larges?"

"Larges! Yes!" Sabbath had just recalled that he hadn't any money. *Larges* sounded like *largesse,* but he could expect none of that in this time when nobility and service meant nothing. People were all equal here in this time, at least insofar as there was money in one's purse. His cross had sold for just enough to buy a sword and sheath. His only other possessions were the stolen clothes, a raincoat of Jennifer's that was fashionably large on her but too snug on him, and Jennifer's laundry bag, which he was going to fill with heads. "Yes, two of your largest pizzas, for free."

"Fuck off, fruitcake," said the cashier. Sabbath has been surprised that his clothes hadn't attracted more attention on the streets, but now he understood that the passersby had taken him for some sort of eccentric vagabond.

"Your master Ray will surely understand. Consider it a tithe. It shall fuel my limbs for holy combat!" And with that, Sabbath put his left hand under his coat and drew his sword several inches for the enlightenment of Ray's clerk. "Believe me or not, but if you do not, I will run you through and take what I need." Somewhere by the base of Sabbath's skull, something whispered, *Want, not need.* It was a reprimand.

The cashier stared at Sabbath for a long moment, then turned and said something over his shoulder. It was in a language Sabbath did not understand, but it sounded broadly similar to Latin. *Obtener* and *fuste* . . . Obtain, or get, the—

Sabbath ducked as the two-by-four swung at his head. The cashier cursed loudly in his language, and several others joined in. Sabbath's hand reflexively went to his sword, but with gritted teeth, he kept himself from drawing it forth and gutting the madmen swarming him. Then the noise was consumed by a rush of wings, and the whole universe stopped, as if eternity held her breath.

Abathar's voice cut through the frozen amber of time. "Thirty-five dollars, yes. Paid in full, plus a forty percent tip," he said. "For all of you." Satisfied, the cashier and the bakers moved back to their positions behind the counter. "I'll have a side salad, please," he added. His gaze turned to Sabbath, who was still in his stance, his sword arm ready to swing out. "You're with me. We'll eat in. Sir Hexen, the sins you hunt integrate perfectly into this society, and do their dark work unnoticed by the worldly authorities. You, on the other hand, stand out in the manner of a village idiot."

"Ah, is that why you have me take their heads? If I gain the majority of them, will I too be able to go unnotic—?"

"No," Abathar interrupted. "Try to keep a lower profile as you perform the task God has commissioned for you. I shall not save you every time. There are souls need weighing." Sabbath looked down at his raincoat and shrugged.

At the table, Sabbath ate with both hands. He glanced at Abathar and said, "What is . . . that?" twirling a finger as best he could toward the area under Abathar's chin.

"It's a necktie. A bow tie, specifically," Abathar said.

"Odd-looking device," Sabbath said.

"The timber could have caved in your skull."

"I cannot die, save on the Sabbath. By modern reckoning it is early Monday."

"According to your witch mother," said Abathar. "Only God knows the time and manner of a man's death. Your mother—"

"*What* of my mother?" Sabbath's blood was hot. Could he slay an angel? His fingers trembled, eager for the hilt of his sword.

"Consider this, at least," Abathar said, still calm. "Even if your mother was right, and you could not die now, early on a Monday morning, you could be incapacitated, and die of your wounds six days hence, or in the conflagration to come. Is that how you'd meet the Lord, Hexen Sabbath? Mumbling to yourself like an idiot, in a soiled garment, your head throbbing, covered in drool—"

"I don't plan on anything like that happening to me," Sabbath said. It had not occurred to him that he could be so grievously injured and yet not die. Then his mind prodded him: in this time, wounds that would be fatal on the battlefield could be treated, even healed, in a hospital. Blood could be taken from one man and given safely to another, and sepsis brought to heel with a tiny pill. Even a man whose brain had died could be kept alive, after a fashion, with mechanical bellows serving as lungs.

"Sabbath, do you plan on spending the week Our Lord has given you in this modern realm stuffing your face, thieving, and fornicating with women outside the bounds of matrimony? You are here to defeat the seven sins, not embrace them, and not to quiz me on matters sartorial," Abathar said, an edge in his voice.

"Ah," Sabbath said. A slice disappeared into his mouth. "I asked you my question as a test. You'll answer questions, will you? We can have a bit of a conversation, man to man. Or mortal to angel." Abathar's eyes narrowed, but Sabbath continued. "So, you perhaps think I am just an oaf with a good sword arm and a disregard for the social niceties. However, one does not become a knight of the realm, one does not earn my rank—" Sabbath wiped his fingers on his PVC shirt. "—without some education in theology. And I must say, theologically speaking, the quest you have set me on is like unto chasing geese. Why me, a soul ten centuries gone? Surely there is some contemporary servant of the Lord more capable of navigating this monstrous city—one with a soul as corrupt as mine! I've walked ten blocks in this city, and I'm sure I've crossed paths with a dozen such rutting pigs. A thousand such men, whom you could field as a legion. And that leaves aside the question of what it even means to defeat the seven deadly sins. Or why they have manifested as men—"

"And women," Abathar said.

"—rather than simply being born in the hearts of men, as has been true for the history of this fallen world."

"Sabbath—"

"Or what the point of destroying the world is! Surely Judgment Day is in the hand of God, not Satan nor the simple fact of sin."

"Your sword," Abathar said. "Give it to me."

"I won't . . . ," Sabbath began, but Abathar had the sword in his palms as if it had just been presented to him.

"A quality Carolingian. It's been in many hands across these ten centuries." He glanced down at it. "Shark leather. Tell me, Sabbath—imagine you were out for a swim in the ocean, and as you bobbed along, a fin broke the waves and cut water toward you. The nose and great toothy mouth of a shark rears up, and then, as this would be a miracle of the Lord, the fish begins to speak. Let us say, Sabbath, this is a female shark. Perhaps you do not know this, but sharks are all but unique among fish in that they give birth to live young. This particular shark, who accosts you now in the black waves off Whitby, asks you a question. She asks, 'Why do you, Hexen Sabbath, own a sword wrapped in the skin of my poor lost son?'"

"I . . . well, it's simply a matter of the grip. I've never fished a shark out of the ocean, and truth be told, I am not a strong swimmer. The smith, I presume, purchased the shag—"

"Why do you need a sword with a shark leather grip, Sabbath?" Abathar interrupted.

"To better handle the blade. A man's palm gets slippery."

"Handle the blade to what end?"

"To kill Danes!" Sabbath said.

"To what end?"

"They invaded my country, Abathar! You know this."

"But the shark does not," Abathar said. "'Why would the Danes invade your country?' she would ask."

"Well, it's . . . it's complex. King Edgar died early, and Æthelred was a weak king. Among the Vikings, pagan rebels were defeated by King Gormsson, who sought to bring the light of Christ to his realm. Those dark-hearted pagans, their lands taken from them, set sail for and sacked Ipswich in order to, well, enrich themselves."

"What's a pagan? Who is Christ?"

"A pagan is a country fool who worships trees and leaves and murders children to lay a cornerstone of their temples.

Christ is our Lord and Savior, God made flesh! I am a Christian; I worship the triune God!"

"So you're a Christian, then, attacked by pagans."

"Yes! Well, no . . . that was before my time . . . the Christian Danes saw how well their fellows did and embraced the idea of the invasion of the British Isles themselves," said Sabbath. "I know that now, thanks only to the gift of knowledge bequeathed upon me by you. I had been told that our enemies were still pagan."

"Christian against Christian, then?" Abathar said. "One Christian army looking to conquer the land of another, and the defenders eager to send their fellows in the faith back to their widows in pieces?"

"Well . . . ," Sabbath said. "Yes. That is how it went. But not for me. I would not strike the killing blow against the youth at my feet, who called himself a Christian. I died rather than kill him."

"Well, why did Christ allow that?"

"You tell me!" Sabbath demanded, slamming his fist against the table.

"I'm not the one asking you, Sabbath. I'm the shark!"

"You can't expect me to explain a hundred years of tumultuous history and kingly chess-playing to a fish just because her skinned offspring played some minute role in the creation of my sword! No matter what I said, she wouldn't understand!"

"Exactly, Sabbath," Abathar said. "Exactly." He turned to his salad and chewed on a lettuce leaf thoughtfully, silently. Sabbath found the weight of his sword tugging against the interior of his coat again.

Sabbath bit into the crust of his pizza and glared.

"Would it make you feel better, Hexen Sabbath," Abathar ventured, "if I told you that this sort of thing happens all the time? Perhaps in your era, a Roman centurion who knew Christ himself and was blessed by him found himself in a strange new world of modern invention and social mores, not one thousand but more than fifteen hundred years from his time, and had to collect seven heads of his own."

"Well, if that fellow is still available, why don't you summon him forth?" Sabbath said.

"He's not . . . available," Abathar said. "He succeeded in saving the world, but failed after a fashion. Sabbath, beware temptation. Focus on your quest." Sabbath opened his mouth to speak, but Abathar was gone.

The office building, down at the corner of the Bowery and Spring Street, was only a ten-minute walk for Sabbath. The tattoo on his forearm burned with need, and it was important that his limbs be lively, so he moved at a fast trot. Sabbath knew that New York was the city that never sleeps, but he was still somewhat surprised to find the doors unlocked and the lobby unguarded.

"A trap, surely," Sabbath said to himself. His voice echoed in the marble vestibule. For a moment, he thought of the Roman centurion, a man out of time much like himself. Was Abathar telling the truth, or playing a game? Could angels even lie, or did whatever one said become the truth of history itself? A dozen questions assaulted him, and as he brushed them away, a hundred more took their place. None of it mattered; the only thing to do was follow the sign. By the elevator, it stood, and it read INTERBOROUGH DEPARTMENT OF TRANSCOUNTY OPERATIONS AND REGIONAL DEVELOPMENT (LKGN). SUBBASEMENT FOUR.

Wary, Sabbath decided to take the stairs. Elevators felt too much like the worst elements of a mine and a tomb, combined. He also felt more capable of battering down even steel hinges than shouldering his way out of an elevator should he get stuck between floors. The stairwell was hot and dark, illuminated only on the landings, and then by a single red light on each basement level.

Hell, Sabbath thought. *I am walking into Hell. Perhaps I was not lifted up from death eternal after all; perhaps this is just more anguish for my sins.* Then he reached the fourth subbasement, opened an unmarked door, stepped through it, and thought, *Yes, this is Hell.*

The twenty-four-hour cubicle farm stretched as far as Sabbath could see, and in each cube there was a man or a woman hunched over either a computer keyboard or a pile of papers. The fluorescent lighting painted all the workers, regardless of race or color, a sickly bluish gray.

Like bees crawling among the honeycombs, Sabbath thought, *surely Sloth will not be found here.* He took in the scene as an archer might, selecting one man to focus on, then another. Only then did he see that these workers were not actually working at all. One might click on the mouse or stab at the keyboard with a single finger, while another sighed and turned a page from the right side of an open folder to the left, but there was no labor here. It was a show, a fraud.

Only one worker met his eyes, and with a sneer, she raised a pen and pointed to the wall behind him.

A row of seats lined up against the wall, and near them a short pole on which stood a red container. TAKE A NUMBER.

Sabbath wondered if the number wouldn't be *666,* from the infamous verse of Revelation, but it was only *74.* He felt lucky until he saw a peculiar lit sign hanging over the cube of the woman who had directed him to sit.

NOW SERVING NUMBER 02

Sabbath was about to bark out an order, but recalled where he was in more ways than one—this was either some form of metaphysical trap or trick contrived by God or Abathar or perhaps Satan himself, or it truly was the twenty-first century, and shouting *You there, woman! Attend me now!* would not do. Further, she was extremely large in her own right. If it were to come to a fight . . . no, he could not strike a woman down, not even for the Lord.

So he took a seat and kept his eyes on the woman, but she did not look at him again. Sabbath's mind cleared, which was a relief. The nagging questions and concerns about his quest, the state of his soul, the intriguing possibilities of a few more sinful dalliances with Jennifer, all left him. The chair in which he sat was not designed to be comfortable, but for a man used to wood and stone and only occasionally a rug, it was a delight. The basement was warm, like the sweet spot neither too near nor too far from the fire. Sabbath's limbs grew heavy, as did his eyelids, and indeed, he would have fallen into a long sleep but for . . .

The clicking.

The woman had begun to click the button of the retractable pen in her hand. *Click. Click. Click.* She stared emptily at her computer monitor and clicked the pen slowly, like it was the beat of a sleeping babe's heart. It was exactly wrong somehow, and plucked at the back of Sabbath's neck.

"Woman," he said, but she did not seem to hear him.

Louder, he said, "Woman! I am number seventy-four, but I am the only one here! I would see your captain now, and have words with him."

She just looked at him, then put down her pen.

"That sign!" Sabbath said. "Why does it not move, as signs in this age often do? When will it read 'Now serving three,' much less number seventy-four?"

The woman shuffled some papers on her desk. "It is," she said finally, "what it is." What that *it* was, was a battle of wills, Sabbath understood. He stood up and drew his sword to no reaction from either the woman or any of her fellow workers. He sat back down, placed the point of the sword against the tiles of the floor, and slowly *scraaaaped* it till his arm was fully extended.

That got the attention of the woman, who glared at him, and several others, whose heads peeked out over the top edges of their cubicles like men stationed behind the crenellations of a castle under siege.

Sabbath smiled and drew the sword back to him, pressing its tip even harder against the tiles. The scratching sound echoed throughout the basement chamber, and made Sabbath's marrow quake in his bones, but he had the woman's attention.

"Sir," she said. "Someone will be with you soon."

"Who? You?"

"No," the woman said.

The woman inhaled deeply, like a horse about to charge, and clicked her pen again. It sounded like a mallet splitting open a Danish skull. Sabbath dragged his sword against the floor as though it were scoring an enemy's rib cage.

"Sir, please be still," the woman said. "Someone will be with you soon. We are all very busy."

"Busy doing *what*?!" Sabbath demanded.

"We are confirming signatures, if you must know. Do you know how many times a day one must sign one's name in this society? With almost every purchase, with nearly every financial transaction. Do you think nobody double-checks them?"

Abathar's wisdom whispered to Sabbath that, indeed, nobody double-checked the many signatures men and women scribbled out to buy and sell in this odd new world. Nobody human did, anyway. "Check this signature, then, madam," Sabbath said. He planted both hands on the sword's grip and scratched his name into the tiles, signing the floor with a mad flourish. It sounded as if every kestrel in England had been struck down by a single hunter's arrow at once.

In a flash he arose and with a warrior's cry lifted his sword high over his head. He rushed the woman but at the last moment turned on his heel and swung a wide arc, slicing open the red canister. Paper tickets flew everywhere and fluttered to the ground. Sabbath fell to his knees and scrambled to collect as many slips of paper as could fit in his wide hands, discarding some at a glance only to snatch up others.

"Huzzah!" he cried finally. "A two! I am number two!"

He spun back toward the woman, the ticket outstretched in his left hand as he reclaimed and resheathed the sword with his right. "I'll see your leader now, I swear it."

"Number two," said the woman. "Number two, you just committed a felony." She yanked the ticket from his hand and tore it to pieces, then deposited them into a wastebasket in her cubicle. "You're going to sit back down. You're going to wait for the police to arrive. They are going to arrest you, book you, hold you until a judge is available to arraign you. That might take a few hours; it might take a few days. And then, if they decide to release you on your own recognizance, which given the looks of you, is a lot less likely to happen than a seventy-two-hour stay in a rubber room in Bellevue, you can come back here, and if we happen to have replaced the machine by then, and if it's not a federal, state, or municipal holiday and this office is open, you could come here, wait in line, take another number . . .

"And wait," she said.

"So go and wait," she said. "Number two, you go and wait."

Her lips were flecked with spittle. She licked them clean with an ophidian tongue, black and forked. She was no woman.

Sabbath drew his sword and pushed it through the flimsy board of the cubicle wall. The woman opened her mouth again, but instead of a rant, out came blood, blacker than Sabbath had ever seen. She slumped forward, challenging his grip and wrist with her weight, then growled as her eyes flickered. "You . . . won't . . . win . . . sinner—"

The thump from her falling backwards onto the floor

only partially drowned out the sound of applause coming from behind him.

"Sabbath comma Hexen," said Sloth, who was standing in the open doorway of his office. "I've been expecting you, and you have not disappointed me. Perhaps you have disappointed someone else. Come in, take a load off, we'll have a chat about your future. . . ." He yawned and turned to shuffle back into his office, beckoning for Sabbath to follow.

The office was simply appointed, though compared to the cubicles, it was luxurious, with a large metal desk, an assortment of bookshelves largely empty of books, and, best of all, a buttery brown leather couch large enough for a man to sleep on. Sloth himself was no warrior; he was a round little fellow, bald except for a Bundt cake of hair ringing the back of his head. His suit was threadbare, and tie done up rather too casually. Abathar would most likely send such a man to Hades on general principles, but this was no man. Sloth radiated an aura of unearned ease just by sitting back in his Aeron chair and smiling a greeting at Sabbath.

Sabbath let his sword arm hang, and gratefully sat on the couch opposite Sloth's empty desk. He wanted to lie down on it, but knew he must not. It was just so . . . inviting somehow.

"Oh Lord," Sloth said, his voice slow and syrupy. "Meetings, meetings. It never ends, eh?"

Sabbath's eyes had been drooping, but one opened wide now. "A . . . sin, calling upon the Lord. You risk much," Sabbath said.

Sloth shrugged with his whole body, undulating like a jelly. "You might say we dare all, but I will tell you that we don't dare much. And you have no right to rebuke me, killer."

"She wasn't real; she was a thing of dark spirit," said Sabbath. "Her blood was black."

"It's the thought that counts," said Sloth. "Or do you mean to tell me that you wouldn't have killed her even if she had been a human being?"

"The end of the world," Sabbath said. "Judgment Day. Fires like the sun itself, in the hands of man—"

"Very dramatic. But I know your type—they don't send monks or eunuchs against us, Mr. Sabbath," Sloth said. "Oh, may I call you Mr. Sabbath? I do like your name. It is the day of rest, after all. It is my day."

"You may call me Sir Hexen. Do not besmirch the name Sabbath. It belongs to the Lord."

Sloth snorted. "It *did* belong to the Lord. Now it belongs to football games, to putting off chores for one more week, to lazing about the house. No, no Sabbath, Sunday belongs to me. Indeed, when you were alive, in your own time, you and I spent quite a fair number of Sundays together. Not much of a churchgoer for a knight and a Christian, were you?"

"I served Christ in my own way," Sabbath said, ". . . my own way." He tried to stifle a yawn, but could not.

Sloth nodded. "Indeed, you did. Blindly at times. Blindly now." Sloth stretched and unleashed a yawn of his own. "Tell me, what was one thousand years blasted by the fire of God's love actually like, as an experience?"

"I . . ." He could not remember, except that it was unpleasant. "I have no words."

"That's your mind refusing to let you relive the experience. The human brain isn't designed to experience more than a lifetime of memories. You've had ten times that, nearly all in torment and darkness. The Lord had no mercy on you, despite your many murders on his behalf."

Sabbath blinked hard and struggled to open his eyes. "But now . . . I have a chance . . ."

"Oh, you do? Think, Sabbath, think. What did the angel tell you? That once every seven hundred seventy-seven years, my colleagues and I get together to end the world. And yet, how long were you . . . indisposed?"

"One—" He yawned. "—thousand."

"That's right. Do you understand?"

Sabbath shook his head, then rested it in his arm and nestled against the armrest of the couch.

"I'll spell it out for you. In the thousand years of your punishment, we sins had come together, and, sad to say, we were put down. By someone else, someone who wasn't you. Or perhaps I should say who *isn't* you. You see, if you could be plucked out of time at any point, why did the Lord not give you a break and send you against us then? Do you even know what a nuclear warhead looks like? What it can truly do? Do you know how close the world has been to the brink of total nuclear annihilation already?"

Sabbath muttered, "No . . . no, I . . . I don't." He rubbed his eyes and yawned again, not bothering to cover his mouth. "I asked Abath . . ." His exhaustion slackened his jaw. He couldn't speak. His chin rested on the top of his chest. His eyes were slits. He could listen, though, listen to the voice that soothed no matter what it said.

"It's easy, so easy. The missiles are guided by men, and they are detected by men, despite all the technological wonders in this era. All I need to do is put a few Russian radar operators to sleep, and the great cities of that nation will be nothing but steaming slag. It would hardly matter, though, as the Russian nukes are far from the urban areas. Those lads will be awake and plenty ready to reduce Manhattan to a cinder floating in the boiling waters of the Eastern Seaboard."

"Hurh . . . whu . . . ," Sabbath said, his tongue heavy. Water, yes. The water was always so restful.

"No, you don't understand at all. For you, a catapult sending a mass of flaming peat over a castle wall would have been a weapon of mass destruction. Why would the Lord send you to face me now, when he could have sent you seven hundred and seventy-seven years ago? When the world would have made more sense to you, when you wouldn't be so . . . at sea."

Sabbath snorted. Sloth's voice sounded far away. He thought of the sea, his beard salty and wet, his body buoyant and relaxed.

"For that matter, he could have spared you all the travail you've faced so far, simply by allowing his former champion to contend against us again. That warrior already has a record of success against us seven sins.

"Think of it, Sabbath. Why are you here? Why is the Lord God making *you* work so hard on his behalf? For longer than a lifetime, after a thousand years of endless discomfort and pain, he calls upon you again to serve him like chattel. He could have let you sleep." Sloth was up now, toddling around his desk toward the couch. Sabbath snored loudly. Sloth gingerly removed the sword from the man's grasp. Sabbath dreamed of the sea, of the black waves of Whitby.

"The Lord God," Sloth said, hefting the sword with a grunt and a momentary loss of balance, then placing the tip of it against Sabbath's heart, "should have let you rest in peace. But never fear, dear warrior. I will be the one to do it.

"May every day be your Sabbath, Sabbath. Rest in peace." Sloth leaned against the sword, pressing his sternum to the pommel, and Sabbath grunted under the pressure. In his dream, something cut toward him, slicing through the water.

"Hmm, the point of this blade," Sloth said, "seems blunted." He sighed dramatically. "I'd best redouble my efforts. . . ." Sloth straightened up, rolled his shoulders, inhaled, and—

Sabbath's eyes flew open. "Aaarrrgh!" he bellowed. Like the shark he had dreamed of, Sabbath reared up, mouth wide, body thrashing. Sloth tumbled backwards, the sword unbalancing him. He tried to lift it to defend himself, but Sabbath grabbed the sin's elbow and wrist, and wrenched Sloth's arm nearly from its socket. The sword fell to the floor, where it landed quietly on the soft carpet. Sabbath dived for the sword, and was up and facing Sloth before the sin even had the chance to react.

"No, wait!" Sloth said. "You don't understand. Take it—"

Sloth's head hit the floor wetly, his portly body following a moment later.

"Easy," Sabbath said.

It was easy, Sabbath thought. *Too easy, in a way, but I could not have succeeded without Abathar. . . .* The workers hadn't barricaded him in the office, nor had they formed a troop to contend against him when he exited the office, though he was soaked in the blood of Sloth and carrying the sin's head like a parcel in the crook of his right arm. They all just stayed in their cubes and raised their heads, like contented, only half-curious pigs in a sty.

"Devils," he said. "Look at you all. I have your man here." He held the head aloft. Black blood spilled from the base of the neck like coffee from an overturned mug. "He sought to beguile me, lull me to sleep. He thought he could stay me from my holy task. What is sloth, after all, but the sin of omission, of dejection, of refusing to do what one must?" They all peered at him silently. "What Sloth did not understand is that though I had often shirked my duties, or gave myself to the simple pleasures—"

Someone in the back yawned.

"—the blade is my greatest pleasure."

With a shrug, Sabbath slipped the duffel bag off his shoulder and onto the floor. He dropped Sloth's head in, took a moment to zip the bag up, then drew his sword as he stood.

"My greatest pleasure," said Sabbath, "though I am afraid

a few of you I'll have to leave . . . clean. My sword has a blunt pommel, perfect when a bludgeoning will have to do. You see, I need your clothes. The garments I'm wearing are stained."

4

Then when lust hath conceived, it bringeth forth sin: and sin, when it is finished, bringeth forth death.

—JAMES 1:15

"You killed a woman," Jennifer said. "She yelled at you and you stabbed her with a sword I procured for you?" Her voice was even, but on the verge of cracking. "Is her—?" She glanced down at the bag at Sabbath's feet.

"No, just his." They were standing in Jennifer's studio apartment, situated directly over the Above Below Arts gallery. Between the two of them and the sword and bag, there was hardly enough room for anything else. It was a single room dominated by an ancient claw-foot bathtub on one end, and a futon couch against a wall. No kitchen area at all, save for a shelf of dry goods and a hot plate atop a pillar of cinder blocks. "She was not a woman. She was a black-blooded devil. They all were."

"The cops are going to find the bodies, Hexen!" Jennifer cried out. She clamped her hand over her own mouth, then hissed through her fingers more quietly, "Surveillance cameras—they'll track you here, surround the place. We bought a sword; they were hacked to death with a sword two hours later. These were people, weren't they? They didn't just show up yesterday, fully grown, did they?"

"What do you mean?"

"I mean, they're not like you!" Jennifer's hands were balled into fists. "You just dropped into town, naked and crazy, but if this 'Sloth'—" Her hands went up, her fingers flicked quotation marks in the air, then made fists again, which she shook. "—worked for the city, that means he was on payroll. He had identification, a pension, a Social Security number. He was a person, with parents, and maybe a wife or husband—"

"Husband?" Sabbath laughed.

"Yes!"

"Oh, I see . . ."

"And they'll want to know where his head is! And it's here, in my fucking three-thousand-dollar-a-month illegal apartment!"

"Draw me a bath," said Sabbath. He wore an ill-fitting button-down shirt and too-tight khakis, but there was plenty of ichor in his hair and beard, and even staining his ears.

"Do it yourself, and then go!" Jennifer said. "Take your costume with you. I'd throw it in the river or find an incinerator if I were you. Dispose of the evidence." There was a small flat-screen TV on one wall of exposed brick, its brace screwed into the mortar. Jennifer snatched up the remote and turned it on. "Thin walls," she said as she cranked up the volume on some home-improvement program. She stomped on the floor, and it echoed. "Thin floors too. I'm literally not allowed to have any bookcases." Sabbath fiddled with the knobs, stopped up the drain, and stripped as the tub filled.

"You're actually taking a bath and not a shower?" Jennifer asked. Sabbath said nothing as he eased himself into the water. He closed his eyes, sighed deeply, and placed his tattooed arm on the rim of the tub.

"They didn't fight back," said Sabbath. "They stood up as one, then fed themselves to the sword. The first few I eagerly struck down. I suspected some sort of trick, and they were devils. I couldn't let them live. But . . ."

"But?"

"They lined up for it, like docile sheep, but with foreknowledge of their fates. They didn't raise a hand against me, not even one. I was nearly pushed out from their room as they crowded me, almost eager to be split open. I cleaned my blade as best I could with some scrap of clean clothing I pulled from the back of one of them. There was no sport to it, and no purpose . . ."

"You feel sympathy for them now?" asked Jennifer.

"I feel sympathy for myself," said Sabbath. "They were devils, using me to return to Hell."

"Well, I hope they just vanished or something after you left," Jennifer said. "To cover their tracks."

"The sins endeavor to end the world in six days. Why would they care about their 'tracks'?" Sabbath asked.

"They could be found out, arrested by the police, maybe even gunned down, or . . ." Jennifer trailed off. "Well, I guess that would have happened by now were it going to happen, huh? It really has to be you, doesn't it? Nobody else, no assistants or sidekicks?"

Sabbath didn't answer. He was asleep. His tattoo was still active, the glowing lights—now only six—pulsed on the map of Manhattan and the outer boroughs. Jennifer turned down the volume on the television, took out her smartphone, aimed it at Sabbath's arm, and began to record video. . . .

"Bagels are wondrous," declared Hexen Sabbath between bites.

"They *are,*" said Jennifer. "Brunch in general is wondrous. Brunch and the smartphone are the two great innovations of the modern world, Hexen." Jennifer had her phone in her hands, and aimed its camera lens at the vegan eggs Benedict before her. "I'm glad you're open to new experiences. I mean, what did you eat for breakfast, back in the day? Just eggs?"

Sabbath snorted. "At times. When we could get them from the peasants. Barely bread, and when on a feast day, white bread like this." He brandished the remnant of his bagel. "But not with creamed cheese!"

"Cream cheese," said Jennifer.

Sabbath ignored her correction and continued. "Cabbage and beets, occasionally a bird. It was good to be a knight. You, my dear, are eating like a very eccentric queen," he said. "As are all of these people."

"It's a very Instagrammable breakfast, that's for sure," she said.

"I've noticed several people waving their phones at their plates," Sabbath said.

"It's all about social media these days . . . uh, do you know what that is?" Jennifer asked.

Sabbath looked thoughtful for a moment, his gaze directed at a corner of the ceiling, and then he grunted.

"I need to get more active on Instagram and Ello. The Above Below needs exposure, buzz. So I'm trying to send out more lifestyle pictures to get people interested."

"Buzz," Sabbath repeated; then he pushed the rest of his bagel into his mouth, as if no longer interested in talking. "Are you sending out pictures of your faux eggs because the paintings in your gallery are all plain white canvases?"

"Yes," said Jennifer. She looked up from the screen to glare at Sabbath. If he understood the look, he ignored what it meant.

"An image of your breakfast will sell your white paintings?"

"The *Ylem* exhibit opens to the public Saturday night. I've not been getting many pre-public appointments, so I need to make a splash. I hope you'll be able to . . ." She frowned.

Where would Hexen Sabbath be Saturday night? Dead? In prison? Slicing somebody's head off? Jennifer's face changed as if suddenly sick. She gulped hard and put a hand to her stomach.

"Jennifer?" Sabbath asked. "Are you all right?"

"I'm fine. It's just so strange. So hard to believe . . ."

"What is?"

Jennifer wasn't a very good liar. She said, "That a week from now, there might be nuclear missiles just over the horizon. . . . I just hope you'll be free to attend the opening."

"Don't be concerned. I stand between this world and that fate. I will not falter."

"You're on a mission from God," she said.

"That I am."

Jennifer frowned. "It's from a movie. You know, *The Blues Brothers*?"

Sabbath shrugged expansively. "I'm familiar with the . . . idea of movies more than any particular ones."

"I'll have to show you how the TV works when we get back to the apartment," she said. She tapped away on her phone, finding the video she took the previous night and uploading it to Instagram.

> GALLERYGRRL86:
> CAN ANYONE TELL ME HOW THIS WORKS?
> #TATTOO #TATTOOSOFINSTAGRAM #INKSPIRATION
> #INKSPIRINGTATTOOS #BUTISITART #CYBORG

Jennifer slipped the phone back into her purse, and was almost entirely unaware that it began to buzz as the video was liked, commented on, downloaded, and shared across multiple social media platforms.

"Do you eat so well every morn, Jennifer?" Sabbath asked.

"Brunch is usually a weekend thing," Jennifer said. She faltered again, then blurted out, "Maybe next weekend, on Sunday, uh . . . after church if you need to go . . . we can try dim sum. Don't zone out on me again, Hexen, I'll just tell you that it's Chinese—bite-sized savory pastries and dumplings and whatnot. Some with meat, some vegetarian."

"Let's go after this," Sabbath said.

"You can't still be hungry. You've had four bag—"

Sabbath presented his forearm. "Is the dim sum close?"

"Well, there's more than one choice, but most of the dim sum places I like are . . ." She traced a circle on his flesh with her fingernail, and one of the six glowing dots traveled over her knuckle. "Uhm . . ."

Sabbath met her gaze. "Is there another place to which I can return after I meet this foe?"

"Yeah, there's still a no-tell motel in the Meatpacking District," Jennifer said.

Sabbath slipped into that trancelike expression again for a moment, then came out of it with a wide smile on his face.

"Yeah," said Jennifer. "I'll write down the address."

"So, Jennifer, how are you familiar with this establishment?"

"Hexen, in this town, the choices are an apartment so small that sex means your guest is having a good time in the hallway, or splitting an apartment with five roommates. So sometimes a girl's gotta do what a girl's gotta do, especially if her boyfriend is married and writes for *Artforum*." Then she added, "Ex-boyfriend. It was a long time ago. Thus, it's back to social media for promoting the gallery for me."

Sabbath had been looking down at his arm as Jennifer spoke, and he didn't raise his head now. "I have a sense of what sin I face next. . . ."

"Which is it?" Jennifer asked.

"I'd rather not say." He collected his duffel and his coat and left without another word.

Sabbath was learning the city. This time he wasn't amazed when English vanished from the signs and the pictographs of Chinese asserted themselves on storefronts, billboards, and even street signs. Perhaps the tattoo Abathar had gifted him had something to do with it. He strode into Chinatown like a long-term resident, brushing past more than one bemused tourist consulting a phone or unfolded paper map on his way to the Red Lantern Massage and Health Institute. He wasn't sure if he was dressed properly—under the big coat he wore a T-shirt featuring John Lennon wearing a T-shirt that read NEW YORK CITY, something Jennifer had dismissively referred to as *jorts,* and a pair of sandals, all of which the girl had purchased for him with the few dollars she had. "It's better to look a little ridiculous when you're walking around downtown," she had said, and then she tugged his beard.

In the waiting area, Sabbath was chagrined to discover he was the only man not in a button-down shirt and necktie. All the other patrons had decided to dress a bit like Abathar had. An older woman sat behind a window carved into the far wall, and waved for him to approach her. A room within a room; he'd never seen a thing like it. He touched the lintel curiously as she frowned up at him.

"Name?"

"Hexen Sabbath," he said.

"Hmph." She wrote down something, but it wasn't anything he could read. "Half hour or one hour. Fifty dollars for half hour, seventy-five for one hour."

Money, Sabbath fumed. He'd had a fairly solid idea as to what sin he was to confront, but he didn't expect to have to pay. Wasn't Lust insatiable, always eager to consume? Perhaps he had misunderstood the map and was to deal with Greed, or perhaps this personification lusted for money. But if so, fifty dollars didn't sound like a lot, except that it was a lot more than Sabbath had.

"I'll pay after receiving the massage," he declared. "After all, what if I am not satisfied?"

"If you're not satisfied, that would be your own fault."

Briefly he considered withdrawing his sword and running the woman through, as he had done in the cubicle farm the night before. He was reasonably sure that this receptionist was also a demon, would also spill tar-black blood, but the other men in the waiting room were likely mortal. He would have to be stealthy to avoid the police.

"Buddy, just pay up!" said one of the men. He didn't even look up from his phone. Sabbath turned to him, grabbed one of the lapels of his suit jacket, and yanked him out of the chair.

"Buddy, you say! The one paying here shall be you!" he bellowed in the man's face. Sabbath was a few inches shorter, but his grip was iron, and the fellow could only squirm, shocked, until a velvety, feminine voice interrupted.

"Gentlemen." She was the agglomeration of what men imagined. Tall with thin limbs that moved like swaying branches, wearing a dress with a neckline that went down to her navel, and that showed off a pair of breasts that defied physics. Long black hair framing a pale narrow-eyed face and Cupid's bow lip. A gaze that made the rest of the universe fall away—it was just you and her, forever and ever.

She walked forward and rested her hand on Sabbath's shoulder. Almost against his will, he loosened his grip on the man he'd been accosting. He didn't worry, even for a moment, that he'd have to duck or eat a punch in response. The man had eyes only for the woman between them. If Sabbath was enamored, this mortal was enslaved.

"You're an eager old goat," she said. Sabbath's heart pounded in his chest. She was talking to him. Not to any of the modern men in their suits and ties in the antechamber, to him!

"Two out of three," he managed to mumble in response.

"Come with me," she said. "I am the owner of this establishment, and a mistress of all the arts of sensual administration. Normally, I work only with my regulars, men and women and others with whom I've cultivated extensive relationships built on mutual trust, affection, and generosity." She touched his jaw with a feather-light finger and traced a line down and then back up it, as though drawing a smile even wider than the one Sabbath was wearing now. "For you, I'll make an exception. Follow me."

The woman led Sabbath down a narrow hallway punctuated by a large number of doors, which he mostly ignored as his gaze was drawn to the sway of her hips, the curve of her ass. The woman's room was in the far corner, and with a smile she opened it and ushered Sabbath into a significant suite of rooms. The theme was chinoiserie and Marquis de Sade: flowers and birds on the wallpaper, chaises longues with cuffs built into their legs, and a rack placed next to them for convenient observation and manipulation of whoever might end up being hung from there. Smaller racks nailed to the far walls held floggers, paddles, lengths of rope, penetrative sex toys, peacock feathers, and other implements Sabbath could only imagine were used for sparring practice.

"This way," the woman said, leading him into the suite's bedroom, with its gigantic four-poster bed and an array of pulleys and winches descending from the ceiling.

"A true temple to the spirit of lust," Sabbath said in awe. He barely felt the weight of his duffel bag leaving his shoulder, almost didn't hear the sound of a heavy wardrobe door opening, then closing, and then being locked.

"Indeed," said the woman, her tongue licking Sabbath's ear. "A temple worthy of you."

"I am here to kill you . . . ," Sabbath said, "but . . ."

"Not yet."

"Yes, not yet," said Sabbath.

"Tell me, do you have a wife, a girlfriend?"

"Of course not," said Sabbath, an image of Jennifer nothing but a fleeting wisp that melted in the heat of his mind. The woman drew her long fingernails across his chest, then sank to her knees before him, her grip finding his crotch. She freed his cock from its restraints professionally, almost clinically, then swallowed him whole, her nose buried in his pubic hair, her hands clutching his meaty thighs.

"Fuck yes," Sabbath growled to himself, his mission forgotten. He took two fistfuls of her hair and started to thrust into her mouth. Somewhere deep within, Sabbath recalled Abathar, and the angel's claim that Sabbath would be immune from the influence of the sins he faced. And Abathar was right—Sabbath could stop at any time he wanted, and twist Lust's head from her neck. He just didn't want to, not yet. He'd save the world in a few minutes. Even a savior had needs.

Lust's fingers snaked their way around to Sabbath's rear, entered him, and pressed hard against . . . something. Everything went black.

When Sabbath regained consciousness, the woman was under him, her body a miracle of curves and lines. Too far below him. He was hanging from the ceiling, his wrists and ankles bound to thick cuffs, and he was . . . spent, dripping sweat onto the woman on the bed. She smiled at him.

"Lust!" he cried.

"Hmm?"

"Foul demon of lust!" Sabbath said, testing his bonds. The chains clinked and he swayed, but the cuffs, and ceiling, held.

The woman twisted up her face, bemused. "I'm not Lust. *You're* Lust!" Suddenly, she was on her knees, and with her right hand she reached up, took Sabbath in hand, and squeezed. "You!"

Sabbath clenched his teeth and screamed through them, sounding more like pig than man.

"You are the lecherous old goat! How many women have been under you experiencing no pleasure at all, even as you found your own release? How many whores? How many peasants did you make whores by sprinkling a few coins around their bodies as they slept off your attentions?"

Sabbath exhaled deeply when she let go of him. The woman snatched up a red lace pantie from the hardwood floor, balled it in her fingers, and shoved it up his throat. Then she slid off the bed and began to pace the room.

"I usually wear a thong. Men are titillated, though even housewives wear them now. For you I selected lace boy shorts, just so I could have fabric enough to gag you, Hexen Sabbath." She glanced over her shoulder and looked up at him. "We already know everything about you that there is to know."

Sabbath said something desperate and angry into the gag. In response, she snatched up a riding crop from the nightstand and with a wicked overhand swing smacked him between the legs with it. He howled for a long time.

"That's exactly the sort of noises I don't wish to hear," she explained when he was done. "You are going to listen to what I have to say, O Demon of Lust."

The woman sat on the corner of her bed, twirling the crop slowly between her fingers. She crossed her legs and peered off into the middle distance, not looking up at Sabbath even when his twisting and pulling made the chains clank, made the ceiling creak.

"The seven deadly sins," she said, more to herself than anyone else. "Obviously conceptualized by a man. Look at this. . . ." She ran her free hand over her face, her neck, her breasts, and down below. "Why is Lust a woman? It's the men of this species who are lustful. Lustful for cunt, for money, for power. And what a mess they have made of this planet from their lusts. All male endeavor, from war to art to the idiot lie of romantic love, are all fueled by lust. Every man wants a harem of women—or men, or a sampler plate of both and those in between—who are entirely devoted to him and repulsed by every other body in the world . . . unless the man wants to see the occasional show. Monogamy and marriage are just the end result of iterated prisoner's dilemma games." She glanced up at Sabbath, waggled the crop at him. "Men always think women are stupid, but you're the stupid one, you disgusting pig. See how easily you were defeated?"

She leaned back onto the bed, arching her back, luxuriating, writhing, and slipping her whole body onto the mattress. She peered up at Sabbath, her prized and mounted prey. "We should have done this long ago. I don't mean the Seven of us. I mean women. Find the worst of you lot, give you what you think you want, and then imprison you, and kill you. Had women a sense of sisterhood, instead of endlessly competing against one another for cock—or for cunt, for that matter—it wouldn't have had to come to this, Hexen Sabbath."

Sabbath found a sharp-edged tooth, one chipped long ago, and with his tongue started worrying the lace of the gag against it.

"I'll need to shower soon. There's a presidential debate tomorrow. We're backing a candidate, and as far as the other candidate, well . . . that candidate and I will be making the beast with two backs." She put a finger to her chin and added contemplatively, "I'll have to pack a strap-on harness. And do my makeup. I'll be all over the internet by Wednesday midnight. Our candidate will be the only one to show up at their assigned lectern. The other will be rather embroiled in scandal. . . . Her opponents often smeared her as a lesbian." She shrugged. "All men are lustful goats, rutting beasts, but women certainly don't mind giving in to their passions now and again."

Sabbath quietly chewed through the pantie as the woman continued her speech. "You have come to the wrong place if you wish to challenge Lust, fool. You should be battering down the doors of the halls of power, or even the humble apartments these animals live in. How many women had their lives ruined by the lusts of men? You see us as nothing but slaves and incubators, and then tell us the great lie—that we women are some unfathomable mystery that only art and culture can plumb. Lust is an ugly emotion that hides like a dark worm within the apple of beauty."

She reached over to the nightstand, upsetting a small bottle of personal lubricant to collect her phone. "It seems silly to take a photo of you all trussed up and suspended, Hexen Sabbath, as in six days' time there will be nobody left to enjoy it, but I do like to please my social media followers with unusual photos. I'm not the only one with such a diverting and illuminating hobby. In fact—"

Putuaah! Sabbath spat the pantie from his mouth. "Silence, woman! Your mouth was made to service my cock, not propound some philosophy!"

It was a risk Sabbath had to take. When you throw a right-hand punch with someone, they'll tend to throw a right back. Call them a jackass, and they'll respond, *You're the jackass!* This Sabbath knew well. He hoped that disparaging

Lust's mouth would bring her fury toward destroying his mouth, and not another vital part.

In less time than it took for Sabbath to think, the woman was up on the bed, the long-nailed fingers that had just so recently been leaving a cross-hatching of scratches along his back slashing at his face. He jerked his head, found the flesh between her thumb and forefinger with his teeth, and clenched as hard as he could. She screamed like a cat being skinned alive and flailed at him with her left hand. Sabbath began to grind his jaw, teeth working through muscle and tendon to find teeth.

The door flew open. The receptionist filled the doorway, a shotgun in hand. She leveled it at Sabbath.

"No!" Lust screamed. "You'll kill us both with that! I need this body!"

The receptionist raised the gun a bit higher, then pulled the trigger. A roar filled the room.

Jennifer was about to make a joke about *Men in Black—Just a little bit early, and ten years too late for Halloween, eh, boys?*— when she realized that the two men, one black and one white, standing outside the Above Below Arts as she walked up to the door weren't cosplaying. The black suits were just a bit rumpled, and the men older, and haggard—like uglier versions of television secret agents: cheaper sunglasses, larger earbuds, receding hairlines. They smelled like coffee and impatience.

"Evgenia Zelenova," one of them said. It was a question in the form of a statement.

"You can call me Jennifer," she said. "I own this gallery. What's up?"

The man who had spoken turned to his partner. "She says she owns this gallery." The partner shrugged. "Operative word being 'gallery,' I guess." Then he turned to Jennifer. "You can go in; he's waiting for you." He unlocked the door with a key Jennifer had never seen before.

He filled the narrow gallery space. It took a long moment before Jennifer even realized that there was another suited man at her desk, and a fourth poking around the kitchenette with a cup of coffee, because *his* aura consumed just that much space.

"What are *you* doing here?" she managed to choke out. It was just a few weeks ago, over drinks with friends, that a tipsy Jennifer had promised to give Thomas Aldridge a piece of her mind should she ever run into him on the streets, but now that he was standing before her, all she could express was confusion and disbelief. "Shouldn't you be, uh . . ."

"I'm in town for the great debate," he said. "Back in town. This is my town, you know."

"I know," she said, quiet now.

"This is my town," he repeated. He walked toward her, or at least in her direction, as he took in the paintings on the walls. "This is a nice space. Up-and-coming location. How can you afford it?"

"It's been rough," she said. She thought about asking Aldridge for a loan—or, hell, a gift. He'd probably demand a blow job or something. The Secret Service agents could be trusted to be circumspect. They'd worked for Kennedy and

Clinton, after all. Maybe she could snatch his balls bald, and change the course of history. . . .

"Real rough," he said. Then he changed the subject. "Do you follow me on social media?"

"Uh . . ." She didn't have to. Everyone was constantly passing around his social media messages. It was nightly news, fodder for late-night comedians and barstool rants. Her useless uncle Vitaly sent them along on a family-wide email chain. There was no way to escape his social media presence. *Say something, say something,* Jennifer commanded herself. *Tell this asshole off!*

"I don't follow you either," he said. "But my daughter, she likes art. It's a good hedge in a volatile market, she says. And she likes going to parties. I used to go to parties all the time. But she still likes parties, and art. I don't understand half of her collection, really. I like pretty pictures."

"Well, there aren't any here," she said.

He nodded, his jowls nearly alive. "No kiddin', sweet cheeks."

The blood rushed to Jennifer's face. "Y-you need to leave!"

He took a step forward, his finger in her face. "No, I don't need to leave. You know why? I bought this building. You're standing on my floor, in my building, on my block. I've got big plans for this area. Big!"

"I have a lease. . . ."

"You have a lease," he said, nodding again. "You have a lease that says I can evict you in seventy-two hours if you're more than three months behind on your rent."

"I'll have to check my copy to confirm that," Jennifer said. She could count to three, though—she hadn't paid

October's, nor September's, nor August's, but it was still October. Wouldn't he have to wait until the first of November to throw her out? "This show opens in a few days. You'll have your rent then, after we sell the pieces."

"You're going to sell these?" he asked, gesturing at the canvases. "I can buy a thousand just like them for a tenth of the price at Soho Art Materials right now." He turned to the agent sitting at Jennifer's desk. "Hey, Lou, can we get the Secret Service van to go down to SoHo?"

"No," said the man. "And I'm Mario."

"I'm Lou," said the man standing near the kitchenette.

"Can you believe these guys," Aldridge said as he leaned in close to Jennifer, taking a conspiratorial tone. "Whoever heard of a black guy with a name like Mario?"

"Uhm . . . Mario Van Peebles . . . ," Jennifer said.

"Mario Cooper, the former deputy director of the DNC," said Lou. "He was on Bill Clinton's first campaign; Bubba was one of my protectees."

"There was that singer, Mario. . . . He's black," said Jennifer. "He was in a movie too."

"It's common," said Mario, his voice hard. "It's a common name among African American men."

Aldridge waved the entire conversation away; it was of no concern. "Let me give you a lesson in business, Jenny. When you want to make a deal, you need something to offer. I can offer you something—like forgiveness for arrears and a long-term lease with a rent of zero. Zero point zero zero. And what can you give me?"

"Uh . . ." Jennifer was tempted to offer her spit, in his face, but she found that her mouth was dry.

"Not blank canvas paintings. Not these," he said.

Jennifer found herself nodding.

"But like I said, social media. My daughter, she loves social media. She saw something very interesting before." He waved one of the Secret Service agents over. "Mario, come here." Lou stepped forward and withdrew a phone from his pocket.

"Where is this image from, ma'am?" Lou asked Jennifer. The phone's screen showed her own Insta post of Hexen Sabbath's tattoo.

"Do I need a lawyer?" Jennifer asked, regretting that she asked before she even finished.

Lou shrugged.

"There's nothing illegal about posting to the internet, honey. I just want to know where this came from."

"We already know where it came from," Lou explained. "We are the federal government."

"I get all the intelligence briefings, anything I want," said Aldridge. "Like I got this building. And what I want now is to meet the man with the magic arm." He pointed to the screen.

At that, Jennifer smiled. "I bet you would. He'd like to meet you too." An angel who weighs the souls of men and finds them wanting, that's what Sabbath had said. She could use an angel now herself.

"So, bring him here, and I'll meet him, and then we can talk about your lease," he said. "And if he's not available, maybe the guy whose arm it is? He looks like he'd have a powerful handshake. I'd like to shake his hand—"

"I don't know where he is," Jennifer blurted out. It was

true too, so she hoped it was believable. "I sent him away"—also true—"and for all I know, he's fucking some other girl right now." That was a possibility that stung, even if it too had the ring of truth to it.

"So you fucked him," Aldridge said.

"I didn't say that—"

"You fucked him," he said more forcefully. "You *fucked* him. If you fucked him, you can find him again. He may even come back, sniffing around, himself." He sniffed the air grandly and smiled. "Bring him back here. I'm a very busy man, and have a lot to do this week, but I'll attend your opening. It'll be in all the papers, all over the news. There will be a line around the block, and I guarantee you'll sell out. I just want to meet him, okay?"

"Okay," said Jennifer. *Just leave, just leave!* She was a prisoner, howling in the dungeon of her mind. Twenty-eight years of female training, and she couldn't even bring herself to smile at the man who might be the next President of the United States of America.

The man with the nuclear codes . . .

He continued to smile, though. "Okay, we'll see you Saturday night. Try to dress up a bit; it's going to be big league here with me present. Try to—" He made an hourglass gesture with his hands, framing Jennifer. "—show off what assets you actually have for once."

Jennifer stood like a statue till they left, not even turning around to see them walk out the door. The bile rose in her throat too quickly for her to make it up the steps; she ran for the wastebasket by the reception desk, but vomited a puddle on the floor next to it instead.

Sabbath landed on the bed, hard, with Lust's ribs breaking his fall. Plaster and dust showered them both. The woman with the shotgun cursed and tried to work the lever action. He was free, but still cuffed, with lengths of chain and rope hanging from his wrists and ankles. He scrambled to his feet and shot out an arm, sending the chain like a whip to knock the shotgun to the floor. Lust howled and threw herself onto his back, her strong legs wrapping his torso, her arms snaking around his neck. She had teeth too, and they found his ear. He shouted and flailed, trying to whip her with the chains. The receptionist scrambled for the shotgun and picked it up, but Sabbath turned on his heel, showing his back and using Lust as a shield.

"Shoot his legs!" Lust shouted, spitting Sabbath's blood onto the walls. Sabbath's knees buckled for a moment; then he sprang into the air, smacking into the receptionist and slamming her into the wall. Lust lost her grip. He shook her off and snatched up the shotgun.

"Do you even know how to use that, you idiot ape?" Lust said as she separated herself from the heap of her receptionist. Sabbath peered at her silently, then glanced down at the gun, looked back to her, and then ran for the wardrobe, shotgun held high over his head.

Lust sprang after him. It took only two strong blows from the stock to open the locked doors. She tried to pull the gun away, but Sabbath let go, sending her awkwardly tripping backwards. The sound of the duffel bag unzipping filled Sabbath's good ear, and made him smile. The sword being unsheathed was loud enough for his bad ear.

But he hadn't heard Lust take two steps forward or put the barrel to his head. The lever action being worked got his attention.

"Hexen Sabbath," said Lust. "Do you know how many times over the centuries I've fucked with a mouthful of blood, with bruised and broken ribs, with bruises and marks all over my body? My *many* bodies? Sometimes I even enjoyed it. This changes not one detail of my plan. Tonight I fuck my beloved leader's opponent, and tomorrow the world learns what a whore she is. But first, I blow your head off."

Sabbath kicked Lust in the knee. Her leg bent backwards with a satisfying crunch. She howled and raised the shotgun; he raised his sword and parried the gun away. With a grunt and a popping sound, Lust flexed her thigh and repositioned her knee. She shook her hair out of her face, and her wounds were gone. She inhaled deeply and raised the shotgun. Her head, trailing a stream of black blood, flew across the room, hitting the far wall and leaving a sudden Rorschach test blot on the paint. Sabbath walked over, picked it up by the still silky hair, and carried it over to the duffel bag. The receptionist had the shotgun now, plucked from the hands of her mistress's headless corpse, and she pointed it nervously at Sabbath.

"If I run you through, woman, would you bleed black oil?" he asked her, the point of his blade aimed between her eyes.

She dropped the gun and scrambled amidst the debris

of the room for a piece of broken glass. “No . . . no,” she said, slicing open her palm. She held it up. “See? Red! Red blood! I’m human, like you! Do you see?”

Sabbath wondered if he shouldn’t kill her anyway. She’d be a witness. She clearly was a whoremonger in her own right. The Lord would be pleased, he thought, for her soul to be consigned to Hell. He sighed sharply. He’d had enough killing for now.

“Clean up, and tell nobody what happened here.” He sheathed his blade, put it in the duffel along with the head of Lust, and left.

5

Cease from anger, and forsake wrath: fret not thyself in any wise to do evil.

—Psalms 37:8

Jennifer decided to be rough with Hexen Sabbath's ear as she stitched it together. If he knew that she was purposefully taking her time pulling the needle through the skin, he didn't show it. He didn't thank her either—not for the first aid, not for the tiny motel room she'd paid for in cash, and not for bringing with her yet another change of clothes, and food as well. He sat, chewing gas station beef jerky, but Sabbath was otherwise still and distant, submitting to her ministrations.

"So . . . ," said Jennifer, "she said that men were the lustful ones and were to blame for the world's sins and the oppression of women? And you killed her."

"Yes . . . ow!" Finally, a reaction.

"And you ended up hanging from her ceiling in some sort of bondage contraption how exactly?"

"Well . . . ," Sabbath began. "She was Lust, the incarnation of the passion of the body. Her nails burned like brimstone, her lips like coal."

"So you fucked her."

"I . . ."

"You fucked her, you fucked her!" She was sounding like her new landlord, but she didn't care anymore.

"She . . . fucked me?" Sabbath asked. "With her mouth."

"Oh, her mouth! That's doesn't count, right. What are you, in high school?"

Sabbath had faced hordes of Vikings and trampled on the guts and bones of dead men without blinking, but now, under Jennifer's withering gaze, he cringed. "I was not in control," he said. "I wasn't. These sins, they tempt and manipulate. I'm supposed to be immune, thanks to . . . thanks to . . . Did you say high school? Is that when you—?"

"Thanks to your own debauchery," Jennifer interrupted. "Not hers, yours. You were so debauched that even the spirit of Lust couldn't keep up with your big dick in her mouth, right?"

"Well . . ." That sounded better than what had actually happened. "Yes, ultimately, I was immune," Sabbath said. "I could have been made her slave."

"Ultimately, you were immune, eh?" Jennifer said.

"Yes," Sabbath said.

"Sure you were, sweet cheeks," Jennifer said. She stabbed him again with the needle.

Sabbath made a low rumbling sound in his throat. "Sweet . . . cheeks?"

"Yeah." Jennifer told him much of the story of her encounter with presidential candidate Thomas Aldridge at Above Below Arts, leaving out only that he had seen Sabbath's mystic tattoo on social media, and that he had tasked Jennifer with bringing Sabbath to him.

"What do you mean, 'running for president'?" Sabbath said. "Preposterous!" He frowned as the knowledge of contemporary politics flooded his mind, but something else in his face, his eyes, suggested that he was rejecting it, like bad blood poured into his veins. "A system in which wealthy people just agitate the masses until one becomes ruler . . . and then a few years later, they do it again?"

"And they step down if they lose, yeah. Peaceful transfer of power," Jennifer said.

"But what about stability? How can a nation be guided if there's constant change of power? How can alliances be solidified and sustained without noble families and their interconnections?"

"Whatever, Hexen, the system works," Jennifer said. "Mostly. The president doesn't have all the power anyway. We have a legislature, and an independent legal system, and the states and cities have their own governments, and there are groups like NATO and the United Nations, so presidential power isn't everything."

"What power do presidents even wield, if they surrender it willingly and are not pushed into exile?"

"Heh," Jennifer said. "For one thing . . . the nuclear codes." Maybe she hadn't even meant to say it, but she could tell from their prior conversations about films, condoms, and mass transit that for an eleventh-century man with a magic tattoo, Sabbath knew more than he should.

"He sounds like the sort of man who could find himself entangled in the plans of the seven deadly sins," Sabbath said. Then he smiled. "Five."

Jennifer finished stitching, wrapped the leftover thread

around her finger, and snapped it free from Sabbath's ear. She smiled when he winced. "All right, you're done. You should probably rest a bit. Be careful of the bed; who knows what's happened on those sheets. You might get infected with . . . something, given all the scratches you're sporting."

"You're not staying?" Sabbath said. He reached into the plastic bag at the edge of the bed and pulled out the T-shirt Jennifer had purchased for him: white, large, with the popular I ♥ NEW YORK logo emblazoned across it. "You people really enjoy your own city."

"They're for tourists," Jennifer said. "They're cheap, like this room. And, no, I'm not staying. Look, Hexen, I get it. You're on a weird magical mission and you're chopping off heads and if you chop off enough, God will let you into heaven? I don't know how your tattoo works or how you got your hands on a perfectly preserved Canterbury cross, but you're dangerous and you don't have any respect for me. You just sat here and casually admitted that you had sex with a woman a day after having sex with me, and that you killed her. You also killed another woman—"

"That was a demon!" Sabbath interrupted. "And today, I let a woman go free. She showed me her blood. It was red, it was human."

"Oh good, so the women you kill just happen to be demons or something? But you only fuck the hot ones? What if you decide that I'm a demon?" Jennifer said.

"You're not one," Sabbath said. "I nipped you on the breast during sex, Jennifer. The mark was red. If you were a demon, it would be black. Black blood."

"So, do you plan on just giving every girl you meet a hickey before you decide whether or not to kill them?"

Sabbath held forth his forearm. "I have five more to kill, in as many days. This I will do, to gain a heavenly reward. I'm pleased, Jennifer, that instead of living a life of piety and timidity, I get to do what I am the very best at and still ascend the ladder to Heaven. . . ."

Jennifer scowled. "How do you know it's God? Okay, let's say the supernatural is real and you were really sucked out of your own time and brought here to kill a bunch of people," she said. "How do you know it's God who brought you here?"

"Who else could it be?" Sabbath asked.

"Aliens? Satan?"

"It wasn't!"

"How do you know!" Jennifer demanded. "How do you really *know*!"

Sabbath told Jennifer of Abathar, and in halting words described the experience of the angel revealing his true form, and of the undefinable something he perceived even beyond the endless light and power that Abathar represented. He trembled as he spoke, stammered uncharacteristically, and more than once his breath caught in his throat.

Jennifer, her arms crossed over her chest, eyes blazing, didn't falter. "Still could have been Satan, right?"

"How dare you . . ." Hexen was seething.

"When has God ever commanded men to kil—?" She stopped herself.

Sabbath burst out laughing. "Oh, Jennifer! This world!

None of you know the first thing about Scripture or statecraft, do you?"

"Fine, Hexen. Save the world. Kill five more people. Maybe ten. Whoever gets in your way. Just stay away from me. I'll be happy if I wake up on Monday morning and it's not nuclear war. I'll even light a candle for you, okay. Just don't . . . don't come around the gallery anymore."

Sabbath opened his mouth to speak, but the motel room was small enough that it took Jennifer only two strides to get to the door and leave.

Women. Some things do not ever change. Sabbath put his head down on the pillow and immediately fell asleep before he could entertain other thoughts.

It was dark when he awoke, but not dark enough. Sabbath had yet to get used to the fact that there was always light from some source other than the moon, even in the earliest hours of the morning. Traffic lights shining in from the slits of the blinds over the window; orange illumination leaking in from the hallway; distant neon signs twinkling like stars. And from his arm, a blazing red point of light, like a blood ruby.

Wrath, Sabbath knew. *And close.* Sabbath smiled. This would be straightforward. No women, no trickery, no turnabout. Two men—Wrath would have to be a man, no?—fighting. And Sabbath could admit that he was plenty wrathful himself, especially now. He'd be pleased to let the blood in his veins turn to fire, and to add another head to his collection.

Sabbath reviewed recent events as he traced a path across the Meatpacking District. The city was different here, more familiar, with its low buildings and occasional cobblestone paths, and the smell of butchered animals wafting around a corner now and again. But he was still a stranger in a strange land. He didn't have any money; Jennifer had left before he could ask her for some. The sins he was to confront had integrated themselves into this society—it had thus far proved impossible to simply find and challenge them without dealing with various underlings, some of whom were human and others of whom had merely taken on a human seeming. He should expect the same from the encounter with Wrath.

The tattoo led him to Gansevoort Street, and a brick building with tall windows and a prominent black awning. Again, the stench of wealth and money, though in this place, there was something of blood. Sabbath could smell it, could sense that the place had once been a slaughterhouse, home to men with hammer, saw, and tongs, tearing animals apart. The dried meat and tasteless cheese Jennifer had fed him wasn't enough, hadn't been nearly enough.

"Yo!" Sabbath hadn't been able to discern the entrance—so much glass!—but the heavy man near the door waved him over, so Sabbath approached. The man held out a fist, and said, "What's up, brother?" Sabbath made a fist as well and touched knuckles, but was surprised when the man tapped the top of Sabbath's fist with the bottom of his own, then opened his hand. Sabbath aped the move, and after palms crossed, he thought the intricate sign was complete. But the man clasped Sabbath's open hand and waggled his own thumb, then grabbed and squeezed Sabbath's shoulder. Then it was over.

"How you?" he asked Sabbath.

"I am . . . well?" Sabbath tried.

"Yah? You look like you been fighting pit bulls. You a brawler?" The man smiled. "I'm Jay."

Sabbath smiled back. "I've been known to brawl. I'm called Hexen Sabbath." He took the man in. He was huge, and corpulent, but there was clearly muscle under the fat, like a knight gone to seed after retirement. His hands were fast, though, as that peculiar greeting ritual had shown. And his face, brown, had a few pinkish scars like rivers on a map, and his teeth had met steel at least once. "Why do you ask?"

"Wanna make a few bucks?"

Money! "Yes," Sabbath said, too quickly. He couldn't back out now, but also couldn't allow himself to be distracted.

"You ever box? Wrestle? MMA?" Sabbath knew only the first two words. "Yes."

Jay nodded. "Yeah, I could tell. The way you swing your arms. Look at those damn thighs, son." He pointed a big finger and circled the air before Sabbath's face. "You don't take shit from anyone either. Nice scratches on your face. Women trouble?"

"Yes, women trouble," said Sabbath. "But . . . money, you said?"

"We got this little thing going on in the basement," Jay said, sotto voce, leaning in. "A little unregulated pit-fighting. Anything goes. Five grand just for stepping into the cage. Just step on in. You can forfeit and run right out if you want. And if you win, a hundred grand."

The knowledge entered Sabbath's mind. Five grand would certainly last a week, and one hundred could settle Sabbath for a year. And on his arm, the tattoo burned. Wrath was close. But . . .

"What do you mean by 'anything goes,' friend Jay?"

"Like I said, unregulated. Anything goes."

"*Anything* goes?" asked Sabbath again.

"You deaf, bruh. I said—"

Sabbath unzipped his duffel and let Jay see the hilt of his sword.

Then Jay nodded. "Anything goes." He took Sabbath's hand in his, and applied a stamp to the back of Sabbath's hand. The image, pink and incomplete, was remarkably like the tiny red dot pulsing on Sabbath's forearm.

"Just show 'em all that. In, left turn, left turn, down the steps, left turn, down the other steps. If you get lost, the other doormen will point the way."

The building was like a labyrinth, and the men Sabbath encountered at the doors were as large as Jay, but not nearly so friendly, until Sabbath flashed the stamp. Then they'd offer handshakes, backslaps, and in the last case, before a giant steel door, a pinch of the cheek and a kiss on Sabbath's forehead. The last doorman pulled a very large switch, and the walls themselves reverberated with interior gears as the doors separated. From inside the room on the other side, a cheer went up.

For a moment, Sabbath hesitated. The room was dark and hazy; the smoke stung his eyes and nose. The crowd was small yet boisterous. All Anglo or Norman, Sabbath guessed, and every one of them a man—very much unlike the average run of humanity on the streets above. In the center of the room, a well-lit cage with seven sides and made of a kind of crisscrossed wire.

Wrath. It had to be him. Even without the knowledge granted by Abathar, and the tingling of his tattoo, Sabbath knew it was Wrath in the cage, loping a circle along its perimeter, limbs swinging, muscles practically rolling. Had Sabbath ever been asked to imagine what wrath would look like were it a person rather than a mere word, it would have been the man in the cage.

And Wrath didn't even appear angry. His face was confident, perhaps even contemplative. But something in him simmered.

The man at the door touched Sabbath's shoulder to get his attention. "You're on deck!" In response to Sabbath's confused look, he clarified: "First *that* asshole gets to make five thousand bucks." With his chin he nodded toward the cage, referring not to Wrath but to a nervous-looking fellow wearing clothing little better than rags.

"Him!" Sabbath said. "He'll die in there!"

"They usually do," the man muttered. "But if he makes it to the hospital, the money will pay for the ambulance ride. . . ."

Sabbath said, "What!" The crowd was too noisy, their cheers and jeers echoing off the low steel ceiling and walls.

"I said," the man said, louder this time, "he'll do something unusual!"

The ragged-looking man climbed into the cage, and

behind him followed a woman in the briefest garment Hexen Sabbath had ever seen. She held something in her hand—*a microphone!* he suddenly knew—and spoke into it.

"Welcome back!" she said. "And thank you for your patience while our cleanup crew took care of bleaching and drying the mat here in the Heptagon! You know that a few seconds' work from our champion can take several minutes to scrape up afterwards." Some titters rose up from the audience.

"Moving right along, welcome to our co-main event at Luta Livre Definitivo, where truly . . ."

"Anything goes!" shouted the audience, as one.

Wrath was obviously favored to win. He was nearly nude, save for a pair of long shorts. The challenger, in rags, looked as though he had stepped right off the street, which Sabbath supposed was also true of himself, but the ragged man wasn't a fighter. Sabbath walked down the aisle to get a closer look, and was left entirely unmolested as he made it to the lip of the cage. There were no seconds, which surprised him. Even in his own era, single combat was ultimately a team sport, with supporters and friends and an impartial judge to declare a victor.

The moment the woman left the cage and toddled down the steps in her too-high heels, the match began. The ragged man withdrew a pistol from inside his shirt.

Wrath moved.

Something happened.

A shot was fired.

The chest of the man holding the pistol exploded.

He was on the floor, leaking.

A roar rose like a wave from the crowd.

Sabbath wasn't even sure he had seen what happened, or if his mind had just put the sequence of events together from the wreckage. Wrath had moved across the cage in one diagonal step, putting his body outside the line of fire. His right hand had grabbed the gunman's wrist, his left seizing the elbow. Then he twisted the arm back toward the gunman, cranking the joints hard. The gunman probably tensed up then, leading him to pull the trigger and shoot himself in the heart.

The woman with the microphone smiled at Sabbath. "Looks like you're next. Don't worry, we always clean up first. You have a couple minutes if you can think of a place you'd rather be." She smiled once more at him, wickedly.

"What happens to the money that man was promised? Does it go to his kin, or to the other fighter?"

She shook her head and laughed. "You have to walk out of here alive to collect it! Maybe one day it'll even happen!" She walked off, still chuckling. When Sabbath turned back to the cage, Wrath was there, on the other side of the chain link, squatting and glaring at him.

"You're next, bitch?" Wrath asked. It was conversational, but Wrath's voice was deep enough that it carried without his voice being raised at all. Sabbath felt it in his spine.

"No, you are."

"I'm going to fuck you after I kill you," Wrath said. "I'm going to find that girl you been fucking and kill her, nice and slow."

Jennifer! Sabbath knew better than to get distracted.

"You wanna know what I'm going to do after they cart

your dead ass out of here?" Wrath asked, but he didn't wait for the answer. "I've got a dirty bomb. I'll set it off in that girl's little art gallery. The mortals'll think it was the Russians tryin' to kill the next president. They'll be howling for blood, for vengeance. Americans won't be happy till they see flash-fried little Russian babies on their TVs, and crying mamas with half their faces blown off."

"Why are you telling me this?" asked Sabbath. "Why do you all keep telling me what you hope to do?"

"Sins ain't always secretive, son." Wrath cast his eyes out at the crowd, who were paying fairly close attention to the cleanup in the cage. One of the janitors slipped on some sausage-like viscera, and got laughed at for his pain and humiliation. "These bitches love it. They love to revel in their sins." Wrath flashed a mouthful of perfect tombstone-wide teeth at Sabbath. "Just like you." Then he spat in Sabbath's face, rose to his full height, and stalked across the cage without another word.

Wrath was larger than Sabbath, surely stronger, and faster. He was influencing the room, feeding from it. Sabbath had seen camp followers pick over the dead in his time, peasant children eager to find a bit of metal or cloth to sell amidst the rotting corpses, but he'd never seen anyone giggle over the carnage, not as the pair of janitors running towels between the cabling to remove the blood and flesh from the chain-link fence were doing as they worked. It was a joke to them. He wondered, for a moment, if he were to cut them down, would those giggling fools have black blood, or red?

Anything goes.

Perhaps the answer wouldn't matter.

Sabbath opened his duffel.

If anything goes, why wait for introductions?

Sloth's jowly head smacked wetly against Wrath's back. Wrath turned, but Sabbath had already rounded one of the Heptagon's corners; he spun Lust's head by her long hair and let it fly, a sling against Goliath. That head Wrath ducked, but by the time he righted himself, Sabbath was in the cage, sword drawn, swinging.

Wrath was fast enough to dodge Sabbath's slashing. Sabbath screamed, "You want to fuck me! I'll fuck you with this!" He kicked at Sloth's head, leaving a streak across the canvas of the cage.

"I'm going to love this! Everyone is going to love this!" said Wrath, raising a huge fist. "God is going to piss himself laughing at how I disfigure you!" He changed levels, took a knee, and slid under Sabbath's sword. Only then did the mistress of ceremonies finally grab the mic and hurriedly introduce the challenger. "He's got a head for this game, doesn't he, gentlemen?"

Wrath hugged Sabbath's legs and brought him down hard, but Sabbath held on to his sword. He slammed the pommel into Wrath's face, laughing over the sound of his opponent's cracking teeth. Wrath pushed himself up Sabbath's body and snaked his left hand over Sabbath's right, pinning the sword to the mat, and answered Sabbath with a headbutt, then two. Sabbath managed to squirrel his left leg out of Wrath's grip, and grapevine it around his back. When Wrath reared his head back for a third headbutt, Sabbath freed his right knee and swept Wrath off his chest, tumbling after him to land on top. Wrath laughed as Sabbath, shaking his head and letting blood fly from his mouth and nose, scrambled to his feet. He kicked Lust's head out of the way, splitting the face open. Wrath casually reached for the sword Sabbath had abandoned.

Which was what Sabbath wanted. He scuttled backwards to the other end of the Heptagon, leaving a trail of blood behind him, lowered his stance, and waited.

Sabbath had to admit that Wrath was a professional. No posing, no waving the sword in the air for the sake of the crowd, no barbaric yawp or teeth-gnashing. The big man didn't even smile. He just moved, faster than the eye could see.

And slipped on the blood.

Arms flailing.

Sabbath's huge right fist met Wrath's chin.

His left seized Wrath's wrist and twisted the arm till Wrath dropped the sword.

Right knee to stomach. Right elbow to the bridge of Wrath's nose.

Low kick to the left ankle.

Wrath, unbalanced again, widened his stance, tried to brace himself.

Sabbath let him.

He dropped to the mat, grabbed the sword, hugged it close, and rolled, smearing more blood across the canvas.

Sabbath spotted Sloth's head in a corner.

So close. He could hurl it at Wrath.

If Wrath ducked, Sabbath would have time to get up, to ready the sword.

If Wrath swatted at it, Sabbath would have time to get up, to ready the sword.

Sabbath snatched it up.

He threw it at Wrath.

Wrath let it bounce off his chest.

The head came tumbling back toward Sabbath.

He kicked it at Wrath with his shin.

This time Wrath ducked.

Sabbath was up.

Wrath was too close.

Wrath slammed him into the fence, the sword flat between them. Sabbath had both hands on the hilt, and Wrath's big right paw wrapped around them. His left peppered Sabbath's ribs and liver with short hard punches. He ground one knee against Sabbath's thigh.

Sabbath planted his feet, braced his back against the cage, and winced through the punches. All his focus, all his power, was on his two arms fighting Wrath's right, to push the sword up.

Two bodies, slick with blood and sweat. The blade, sliding between a pair of sweaty torsos, leaving thin trails of blood as it climbed. Wrath sensed it and pushed his chin down atop Sabbath's head. Sabbath did not stop pushing the blade upward, even as he clenched his teeth and hissed through them.

Then, a knee to Wrath's groin. Wrath was wearing a cup, and Sabbath's knee rang like a tuning fork, but it was enough to make Wrath grunt, to loosen his grip slightly. Sabbath slid his head back and held in a yowl as the sword nearly opened his nose. Then the sword point found the bottom of Wrath's jaw. He slid back and the blade tore the flesh from his chin.

Then he punched Sabbath square in the nose. It flattened against Sabbath's face.

Sabbath kicked again, finding Wrath's knee.

Wrath jerked his leg back and slipped once more.

Sabbath lunged with the sword. He slipped too.

They fell in a heap, the sword bouncing away.

Sabbath reached for it.

Wrath took Sabbath's arm, threw his long legs over Sabbath's torso, and began to torque the elbow. Sabbath slapped his hands together and tried to pull his arm back. Wrath started kicking at Sabbath's forearms and hands.

The crowd was strangely quiet. The basement room filled with the soft sounds of two men grunting and hissing.

Wrath pulled back his foot for another strike, and Sabbath rolled and followed it, ending up atop Wrath.

But Wrath had the arm, and yanked it, then planted his thighs on either side of Sabbath's head.

He squeezed.

Sabbath's face turned red as he spread his stance, braced himself, and lifted Wrath off the canvas. The crowd inhaled as one. Wrath was huge. A slam wouldn't loosen his grip. Sabbath was using all his energy on a last foolish attempt to escape. It was clear, obvious.

Then Sabbath began to slowly shuffle toward the sword, Wrath hanging from him like a great white octopus.

Sabbath's legs wobbled; then he slammed Wrath to the mat.

The sword bounced.

Sabbath pulled Wrath up again, slammed him again.

The sword bounced.

Wrath squeezed his thighs tighter, pulled on Sabbath's trapped arm.

Three more seconds.

Sabbath yanked hard, whipped Wrath from the floor, slammed him again, and as the sword bounced, Sabbath slipped on a patch of bloody skin and fell forward.

The sword found the side of Wrath's neck, and sank into his thigh. Sabbath fell backwards, out of Wrath's failing grip. Wrath grabbed the sword and took to his feet. From the ground Sabbath upkicked at Wrath's wounded right leg. He staggered and nearly did a full split, but held on to the sword till Sabbath kicked him in the elbow.

The sword went flying.

Both men scrambled for it, sliding on their knees.

Wrath grabbed it.

Sabbath grabbed Lust's head.

Wrath thrust the sword as best he could from his knees.

It pierced the ruins of Lust's skull as if it were going through a rotten melon.

Sabbath leapt to his feet and kicked Wrath in the head.

He took the sword.

With the backswing, Lust's head came flying off the point of the blade and smacked one of the corners of the Heptagon.

Wrath's head hit the opposite corner a moment later.

Sabbath waited for a bell, for applause, for black-blooded demons to storm and climb over the gates, but the hall was silent and the audience still.

Sabbath coughed once, and snorted. He wiped his bloody face on his forearm.

"A-all right," he said. He picked up his sword, stepped to the cage door, waited patiently for the announcer to unlock it, then retrieved his duffel, reentered the Heptagon, and collected the three heads.

"I would like a towel," he said quietly. Then louder: "A towel!"

Someone threw a white towel into the cage. Sabbath used it on his face, and then the blade, which went back into the duffel. He stepped out of the cage, walked up the aisle, and out the door, blood trailing after him like a snake.

"You won, eh?" said Jay. "Nice!" He looked Sabbath up and down. "You know what dudes usually say when they look like you? 'You should see the other guy!'" He laughed at his own joke, then stopped when Sabbath unzipped the duffel bag and offered him a peek inside.

"Brutal," he said. "Well, you get this." He reached into the interior pocket of his coat and withdrew a golden credit card. "Prepaid. Five grand. A bit harder to trace than usual too."

Sabbath took the card and peered at it. "I won. I'm owed more."

The bouncer shrugged. "We don't have the money; nobody was ever supposed to win."

Sabbath stepped forward. "I just killed your master."

"You can kill me too, but the cops will be all over you for it. I'm just a dude with a job standing out in the middle of the street, talking to a white guy who looks like he punched a hole through a wall with his face; I'm not a demon who'll collapse into a puddle of black blood. We got video." The bouncer gazed up at the security camera mounted in the doorway above his head.

"There was a promise made, sir . . . ," said Sabbath.

"Call the cops," Jay said. "What do you think they'll do about your bag full of heads and bloody sword?"

"Well, what shall I do, then?" Sabbath said with a sigh. He was tired of fighting, too deflated even to ball up his fists and experience the joys of revenge against this man.

"You'll probably want to go get stitched up at the ER. You got insurance? If not, you can probably kiss all that money goodbye."

"I . . . I know someone who can 'stitch me up' for free," Sabbath said.

"Baller," Jay said. "Bless you, bless your mama."

Sabbath could not successfully hail a taxicab. It was a long walk back to SoHo. Even with Wrath dead and the sin's head safely on his person, Sabbath was concerned for Jennifer. Four sins remained, and they seemingly knew everything about him, and everything about her.

And Jennifer, she didn't understand. She might believe—in God, and in Sabbath's mission—but she fundamentally didn't understand. These times were full of weak people who somehow all had warm homes and incredible machines to travel in; food so plentiful, it filled metal rubbish bins on every corner; and more changes of clothes than there were days in a month. Abathar's knowledge pushed him toward a subway entrance, but Abathar's wisdom suggested walking instead. He had a card now; he could buy water and pizza, or some other food, and walk along the streets generally unmolested. A bruised and bleeding man was of no concern to most passersby. Sabbath had been rendered invisible. Not a trace of Christian charity remained in humanity so far as he could perceive. In his time, the good men and women of a village or town would come running to assist a wounded man or a hungry one. Even Sabbath would throw a few coins to beggar children, and not just for the pleasure of seeing them scramble and fight for them.

Though, he had to admit, that pleasure did motivate some fraction of his generosity.

The Above Below Arts gallery was dark, as was the window to the apartment overhead, when Sabbath arrived. He searched his mind—would Abathar's gift tell him something like Jennifer's location and mental state?

No.

He imagined that the angel wasn't pleased with extracurricular fucking, and perhaps not even with the affection he had for the girl.

"Oh shit," he heard, and turned. It was Jennifer, who had just come around the corner, and with her was another woman whose smile was as enthusiastic as Jennifer's frown was dismayed. They were both in short skirts and had their faces painted in a way Sabbath found grotesque, as though they were in costume as black-eyed birds with bloodied beaks. The woman next to Jennifer was clearly an intimate of some sort—she stood close to her, had been keeping an even pace. She was a bigger girl, sort of like the wenches Sabbath preferred, with a haircut like a young boy's and clunky glasses. For a moment, Sabbath wondered if she weren't a man, and if skirts were common among both genders, but then a bit of modern knowledge entered his mind, and he understood.

"Oh, is this him? Hey, I'm Miriam!" the smiling woman said, her eyes wide. She walked up to and walked a circuit around Sabbath, looking him up and down as if he were a prize cow. A bold one, Miriam was taller than he was by an inch or so. "Damn, Jen, you're right. He is like Jack Black after CrossFit . . . and a traffic accident."

"Uh, hello," Sabbath said. "How do you do, uhm, miss?"

"What happened to you?" Miriam asked. She peered right into his face. "Close encounter with a Cuisinart?"

"Miri!" Jennifer cried out. She hadn't moved from the corner, and had to shout to be heard. "Forget him, let's go! He's dangerous!"

"Maybe you should go," Miriam said to Sabbath.

"There is danger here, but not from me," said Sabbath. He turned to Jennifer, who was digging in her purse for something. He suspected pepper spray, so stayed put. "They know of you, Jennifer!"

"All the more reason you should go, Hexen!"

"Hexen . . . ," said Miriam. "I would have thought you'd have more than just the one tattoo."

"I'm here to protect you!"

"You're the reason I'm in danger. Go anywhere else, and I'll be fine!"

Miriam ignored the shouted conversation and gingerly clutched Sabbath's wrist and forearm to better scrutinize his tattoo. Sabbath noticed that she was inked as well—a heart between her breasts, the phases of the moon wrapped around her large wrist, and even a vine on her neck, tracing the jugular.

"Nice piece. Saw it on Jen's Insta. Pretty amazing . . . ," Miriam said, mostly to herself.

"Miriam, get away from him," Jennifer called out. "He's a psycho; he kills women!"

Miriam looked up at Sabbath. "Are you going to kill me?" Her affect was flat, but Sabbath understood that she was mocking both him and Jennifer.

"You're . . . intoxicated," he said.

"Intoxicat*ing* would have gotten you further," Miriam said.

"Do I need to call the police?" Jennifer said. She'd finally retrieved her cell phone from the bowels of her purse.

I have three heads in my bag! Sabbath nearly shouted at her. *And you know of two of them! The bag has your name on it!* But Jennifer's friend was hovering near, swaying slightly in her high heels, and she looked at his stitched-up ear, the sliced-up tip of his nose. "No, you do not need to call the police," he said finally. "You don't need them to protect yourself from me, and they will not be able to protect you from sin."

"Theological!" Miriam snorted.

"Your friend is drunk," Sabbath told Jennifer. "It's neither right nor safe for women to walk the streets as you do."

"I don't need a right-wing Women's Safety lecture from

you," Jennifer said. "Just go." Sabbath turned and left without another word, choosing his direction arbitrarily so far as Jennifer could even tell.

"Where the hell's he going?" asked Miriam, too loudly. "To the Staten Island Ferry?"

6

So are the ways of every one that is greedy of gain;
which taketh away the life of the owners thereof.

—Proverbs 1:19

It wasn't that more wine was going to help the situation, but it probably wouldn't make anything worse, so Miriam and Jennifer had some bottles delivered. No reason to live just north of TriBeCa if you weren't going to stupidly waste money and get stupid wasted.

"I need to save the good stuff for the opening this weekend," Jennifer said apologetically after shutting the door on the deliveryman without tipping him. "Old vine zinfandel will have to do."

"Well, at least you bought in bulk," Miriam said as Jennifer slid the third and fourth bottles out of the large paper bag from the liquor store.

"I just—"

"Stop!" said Miriam. She was sitting cross-legged on the floor, holding up her right palm. "No more 'I just . . .'"

Jennifer popped a cork. "Huh?"

"All night, every time you start a sentence with 'I just,' it's been the launchpad for an extended monologue on Hexen Sabbath. I get it: you're not in the habit of fucking weird strangers. But you had just experienced a big scare. It was like he saved your life. Adrenaline and pheromones took over. It's like a duckling hatching and imprinting on the first animal she sees—you're the duckling and his cock was the adorable potbellied pig or whatever."

"But—"

"But," Miriam interrupted. "I am tired of hearing it. I insist on a conversation that passes the Bechdel–Wallace test for once." She shrugged out of her small blazer and left it on the floor as she stood. Jennifer handed her an overfull glass and poured a similarly unbalanced one for herself. They looped arms and drank.

"Tell me about anything else, Jenny," Miriam said.

"I don't have any money," Jennifer blurted out. "If the *Ylem* exhibit doesn't work, I'm done. I'll have to move down to Florida and live with my mother and her doilies."

"There's got to be something you can do," Miriam said.

"Why does there always have to be something?" Jennifer flopped down on the futon.

"Raise your feet." Miriam put her glass down and tugged on the edge of the futon frame. Jennifer whooped slightly as the mattress moved under her, the couch unfolding into a bed. Miriam retrieved her glass and clambered up next to Jennifer.

"There always has to be something," said Miriam, "because one always takes some form of action—even the decision to do nothing is an action."

"Well, sure. Everyone knows *that*."

"You can sit here, let the lights flicker, let the landlord bang on the door, let the cops come with an eviction notice and drag you out to the corner with all your stuff, and that is still taking an action. Remember what you told me once? 'Woman is con—'"

"I remember," interrupted Jennifer. "I was the one who told you all that existential freedom stuff in the first place. 'Woman is condemned to freedom' was on my OKCupid ad. And now I know that art history is only the second most useless degree, Ms. Philosophy."

"No, theology is even more useless," Miriam said. "I was a double major."

"What do you think—?"

"No talk of men, Jen," Miriam said. She had taken off her blouse, Jennifer noticed. Miriam's bra wasn't quite an I-am-here-to-fuck model; it was white, decorated with large flowers, like a grandmother's couch. Nonthreatening. Maybe one more brief fling before heading back to Florida, where the tobacco-spittin' cracker kids harassed her for being a "Ruskie" in school, maybe women were better than . . .

"Put your clothes back on, Miri," Jennifer said. "I'm definitely not looking for a rebound thing."

"That's not what you said last time, after what was his name?" She slipped her top back on and started rebuttoning.

"Brendan," said Jennifer. "Anyway, do angels count as men? Let's talk angels. Have you heard of one named Abathar?"

"Angels do not count as men," Miriam said. "Are you going to send me back on the PATH train after this?" She tried a wide smile as she asked.

Jennifer turned to face Miriam, and didn't offer a smile in return. "I'll put my big comforter in the tub and sleep in there. You can have the futon. Tell me about Abathar, Miri."

Miriam rolled her eyes. "God, Jen. That's cold. And nobody really studies angels in depth as an undergraduate except for religious wackos."

"Aren't theology departments full of religious wackos?"

"Never for long," Miriam said. "They all wash out after two semesters and go to Bible school instead. Anyway, Abathar, Abathar . . ." She was sobering up. "Damn it, you're going to make me reach for my cell phone, aren't you?" Miriam slithered over Jennifer, who was stiff and sad under her, and reached for her clutch. "It's not Judeo-Christian. Maybe some Islamic syncretism . . ." She got her phone and thumbed the screen expertly. Maybe she wasn't drunk at all, but just playacting to have an excuse to stay over.

"Mandaeism!" she said.

"What?"

"Exactly," Miriam said. "It's a gnostic religion—when you have a lot of small tribes and a lot of big ideas, you end up with ethno-religious groups piecing together all sorts of stuff. Mandaeism is a gnostic religion; an Abrahamic grab bag. Not the kind of name a normal crazy person would come across."

"What about . . . an eleventh-century English knight?" Jennifer asked.

"Definitely not," said Miriam.

"Hexen says that he met Abathar," Jennifer said.

"And so the one true religion is a syncretist sect in the

Middle East that doesn't proselytize, doesn't go for intermarriage, and has spent the last eighteen hundred years being shit on by everyone else?" Miriam asked.

"Is that the only option?" Jennifer said. "Do they believe in some kind of End Times Armageddon?"

"End Times Armageddon," Miriam repeated.

"Yes," Jennifer said.

"Well, I think you've confused a couple of concepts here. In Christianity, or most forms of it, anyway, Christ is supposed to return at some point, either before, during, or after a period of great tribulations."

"Like the Rapture?"

Miriam rolled her eyes. "Don't get me started on that."

"What, then?" said Jennifer.

"You tell me! What did that loon tell you?"

"That he has to keep the seven deadly sins from destroying the world with nuclear weapons," said Jennifer, ". . . by killing them. They're people or something, I guess. He wants to chop off their heads."

"Well, is he the Christ, then?" Miriam asked. "He doesn't sound like it."

"Uh . . . no?"

"Well, then it's not the End Times, Jen," said Miriam. "Armageddon is also supposed to be a huge battle between the armies of good and evil, not one guy killing seven really bad people. He sounds like an all-weather schizophrenic to me, even if he has some inexplicable tattoo. Maybe he's a performance artist gone mad. You're well rid of him regardless."

Jennifer shivered, hugging herself. "But a man like that—"

Miriam covered Jennifer's mouth. Her hand was light on Jennifer's lips—a weird mix of flirty and threatening. "No men," Miriam said. "No Hexen." She removed the hand and kissed Jennifer.

Jennifer considered herself less bicurious and more simply bicompliant. When women were forceful and had broad shoulders, she wanted them. And this opportunity would be hard to replicate in a month, when she was sleeping in her childhood bedroom in Kissimmee, with innumerable stuffed dragons and a few Russian Orthodox icons looking down on her bed from the shelves.

Unless Hexen fails . . ., she thought.

But she couldn't do anything about that. She couldn't even bring herself to really believe in it.

"Miri . . ."

"Yees?" asked Miriam, comically extending her vowel, an eyebrow raised.

"Let's make me forget for a night."

But she thought about mushroom clouds as Miriam buried her tongue between her thighs anyway.

Even with his native cunning, and the small doses of contemporary knowledge introduced to his mind as needed, it took Sabbath a long while to find a hotel that would accommodate him. Prepaid debit cards are most often greeted with suspicion in Lower Manhattan, and a battered man carrying a stained duffel bag is simply assumed to be homeless. But the New World Hotel, on the bottom of the Bowery, in Chinatown, so close to where Sabbath had claimed his first two heads, finally took him in. Was Manhattan like an intestine, with all the filth collecting at the lowermost points? He checked his tattoo—and, no, the remaining sins were scattered across the city. One was close, two others uptown, and one was . . . elsewhere. Sabbath couldn't rally himself to go hunting again; he needed sleep.

He also understood that there was such a thing as room service, but knew that the dumpy hotel he was in didn't offer such a thing. In his exhaustion, Sabbath couldn't bring himself to walk back down the three flights of crooked steps and feed himself, though. He would sit here, curled up like an unborn babe in a womb. The room had a private bath—Sabbath had coughed up an extra ten dollars for that—but he'd been in tents while off on campaign that were larger than the room, and that contained more furniture.

But the room also had a television. What if the knowledge of Abathar was misleading him somehow? He could confirm his suspicions, or his hopes, with the TV. Sabbath threw himself on the bed, fumbled with the remote control, and found something called the History Channel. That sounded promising, though fatigue tugged at his muscles and his mind. He fought to keep his eyes open as footage from the Allies liberating concentration camps filled the screen.

When Sabbath awoke, the television was off, the room darker than it should be, and someone was in the room with him. He couldn't raise his arms to fight, couldn't roll off the bed and dive for his sword. His muscles were just dead meat hanging off the cage of his bones.

"Sir Hexen," said Abathar.

"Mmm," said Sabbath. He was relieved. The angel was not good company, but he at least had Sabbath's interests at heart.

"The very state of you," said Abathar.

"Wrath was . . . very strong," said Sabbath.

"I believe you might die soon," said Abathar. "You were not made for these times. You're breathing tainted air, eating foods composed of compounds that literally did not exist when you last walked the earth. Your wounds are deeper than you know, and your body nears its limits."

"Compounds . . . ," Sabbath repeated. Some memory of the TV documentary he'd been watching flickered in his mind. "I . . . why should I strain myself to save this world?"

The room was dark, but somehow Sabbath sensed that Abathar was grinning. "Go on, Sir Hexen," he said. "Go on."

"War is fought in different ways now," said Sabbath. "It's no longer men against men . . . it's no longer even simple rape and pillage."

"Now?" said Abathar archly. "These precise words may not be familiar to you, but you'll recognize the sentiment from the Scripture of your time and language: 'Now go and smite Amalek, and utterly destroy all that they have, and spare them not; but slay both man and woman, infant and suckling, ox and sheep, camel and ass.'"

"Ah yes . . . First Samuel . . . something something . . . ," Sabbath muttered.

"And what of the Picts?" asked Abathar.

"Some few remain," Sabbath said, though something in the back of his mind corrected him even as he spoke.

"No," said Abathar. "In your generation, they died out.

You had a fair amount to do with the end of those noble people in your younger days."

Sabbath roused himself. "If what you say is so—that men have always annihilated one another—then my predecessor in 1239 should have laid down his sword and let the sins have the world."

"If you are so sure, Sir Hexen, so callous, I'll weigh your soul now," Abathar said.

"Have I sinned?" Sabbath asked.

Abathar laughed in the dark.

Sabbath snorted. "Even an angel enjoys a little irony, eh . . . ," he muttered, raising himself up onto his elbows. "If you wish me to save this planet, why not heal my wounds and fill my belly? Why translate yourself here, angel, just to bedevil me?"

Abathar didn't laugh at that.

"Like all sinners, Sir Hexen, you love the world and its poisonous treasures," said Abathar. "This is a fallen place, given to misery and death. But if your desire is to continue living in it, even just for a few days more, I'll withhold my judgment. But be aware—as it stands, even if you do defeat the remaining sins, you shall fall."

"You . . . told me I was immune to the temptations of the sins . . . but . . . ," Sabbath said, "how could the sins influence anyone in this world? What was once unimaginable is now commonplace. Were the gates of Hell to be split open today—" He coughed, sputtered. "—today . . . the damned dead would greatly outnumber the living. . . ."

"You've been watching television," Abathar said.

"Is that a sin now?"

"It probably should be."

There was a knock at the door. Sabbath jerked himself fully awake and reached for the duffel bag, but groaned and grabbed his side.

"Rest, Sir Hexen," said Abathar. The knock came again, more insistent this time. "I'll answer it."

Sabbath squinted as the door opened and light from the hallway flooded the little dark room. He could barely see what was happening and couldn't hear at all the conversation between Abathar and the man who had been knocking on the door. Sabbath's eyes adjusted as Abathar raised his arms and put his hands on either side of the man's head, and drew him in for what Sabbath was sure was going to be a kiss. Abathar inhaled deeply, and the man somehow emptied out. Abathar held what was left of the man in his hands, folded it up twice, and tucked it into his suit jacket's breast pocket like a handkerchief.

"I will not intervene in your behalf again, Sir Hexen."

"Wait!" Sabbath said. "I have a question—at least tell me one thing. Why must I cut off the heads of the sins?"

"You need the practice," said Abathar. And then he was gone.

The morning twilight was fading when there was another knock at the door, this one tentative. Sabbath roused himself, took up his sword, and put his hand on the doorknob. The weapon was a little unwieldy for close work, but it would have to do. When the next knock came, he swung open the door, stepped back and then forward, thrusting the point of his blade.

"Wait, please!" The man was the most unusual-looking person Sabbath had seen in the twenty-first century so far, and walking around Lower Manhattan, he'd seen many odd birds. This fellow was almost aggressively normal-looking. He was an Anglo, with blue eyes and sandy hair going gray. He wore a suit of the sort Sabbath had grown used to over the past two days, but this man's was a shade of gray, and the necktie a shade of blue, that made him instantly forgettable. Sabbath stared the man down, but couldn't commit any details to memory.

"Uhm . . ."

"Let's get breakfast, Hexen Sabbath," the man said, his smile television-wide. "My limo's double-parked downstairs. I don't want to get a ticket."

"Who are you?"

"Me?" The man tapped his lapels with his fingertips, the sword at his throat forgotten. "I'm Greed. And I'm your only friend in this world, I promise."

The limousine was impressive. All cars looked new to Sabbath, but this one—a 1937 Cadillac Fleetwood in metallic green, gutted, refurbished, and double-stretched—was an ostentatious classic. Save for the low roof, the interior was nearly the size of the New World Hotel room Sabbath had rented for the night. He and Greed sat opposite each other as the car motored down toward Wall Street, somehow managing to slip between taxicabs and around tight corners. Greed mixed mimosas from the small dry bar at his right.

"There's a seat belt if you want one, Mr. Sabbath," Greed said as the car turned yet another corner. "I just find it a challenge to mix a decent drink while strapped in." He passed Sabbath a tall glass of orange juice and champagne. Sabbath sniffed at it curiously, shrugged, and chugged.

"My man!" said Greed. "We'll stop and get pancakes at the Stage Door. Anyway . . . do you mind if I just say my piece, Sir Hexen?"

"Go on, Sir Greed."

Greed smiled. "Thank you. Let me just start by saying . . . I'm not like the others. Look out the window." He pointed at the passing skyscrapers, gestured at the black cars choking the narrow streets. "The fact is that Greed isn't a sin. There was a movie some years back that popularized a certain slogan: 'Greed is good.' My understanding is that you're from the past, correct?"

Sabbath started to nod, but it wasn't necessary, as Greed just kept talking. "And correct me if I'm wrong, but in the feudal era, most people lived lives of privation and misery. Greed solved all that. Greed is the motor of creation, of innovation. Have you had a chance to meet any poors?"

"Poors?"

"Poor people," Greed said. Sabbath shrugged. "I've not met too many myself, but I know something about them. Poor people today live lives that even the kings of your time could only dream of. Have you used a flush toilet since coming here?" He nodded toward his mimosa. "You liked the drink, yes? The oranges were imported from another country. Not because anyone went down there and chopped off heads; it's just pure market forces. We want to buy oranges. Someone in Mexico or Venezuela, where oranges grow easily, wants money. We exchange and we both benefit."

"Makes sense," Sabbath said, though Abathar's wisdom had something cynical to say about the notion of *pure market forces* bringing fruit from Latin America to the United States.

"Capitalism unleashed the power of the individual to pursue self-interest, but when we all pursue self-interest, great things happen. People who work hard or who have good ideas or who can manage rather than simply waste their money are rewarded."

"And those who fail?" said Sabbath. He rested a hand on the duffel bag he'd brought with him.

"Well, that's the very thing, Sir Hexen," said Greed, his forefinger pointing triumphantly in the air. "They're not punished. Successful people generate so much wealth, so many untold riches, that even the poor people of this time have food, heated homes, and cell phones with all the world's knowledge in their pockets. Even the homeless people in this city are better off than the peasants of your time. If they sleep in Penn Station, it's because Penn Station is well lit and warm. If they spend all day in a public library, they have a toilet and access to books they actually know how to read. The system works, my friend. Everyone is better off when people are allowed to be greedy, and not hampered by notions of charity or hamstrung by a government working for aristocratic looters."

"I suppose I'd say that you're half right, Mr. Gree—" The Cadillac turned hard and stopped short. Greed threw a hand against a window to keep his balance. Sabbath reached for the seat belt and strapped himself in. "Half right," he said.

The chauffeur slammed the door behind him and quickly hustled into a crowded-seeming restaurant.

"Mr. Greed, I agree, somewhat. Certainly I've met many a noble whose only purpose in life was to eat gold and shit war," said Sabbath.

Greed was peering out the window. "We're not really supposed to park here either," he said to himself.

"But what is this all to do with me?"

Greed retrained his attention onto Sabbath. "What it has to do with you is simple—I support you. Why would I wish to see the world destroyed? Greed isn't a sin. Sin doesn't lead to such wondrous achievements; sin doesn't benefit the world. I'm not *with* them. In fact, I want to help you."

"Help me?" Sabbath said, his voice tinged with suspicion.

Just then, the side door opened and the chauffeur ducked his head in. "Brunch," he said, then stepped aside. A deli worker with a large tray full of pancakes, bacon, and small bowls of fruit salad stood on the curb. She offered the tray to the chauffeur, a beast with sharpened teeth who took it expertly in one enormous hand, helped himself to a strawberry from one of the bowls, then gave it to Greed, who accepted the fruit happily.

"These pancakes here are the best," Greed said. "And I figured it would be broadly similar to something you may have enjoyed back in your era, yes?" He set the tray down on a low table built into the limo floor, and used special spring hooks along the table's edge to snap it into place.

"No, not as such," Sabbath said, but the smell was intoxicating. His mouth flooded with saliva, his belly grumbling. The car started up again. Sabbath sliced his stack in quarters and shoved a forkful into his mouth.

"Glad you like it—Whoa!" The car turned sharply enough to nearly unbalance the pancake plates on the tray. Greed grabbed for his glass and took a healthy gulp of mimosa.

"Mrrhf s'gud," Sabbath said. After he swallowed, Sabbath said, "But we must be clear. Greed is the fuel for the fire of all manner of human misery. If the peasants starve, it is due to the greed of the aristocrats. If a town falls to rape and pillage, that is greed."

"No, Sir Hexen," said Greed. "That's envy; that's lust. The aristocrats compete with one another for wealth and power—it's how the peasants are drafted into war. And the villages falling to rape and pillage; that is clearly lust. Untrammeled sex and violence. There are six deadly sins, not seven."

"I've seen many a knight grow fat on the spoils of war, abandoning their duties to both faith and king!" Sabbath said. He wasn't quite among them, of course, if only because he hadn't yet lost his muscular physique to age and appetite.

"Gluttony," said Greed. "Look at our meal! It's filling, and tasty, and healthy, and we are eating it together in a truly remarkable motor vehicle, cruising down the streets of the greatest city in the world. But are we stuffing our faces, choking on our pancakes in our eagerness to eat them? Are we fighting over them? Are we running down little street urchins? Are we—?" Greed swallowed the rest of his sentence as the car made yet another sharp turn.

Sabbath laughed. "Greed! Enough talk; we'll both die in this bizarre box! What do you want of me?!"

Greed regained his balance. Despite the unique surroundings, and the nervous grin on his flushed face, the sin looked no more distinctive than he had in the hallway. A perfectly average twenty-first-century Anglo man. He could have been anyone, and perhaps that was the point of this incarnation.

"I want to help you!" Greed said. "You said it yourself: greed is seen as a sin, thanks to envy, gluttony, and lust. I want you to eliminate the six deadly sins. I have no interest in ending this world. Why would I? I love the world and everything in it."

"Why don't you do it yourself?" asked Sabbath. "Or hire someone? I'm sure you could afford to hire an army." Greed smiled weakly. "Ah, you're miserly as well as greedy, is it, O Sin?" Sabbath said.

"I don't want to get my own hands dirty, it's true," Greed said. He hesitated for a moment. "And let's just say that without me, the other sins would not be on your radar. You know what radar is . . . ?"

Sabbath nodded. "I do . . . now."

"I'm supporting a presidential campaign. The candidate of our choice, Mr. Aldridge, claims to be very wealthy, but in truth, he's on the verge of destitution. I gave him a cash injection when he needed it."

"And where did you get the money to do that?" asked Sabbath.

"Wall Street!" Greed said. "We're here. It's a miracle, truly. The use of money to make money. Bets on future prices, swaps of interest payments—Party A may offer to pay me a fixed amount, while I offer to pay them interest based on the market. Do you understand what credit default swaps are? If a firm comes up against some hard losses and is unable to pay its debts in a timely manner, I can benefit from a sort of insurance payout, even if I don't own any of the underlying principal. It's a way of distributing risk across a market. I . . ."

Greed continued, and the knowledge of Abathar filled Sabbath's brain, but even with the whispers of the angel, he could not quite understand what Greed was getting at.

". . . and in that example, even though I have essentially taken out an insurance policy on my neighbor's house, I *don't* walk over at three o'clock one morning and set it ablaze myself, because I've placed a series of bets with other neighbors who also hold insurance policies that the house won't burn down. And so you might wonder if we all aren't just praying for lightning to strike the house. . . ."

Sabbath peered out the car window. Manhattan was a glory, in its way. More glass than he'd ever seen in his life skinned buildings, and somehow resisted the elements. Even when he craned his neck—he was tempted to try to roll down a window and stick his head outside, but the Cadillac was rushing past the traffic too quickly—he could not see the tops of most of the skyscrapers they passed.

Something extremely powerful had raised these buildings, consecrated them to the generation of wealth.

". . . and so when the owner decides himself to burn down his house when he realizes that his debts far outstrip his equity, as he's borrowed against it to buy insurance against my house burning down, we all benefit."

"I . . . see," said Sabbath. "But couldn't that lead to everyone simply burning down their own homes?"

"Oh, we don't live in those homes. We just borrowed money to purchase them from the banks we own. We can't just buy and sell swaps without a stake in the banks. We would never live in such firetraps, after all. Why buy insurance on a house that might be difficult to burn down?"

"And you borrow money from the banks . . . you own?"

"Yes," said Greed. "We own some of all of them, to give us 'visibility' when deals are made with our competitors."

". . . and your competitors . . . ," Sabbath ventured.

"Also own some fraction of every bank, yes," said Greed. "The system works. If any one of us were just a little less greedy, it would all collapse. Same too if any one of us were just a bit more gluttonous or slothful or envious, if you get my drift. . . ."

"Why even attempt to waylay me, then?" asked Sabbath. "If you wish to be the last sin . . . or virtue . . . standing, why not just let me be?" He glanced down at the tattoo on his forearm. "Leave the boroughs of this city, and I'd not be able to find you."

"Well, I mean, we're having this nice conversation . . . ," Greed began. Then the car stopped short again. He jerked forward in his seat, nearly taking a header into his pancakes.

Sabbath dived for his duffel bag, unzipped it, and in a moment was up with his sword. He had to hunch, but there was room enough to unsheathe his sword and thrust it.

Not toward Greed, who curled up in his seat and threw up his arms, but behind him, through the partition and into the front seat. The car skidded, then stopped hard. Outside, horns started blaring, tires screeching.

"Please, don't!" cried Greed. "I'm just an actor! They hired me this—"

"This morning, yes. After attempting to assassinate me yesterday evening," said Sabbath. "Your chauffeur is more than just a terrible driver; he is Greed. While you jabber about universal benefit, he could not help but demand every inch of the roadway, violating every rule and even endangering himself for the slightest advantage." He yanked the sword out of the seat behind him and examined the blade. "Black blood. I'll be right back."

Sabbath threw open the driver's side door, and with a yelp threw himself back into the limo as a taxi roared past. "Passenger side . . . ," he muttered to himself, but the chauffeur opened that door, grabbed Sabbath by the collar of his T-shirt, and threw him onto the pavement. Sabbath rolled carefully, keeping the sword flat against his chest.

The chauffeur, Greed, had a hole in his chest where Sabbath had struck. Sabbath squinted and saw through it. He had struck true, but missed the vital organ he would have punctured on anyone else of Greed's size. This sin had no heart at all. Sabbath shifted to his knees, pointed his sword, and slowly gained his feet. "You're not like the others," he said to Greed. "You don't talk, do you?" Greed answered with a smile. Every one of his teeth was a pointed canine. Deep in Sabbath's chest, his own heart skipped a beat. But the pedestrians around him were not afraid at all. They gathered in a tight circle around the combatants, and to a person had their phones out. They were recording video; Sabbath realized that some of them were transmitting the scene live to a potential audience of millions. Several police cars, sirens wailing, pulled up and quickly formed a cordon. There was even a helicopter overhead now, low enough that Sabbath felt the wind whipped up by its rotors playing with his hair.

Greed wasn't going to give a speech or play a trick or even offer a semblance of a fair fight. This sin had organized the world against Sabbath. The actor came stumbling out of the backseat of the car and inserted himself between the point of Sabbath's blade and the mountainous Greed.

"You don't get it," the actor said. "I need to go viral!"

"If I need to run you through to get to him, I will," said Sabbath. It didn't matter. Greed, a full head taller than the actor, grabbed his arm and flung him bodily to the pavement. The thick wet sound of the man's head meeting the ground was familiar enough to Sabbath, but brought only a chorus of enthusiastic gasps and low whistles from the crowd.

It occurred to Sabbath that he might have to kill his way through the crowd, even the police, to escape alive. *Abathar!* he thought desperately, like a battlefield prayer. But the angel had promised not to intervene again.

Greed charged, taking the blade in his stomach up to the hilt. It meant nothing. He grabbed Sabbath by both arms and squeezed hard, with huge hands and a grip that Sabbath could only squirm in.

Greed opened his mouth. There were teeth all the way down his throat. On his tongue, on the roof of his mouth. His face inched slowly toward Sabbath's. That, Sabbath realized, was the difference between gluttony and greed. A glutton would have simply consumed his face, sucked the flesh from his skull, and swallowed it all before Sabbath even hit the ground.

But Greed wanted more; his appetites were diverse. He wanted the meat, and the energy of the crowd surrounding him, and to inhale Sabbath's fear and agony, before finally devouring him.

But Sabbath wasn't afraid. It was a Tuesday morning. Despite the aspersions cast by the angel, Sabbath knew that his mother was a true prophetess, and that she loved him. He was going to live.

Sabbath relaxed his arms and hooked his right leg around Greed's left. Greed lunged, and Sabbath twisted. They fell together. Sabbath took the pommel of his sword in the sternum, but it made Greed let go as he hit the sidewalk. Greed plucked the sword from his chest, grabbing the blade with both hands, heedless of anything and gaining it before Sabbath did.

Sabbath ran, pushing his way through the cheering crowd, knocking cell phones and grasping hands away from his face. The police began shouting, the sirens screeching again. The helicopter was coming in low. The Financial District reminded Sabbath of London; the high buildings like the Roman wall, long wide streets cutting through a grid of tiny doglegs with low-slung buildings on either side. He couldn't run for much longer; his lungs were burning. He didn't dare stop even for a moment to consult the tattoo on his arm. Greed, and the swelling crowd, were behind him, a crashing wave of shouting and hunger.

"What are you doing?" Jennifer said to Miriam. Jennifer was staring up at the ceiling, her legs and arms spread wide, limbs spilling out of the small tub. Miriam was in a corner, hunched over her phone, toes hanging off the edge of the mattress like a gargoyle.

"Watching this livestream. Some kind of riot near Wall Street," she said. "Don't you care about the news? I start my day catching up with Twitter."

"Not when I turned my back into a pretzel sleeping in the bath all night," Jennifer said. She picked herself up, and gasped as the tub itself shifted and the soft wood of the floor under it creaked.

"That tub is going to fall through the floor one day, Jenny. Anyway, your boyfriend is on Wall Street, in the middle of some kind of riot," Miriam said. "He probably started it." She raised the volume on her phone, filling the room with the tinny sound of a streaming video.

"Oh God!" Jennifer scrambled upright and found the remote control. She turned on the TV and clicked to NY1. "It's just the mayor talking."

"By the time the news vans get through the streets, it'll all be over. This is pre-breaking news. Check it out; two screens, two streams." Miriam had a sleek new Google Pixel that could display a split screen. Small images, of course, but they were clear. In one, Sabbath ran wildly toward the famous statue of the bull on Wall Street; in another, a flood of people pressed up against the camera lens, flowing toward some off-screen goal.

"We need to get down there!" Jennifer said. "Call a cab."

"No way; a ride-share is better," Miriam said. She thumbed her screen, then stopped. "Wait, why are we going down there? Why am I going there? You don't even have a car app on your phone. What can you possibly do to help?"

"Whatever, Miri," Jennifer said. "Lock the door behind you. I'll hail a cab on the street like some kind of Neanderthal woman." She grabbed a pair of yoga pants on the floor, turned them right side out, and furiously pulled them up her legs.

"You're not even wearing underwear—goddamnit fine, I'll come with you!" Miriam said. "Car will be downstairs in two minutes."

When Sabbath saw *Charging Bull* and *Fearless Girl,* he was perplexed, out of breath, and out of ideas, save one. *This is a pagan place,* he thought. *One of magic and sacrifice.* Is that what Greed was—some primal thing, older than Christianity, older maybe than even humanity? The actor had been fed some sort of catechism, but it was just so much excuse-making. Even old King Croesus wouldn't be so bald-faced as to insist that greed was a virtue that even outlaws in rags benefited from.

And yet, here, a mass of people the size of English forces

at Assandun was converging upon him, all somehow committed to greed.

And Greed, who led them, with Sabbath's own sword in his hand, was their God. Sabbath? He was the sacrifice. The helicopter overhead wasn't the divine Abathar come to spirit Sabbath to his reward, but a vulture to claim his body.

They didn't charge, to overwhelm Sabbath like a tide. Instead, Greed's acolytes, some in suits or sharp-angled skirts, others in the denim Sabbath had learned to associate with the toiling classes, and others still hardly dressed at all though it was autumn, surrounded the small green on which Sabbath found himself. Greed stepped forward, casually swinging the sword, still hungry for the spectacle. Those blasted little rectangles of glass were everywhere. Though they were, to a soul, Greed's thralls, the assembled were more deeply enthralled by their phones.

Then they began to chant. It wasn't the modern tongue, and it wasn't the English or Latin Sabbath knew. It, if anything, sounded more like the sound a beast would make, something emerging from darkness upon the face of the deep in the time before God shifted his gaze toward a world covered in black waves. Greed swung the sword, his wrists spinning it about him to the rhythm of the grunting, the keening.

Sabbath had a moment to think. *How can this possibly be happening?* was the first thing that came to mind, his entire being rejecting the madness of the modern age, angels, cars and helicopters and a shark-mouthed sin leading an army of eager slaves to kill him.

Just surrender. There had been so much death already. It was almost as though the sins Sabbath had dispatched had thrown themselves at him, hoping to blunt his blade against their hell-forged bones, to drown him in their own oil-slick blood. To wear him down to nothing so that he would *just surrender* before completing his holy mission. Surrender. The thought was comforting but foreign, like a warm greeting offered by a guard on the borderlands of a strange new nation.

You have to fight again, Sabbath thought. His aching muscles stirred; fire ran through his veins, momentarily easing the pain of his many cuts and bruises. Sabbath *wanted* to fight again. He was hungry for it. That's what the angel had told him. It was Sabbath's wickedness that made him immune from the influence of the sins.

Everyone wanted a show. So Sabbath would give them one. Even if the climax was Greed slicing open Sabbath's stomach, Sabbath would strangle that sin-beast with his own entrails. Give the crowd what they thought they wanted.

Sabbath kept his knees loose and held out his arms, palms up. He put himself in position, between the statues. Greed would have a little trouble swinging a full arc of Sabbath's blade.

"I'm waiting!" he shouted at Greed. "Aren't we all waiting?" He glanced around him and the bystanders. They all were eager for it.

Greed smiled. Those teeth again. And for the first time, he spoke.

"I want you," he said. His voice was a rumble, like a pair of tectonic plates scraping against each other. Sabbath felt it in his bones. The crowd grew still. They wanted him too.

"Come, then!" roared Sabbath. "Come collect your beating!" Greed glanced at the sword in his hand. Then his smile faded. No more fangs, just a pair of lips drawn tightly over them.

I will not die today, I will not die, I will not *die,* Sabbath reminded himself, trying to bury Abathar's warning that he could still spend his last few days on Earth a helpless cripple.

Greed charged. He was many things, but he was not a clever swordsman. He swung the blade like a baseball bat, too eager to slice his foe in half. Sabbath ducked a wide swing and shot under. He squatted, wrapped his arms around Greed's knees, and threw himself backwards onto the cobblestones. Greed flew out of his arms and landed with a thump and a shriek behind Sabbath, and on the statue.

Greed had gotten a horn in the base of the neck. Sabbath scrambled for the sword, his rib cage a vest of pain. Greed put his hands against the bull's head and plucked himself off the statue's blunt horn. The puncture wound was ugly, but not fatal. Sabbath slid behind *Fearless Girl* to give himself a moment to catch his breath.

Greed touched his neck. "More," he said. His voice hadn't changed at all. It wasn't coming from his lungs, his throat, his mouth. It was in Sabbath's mind. Greed's words echoed in the minds of the assembled, who were watching like bored aristos casually taking in a morning's sparring practice.

Sabbath didn't feel more confident, though he'd won

first blood, though his sword was back in his hand now. He'd hit the ground hard. Greed didn't seem fazed by his wound.

"Do everything you can, Sir Hexen. Every scintilla of effort, for me. Aim all your focus and energy at me—"

A car horn blared. Not unusual in Lower Manhattan, but this one was insistent; the driver was leaning on the steering wheel, eager to be heard over the whooping of the helicopter. For a moment, Sabbath wondered if it wasn't the police, here to take him in. In the split second of hesitation, Greed charged. Sabbath was still fast. He winced as he sliced into Greed, and Greed kept coming, pushing himself up the blade, reaching out to embrace Sabbath.

Then Sabbath understood. He let go, planted a front kick in Greed's stomach to push himself backwards, out of range of Greed's grasp. He couldn't give Greed what he wanted. Instead, he rushed into the crowd, tearing phones from hands, smacking faces, practically swimming into the throng.

At the other end of the block, inside a late-model Prius, Miriam shouted at Jennifer over the sound of the horn. "Well, there's one stream gone! And another! Your boyfriend is really going apeshit on everyone!" She was in the front passenger seat, and so had to turn and extend her arm to show Jennifer, in the back, the phone. But Jennifer's head was down; she was peering at her own phone.

"I've got the aerial view," Jennifer said, "from a legitimate news source. Oh . . . God . . ."

The driver stopped honking for a moment, then redoubled his efforts on the horn. He tried to rev his engine, but the Prius didn't make much of a sound. He edged forward, waved his arm, and bellowed for people to get out of his way. Miraculously, they started to. Then the crowd broke into a wild run. Sabbath hit the windshield hard.

"Hexen!" shouted Jennifer. The driver beat on his horn again, then stopped and turned to Miriam. "Out! You and her go!" Miriam opened her mouth to object, but Jennifer was already out the door. Miriam opened the passenger-side door and slammed it into Sabbath, who winced and staggered.

"What the hell is going on?" both women demanded of him. Miriam put her camera in his face, and Sabbath grabbed it and threw it into the mass of people following him.

"My phone!"

"I need to get away from this place," Sabbath said. "Greed draws his power from adulation, from the crowd."

"How do you know that?" Jennifer reached for the handle of the car door, then yanked it back suddenly as the Prius sped away, in reverse, the driver still beating his fist against the horn.

"You learn things about a man when you fight him," Sabbath said. He nodded toward the approaching figure. Greed had found his smile again, and was flashing fangs enough to rival a thornbush.

"What about my phone!" Miriam said.

"Forget it, let's go!" Jennifer said, grabbing her hand.

"Why did you even bring us here!"

"Do you know this part of town? We need a quiet place."

Miriam laughed harshly, like a dog spitting something out. "Good fucking luck!"

"Miri!"

"Wait, I do know a place . . . but you owe me a phone. Come on!" Her hand still in Jennifer's, she ran, pulling Jennifer behind her. Sabbath followed as best he could, with Greed, and his worshippers, casually strolling behind him.

They ran up Broadway, Miriam pounding the asphalt, Jennifer barely keeping up. They had to wait for a few precious moments on the corner of Exchange Place for a limping Sabbath to catch up to them.

"Three more blocks, then another turn," said Miriam. "Don't get separated."

"They're still coming," said Jennifer. Greed hadn't quickened his pace, and had even lost a few of the quiet mob following him, but his stride remained confident, inexorable. He even waved, then pointed a long index finger at Sabbath.

"Don't panic, we're close," said Miriam, "and the place is probably empty."

Nobody was patronizing the Museum of American Finance that morning. Sabbath's sword convinced the ticket taker and the docents to have their lunch breaks both early and simultaneously.

"It's so strange, we haven't attracted police attention at all," Jennifer said as she looked around the museum. There were an array of exhibits and informational standees, a wall of currency, a small couch made of hammered coins, a statue of Alexander Hamilton, and a pair of winding staircases that dominated the middle of what was once a marbled lobby.

"Of course not. If that really is the personification of Greed out there, he owns this part of town. The state is subservient to capital," said Miriam.

"Indeed," said Sabbath. He was looking at the currency display. "Paper money, for use by anyone at all . . . ," he muttered to himself.

"You're very sure of yourself for someone who didn't even believe any of this a few minutes ago," said Jennifer.

"I pride myself on being an adaptive thinker who is open to new experiences," said Miriam. "We need to set up an ambush. He's here."

"This is where you chose to die and be consigned to Hell," Greed said as he entered. The crowd behind him did not follow, but rather stayed by the doors and the heavily barred windows. The view was inadequate, but Greed needed space to perform, and followers would just cramp his style.

"Fuck this," said Jennifer, pulling her pepper spray from her purse.

"Women, go," said Sabbath. He readied his sword and positioned himself between the pair and Greed.

"I've got to see this," Miriam said. "Jen, gimme your phone. Your boyfriend chucked mine somewhere."

"No . . . ," said Jennifer. "I . . . we shouldn't . . ." But she was reaching back into her purse for her phone as she spoke.

"Jennifer, don't," said Sabbath, glancing around to see where he could catch a glimpse of her.

Greed grinned. "Very good." He walked toward Sabbath, casually considering the blade pointed at him.

"Girls . . . I am not going to win if you stay . . . ," Sabbath said. He started edging backwards, toward the staircases.

Miriam held up the phone. "No way . . . the irony of it all. This will go viral. . . ."

Greed opened his mouth wide. His jaw unhinged, and to Sabbath it grew larger than was physically possible. The mouth was like a cave, with white stalagmites and stalactites ending in glistening points, an esophagus like a bottomless pit, and a hungry, howling wind that threatened to pull Sabbath into Greed's maw, tear him to nothing more than shredded meat hanging off a set of splintered bones.

That's greed, Sabbath understood now. *A great hole that can never be filled.* He'd experienced it himself. Sabbath had never cared much for riches, but there was greed for other things—women, food and drink, combat. . . .

And acclaim. It wasn't enough to be the bravest, most audacious knight. He had to be universally feared. When Richard II got on his knees and begged, when Sabbath mocked him though the whole kingdom hung in the balance, that was greed. All for Sabbath, nothing for anyone else.

Sabbath couldn't fill the hole confronting him, couldn't find his way through the darkness. This was it, then. Swallowed, consumed, crushed, and dissolved. That would be his hell. Sabbath wouldn't even make it to God's Judgment. In what seemed like the distance, he heard his sword drop to the floor.

And then came the scream. Sabbath thought it had emerged from his own throat.

No, he was wrong. It was someone else.

Miriam was on her knees, cursing and grabbing at her face. Jennifer met Sabbath's eyes, then turned the pepper spray on herself. She blinked, struggled visibly to keep her eyes open, then sprayed herself and let out a howl.

Greed paused for a moment, nothing but a large man with his mouth hanging open. Sabbath grabbed his sword and with a two-handed swing took off his head. Black blood splattered all over the display cases and splashed against the floor like ink. Miriam regained her footing, only to slip and land painfully on her ass, grunting hard and flailing about blindly.

"Fucking kill him already, Sabbath!" Jennifer cried out between heaving gasps.

"I did!"

"Then go get us some water!"

"No, milk of magnesia . . . ," said Miriam. "Don't touch your face. . . ."

Sabbath glanced through the windows. The crowd was already dispersing, and not as one would expect. They didn't walk off in small groups or point into the museum as they left or even behave as though they had witnessed a killing. Sabbath guessed that the museum staff might have a small refrigerator somewhere about, as Jennifer had in her gallery, and soon enough found both some bottles of water and a pint of milk in a break room. He also found a canvas tote bag and deposited Greed's head within.

"You can't just leave the body here," Miriam said. Her face was still flushed. "You were on the internet. That was a news copter up there."

"I don't think the sins wish to be known to the world at large any more than I do," said Sabbath.

"At any rate, we'd get more attention trying to get rid of the body," Jennifer said. "Let the janitor or the cops deal with it. We need to find a place to hide out."

"They know of you, Jennifer. In my encounter with Wrath—"

"What was he? A crooked cop?" said Miriam with a snort.

"A—" Sabbath reached for the words. "—cage fighter." He glared at Miriam, then turned to Jennifer, squaring his shoulders. "He threatened you. The sins know of you, and of your home. We cannot return there. And they know of where I was staying . . . a hotel. Not the one you put me in."

"How did you get the money for a hotel?"

Sabbath dug into the pocket of his jean shorts and produced the prepaid debit card he'd won after defeating Wrath. Miriam hopped to her feet and twisted it in half till it snapped. "This is how they're tracking you, of course." She flashed a mischievous smile. "You two will have to come with me."

"But . . . I need my heads," said Sabbath.

7

When thou sittest to eat with a ruler, consider diligently what is before thee: And put a knife to thy throat, if thou be a man given to appetite.

—PROVERBS, 23:1–2

On the PATH train to Jersey City, Sabbath found himself contemplative. This world was a strange place, and so full of wonder and convenience that he could not even understand how war and strife could continue to exist, save for mankind's propensity for sin. Retrieving the duffel bag was trivial; Miriam had summoned a freelance servant who worked for money that wasn't even paper money, but simply the idea of it, and directed him up to the room. Another servant drove up in his own car and transported them quickly to the World Trade Center PATH station, and then a great snaking train brought them not only underground, but under the Hudson River as well. The train was neither wet nor dark, nor did it smell of fresh water or fish. The world was a wonderland of untold riches and convenience, even for someone as poor as Jennifer purported to be.

Of course, this was just as the actor who had been possessed by Greed had explained to Sabbath that morning over pancakes. There were still profound divisions in society. Miriam had even laughed right in his face when he remarked about how pleasant-smelling he found Manhattan as they took the car trip.

"Next stop, Hexen," Jennifer said. She seemed exhausted. Her face was still streaked red from the pepper spray, but the few other passengers on the subway coach paid it no mind. Her curls were falling flat, and she chewed on her upper lip absentmindedly. Miriam had her arms folded across her chest and was staring at Sabbath, as if trying to see through his skin, to his inner workings.

Sabbath couldn't even describe his inner self to her had he wanted to. These conflicts, assassinations after a fashion, were wearing on him greatly. He needed a healer; he needed men to help him. He needed fucking Abathar to wing on down and explain all this shit to him, and to the girls at least.

"Why do you believe me?" he asked Miriam, his voice dry. The train slowed to a stop, the bell chimed, and the doors slid open by themselves, and fit perfectly into the very walls of the coach. *Amazing!*

And nobody around him appreciated the spectacle, save for a near-infant girl who pointed a stubby finger at the doors and laughed as Sabbath shuffled out behind Jennifer and Miriam.

Miriam's apartment was significantly larger than Jennifer's—a large living room overstuffed with bookshelves, a small kitchen, and three bedrooms and two baths off a long hallway with yet more books lining its walls. "Fuck," said Jennifer, to which Miriam quickly responded, "I told you that you were being a snob with your 'technically New Jersey' shit."

"You live alone?"

"I Airbnb the spare rooms," Miriam said. Abathar's whispers did not deign to enlighten Sabbath on the subject of Airbnb. He lurched to the living room couch and, without kicking off his shoes, lay down and closed his eyes.

"Should I . . ." were the last words he heard before falling into a deep sleep.

". . . put the heads in the fridge or something?" Miriam asked Jennifer.

"This is the strangest conversation I've ever had," said Jennifer. "I guess so?"

"This is what happens when you fuck strange men," Miriam said as she pulled the duffel into her kitchenette. "I'm going to just put the whole bag in. Luckily, I always eat out. Nothing but a couple bottles of wine and some condiments in here."

"It's not like I knew you very well back when we hooked up, Miri," Jennifer said. "We'd hung out, what, twice?"

"I said 'strange men,' not 'strang*ers*.' Women are much less likely to . . . uh, be a serial killer. You're lucky I was your lesbian rebound, honestly. I'm not like other assholes on Tinder. I read a lot."

"After all you saw today, you still think that's what's happening?" Jennifer peered down at Sabbath, who was snoring gently. "Should we tie him up? Call the police?"

Miriam slammed the door to her refrigerator shut with her hip and then snatched a book off one of her shelves.

"Check it out: *Serial Crime: Theoretical and Practical Issues in Behavioral Profiling*," she said, pushing it against Jennifer's chest. "Criminology minor. I had a double minor."

Miriam returned to the kitchenette and poured a couple of glasses from the wine bottle she had removed from her refrigerator. "It's a classic—Hexen Sabbath is a visionary serial killer. He remains one even if he is politically or metaphysically correct. He's driven to murder because of voices in his head, even if the voice in his head really is from God. Which I doubt, even after our, uh, experiences earlier today."

"Because you're Jewish?"

Miriam glared. "Because I'm rational. I mean, he could go to the authorities, couldn't he? He doesn't have to kill or confront the sins directly in order to stop them, does he? What did he say, that Wrath was a cage fighter? Just call the cops and have them bust the fight."

"And Greed? You even pointed out that there were no cops, that Greed controlled the whole Financial District. . . ."

Miriam contemplatively sipped at her wine. She had Jennifer's glass still in her hand. "Sure, but Greed seemed to emerge only in response to Hexen. If he hadn't killed the other sins in the first place . . ."

"So we should tie him up?"

"Take your drink," Miriam said. Jennifer juggled the book in her hand for a moment, and then took a gulp of wine. "No, I don't want him on my couch all day. Besides, how would he go to the bathroom? No, what we would do is look at his tattoo and make nuisance phone calls—police, fire, EMT—at the locations, then watch the news and see what happens, if anything. Flush 'em out."

"That sounds criminal," said Jennifer. "But I guess we're already really fucked, in a way."

"I have several rotting heads in my refrigerator, and we transported them across state lines," Miriam said. "One of my tenants left behind a burner phone—she was French; her usual cell phone didn't work here in America. We'll use that to make calls."

Jennifer sat cross-legged in front of the couch, finished her wine, and examined the tattoo on Sabbath's arm. "Only one glowing dot left."

"Maybe the others are here in Jersey City," said Miriam. "Maybe they're right downstairs." Jennifer whipped her head in Miriam's direction, and Miriam cackled.

"What is wrong with you?" Jennifer demanded.

She shrugged. "Call it a bit of black comedy. We've been through a lot today. If we're not going to do the logical thing and just grab all the cash we have on hand and take a bus to Canada and once there do farmwork till we can afford to fly out to Cuba, I insist on my right to make upsetting jokes. Listen, does the tattoo shift around, or does it just depict Manhattan? Maybe the other sins are just based in Brooklyn or something. If they *are* here, there's nothing we can do about it now. Where's the one dot?"

"Fucking fine . . . ," Jennifer muttered to herself. "Central Park West, maybe. Like the southwest corner of the park." Her voice was toneless.

"Fancy!" said Miriam, resolutely ignoring Jennifer's mood. She walked over to her open laptop and looked up a few numbers. "Damn state lines . . ." Then she punched the first phone number into the burner phone.

Miriam was inventive on the phone, calling in the smell of gas from a hallway, a lame carriage horse spotted from the street, and concerns about an abandoned-seeming cardboard box that she was just sure might contain a jihadi IED—this last reported in a passable Texas drawl.

"That's it?" said Jennifer when Miriam was done. "Prank calling?"

"It's not the greatest idea, but it is the safest. What should we order in for dinner?" asked Miriam. "Also, are you sure you don't want to head to the bedroom for a bit?"

Jennifer was sure she did not. Miriam turned the living room television on to keep an ear out for any unusual news reports while Sabbath slept, but recaps of the previous night's debate between presidential candidates, from Las Vegas, droned on, uninterrupted.

"I feel that you are subtly mocking me," Sabbath said soon after he awoke. It wasn't the gibberish of the politicians that had roused him—though he was more convinced than ever of a need for a hereditary monarchy—but the smell of dinner. Miriam held out the turkey leg, a huge smirk on her face. Sabbath snatched it from her, chewed off a huge hunk of meat, swallowed it, and said, "Despite your insolence, I thank you."

Miriam snickered. Jennifer pursed her lips.

"How are you feeling, Hexen?" Jennifer asked. She was picking listlessly at a small bowl of takeout macaroni and cheese. Her cheeks were sallow in a way familiar to Sabbath. Not everyone could handle war. He didn't know what to say—a jest would be easy, a boast satisfying, and there was nothing to be gained at all from the truth. But he spoke the truth anyway.

"I'm alive, thanks to you, Jennifer," he said. "Greed would have consumed me—"

"And we would have enjoyed watching it," Miriam interjected. "We were positively eager to see it."

"Eager to see something," Jennifer said. "I wanted you to win, Hex."

"So did I, but—"

"But to you it didn't matter, did it, Miriam, so long as there was some sort of spectacle to witness, right?" said Jennifer.

"We are all weak in the face of sin," said Sabbath, holding out a hand. She quieted down, and Miriam seemed less tense as well. "It wasn't that you wanted me to behead Greed that saved us, it was your self-sacrifice, Jennifer."

"Yes, thanks for Macing me," said Miriam. "That's not sarcastic, though I'm sure it sounds it. It was the right thing to do, and honestly I've always been curious as to what it feels like. I missed out on Occupy a few years ago, because I was busy with graduate school and I'm rambling sorry I'll be quiet now." The sentence didn't so much end as it simply stopped when Miriam crammed much of a biscuit into her mouth.

"I'm alive, but I am hurt," Sabbath said. "Rest and food are good, but I think I've broken some ribs. My legs are weak. I dread the thought of lifting my sword again. I have a sense of what your medicine is capable of, and it's not much for someone like me. I have no time for the physical therapy or bedrest a modern doctor might prescribe." He licked his fingers. "I need drugs."

"Like painkillers?" Jennifer asked.

"No," said Sabbath.

"Steroids? Those won't work in time. We have, what, three days?"

"Not steroids either, Jennifer," said Sabbath.

Miriam smiled, her sticky lips coated with crumbs. "Coke or meth? PCP?"

"Something along those lines," Sabbath said.

"I can get coke, but I don't see how it'll help. You need your wits about you, not just to be on a rampage."

"I need both," said Sabbath, "but I think I'll be able to call upon neither if I have to confront the rest of the sins any time soon."

"How do you even know about contemporary drugs?" Jennifer asked.

Sabbath nodded toward the television and shrugged. "I heard a man arguing with a woman about them as I slept. Something about rampaging, drug-crazed people taking over the country. I'll need to go on a rampage if I'm to defeat the remaining sins."

"You don't need to go berserk, Mr. Sabbath. It didn't help with Greed. Jenny outwitted him," Miriam said. "What you need is acid. This morning, before we came down to Wall Street, Jen told me about the angel and the whole business. You need to get back into contact with a higher consciousness, your cosmic self."

Abathar's gift quickly filled him in on the nature of LSD. "I . . . hmm," he said, considering the possibilities.

"That sounds like a terrible idea," said Jennifer. "What sins are left—?"

"Gluttony, Envy, Pride," said Sabbath.

"And what were they like?" asked Miriam. "Like . . . that *thing* we encountered today?"

"Sloth was a government employee." Miriam guffawed when Sabbath said that. "Lust a whoremonger who claimed not to be lust at all, but she bled black as pitch."

"You kill women," Miriam said plainly, but she looked at Jennifer when she spoke.

"She had entrapped me, and was going to kill me. She said that *I* was Lust." No noise from Miriam that time.

"Wrath was a warrior; I defeated him in a fairly straightforward single combat."

"And Greed hardly even seemed human," said Miriam.

"So what might the others end up—" Jennifer searched for a word and found it. "—manifesting as?"

"Pride could be . . . hell, who isn't proud of themselves these days?" Miriam said. "Maybe like Greed, it'll just be a human shell and be surrounded by normal human braggarts. Or it could be some Upper East Side soccer coach with a sack full of participation trophies."

"Envy? A homeless person?" Jennifer offered. Miriam glared.

"Or like Lust," Sabbath said, "perhaps Envy would be someone who inspired envy rather than someone envious." He sensed that Jennifer had made some political claim Miriam disapproved of, but decided the best thing to do was push past it.

"Most homeless people don't envy a bath and a warm

meal and a roof over their heads," Miriam said. "They deserve those things, as a human right, Jennifer." Her voice was acid. An instant later, Sabbath understood what "human rights" were and laughed out loud.

"Let's get drugs and get going," he said. Jennifer turned to her phone and sent a few texts, making arrangements. Jennifer's contacts were all in Manhattan, so a rendezvous point had to be arranged, but Miriam's "friend" was over soon enough.

"No acid," she said when the man, who never entered the apartment proper, handed her a brown paper bag and left. "Shrooms. Time to find out about this God business."

"Shrooms upset my stomach," said Jennifer. "I'll wait till we get to the city and get something real."

"Hexen?" Miriam said, holding out a dried-up cap. He shook his head warily, so Miriam just popped it into her mouth, winced, chewed, and then swallowed. "Blech, I should have eaten it with peanut butter or something." She walked to the kitchenette for a glass of water.

"Gluttony," Sabbath said, looking at his forearm.

Sabbath had to admit to himself that there were many things he just wasn't good at. Even with Abathar's gift providing him the basics of living in the twenty-first century, Sabbath realized that he was so out of place in this new world, he could barely function. He needed Jennifer to guide him back through the PATH station, and it was Miriam who reminded him, more than once, to watch for traffic in both directions when crossing the street, even if he was also supposed to entirely disregard the lighted pedestrian signals. “Everyone jaywalks!” she snapped at him. “But you have to be predictable. Waffling about whether or not to cross the street is a great way to get hit by a car.” They were like a pair of fish, these women, swimming down a stream whose currents they could sense easily, but that he was blind to.

That’s why he wanted to fight. It would make more sense, tactically, to try to bring the sins together in one place, set the building in which they met aflame, and then slice off the heads of the survivors, but Sabbath couldn’t understand what motivated them, what their plans were. The sins seemed happy to explain themselves—they mocked him with their disclosures, and even though his collection of heads weighed down his duffel bag, the sins had thus far made very little in the way of moves against him. Fighting was easy enough, and he was good at it, and he was winning, so that was what he’d focus on.

Sabbath didn’t bother to ask why Miriam hailed a yellow cab instead of summoning a car with her telephone, and why Jennifer paid in cash instead of with one of those miraculous money-cards. He didn’t know why Jennifer and Miriam had a quick and angry discussion about menthol cigarettes, nor why they spent several hours in a tavern where virtually nobody spoke the language he understood to be English, nor why the cigarette he was given to smoke was wet as if it had been dipped and drowned in some vile liquid.

He was especially confused by what appeared to be a king’s wood in the middle of the otherwise relentlessly urban concrete labyrinth of the city, and why Miriam started laughing at all the police cars and crime scene tape on the corner of Central Park West.

"We did this," Jennifer whispered in his ear, which didn't illuminate matters. He looked down at his tattoo—one of the sins was very close.

"Follow me," he said, ducking under one of the NYPD sawhorses. Jennifer and Miriam scrambled after him.

"Perfect!" Miriam said. "The police aren't bothering you. It must be time for a showdown, just like this morning. . . . Where are we going?"

Jennifer shuddered, then laughed sharply, like a seal barking. "Svinya!" she said, pointing. Sabbath noticed that her nose was a bit bloody, and she twitched.

"Of course," said Miriam.

"Could somebody . . . ," Sabbath started. Something was happening to his lungs, his muscles. His aches hadn't vanished, but they had . . . dissolved? For lack of a better description, he felt the pain leaving his body, pooling at his feet, dripping out of his toes, and somehow percolating through the asphalt down into the bowels of the earth, where it leaked like rain on a poorly thatched roof onto the heads of horned imps and demons, sending them howling and flinging their arms up to protect their heads from the acid of his agonies.

". . . Russian for 'pig,'" Jennifer concluded. Sabbath had missed everything. It was very late, but he wasn't tired. He had no idea what he was experiencing now.

"No way am I paying for this. On top of everything else, we're going to do the ol' dine and dash. Who's with me?" Jennifer said. She led the way, striding ahead of Sabbath and through the doors of a restaurant, the name of which Sabbath couldn't read. The letters on the signage and windows weren't of the Latin alphabet.

"Fuckin' cokeheads," said Miriam, mostly to herself. She looked up at Sabbath, her lips pursed. He looked back, and couldn't help but smile. Even his teeth weren't bothering him.

"I . . . ," he said. His tongue felt odd, bigger than a fist, in his mouth.

"We're facing Gluttony," Miriam said. "Svinya is a Franco-Russian fusion place; very elite, very one percent. Jean-Georges lost a Michelin star and . . . oh, you don't understand any of this, do you."

"Is it time to fight?" Sabbath managed to say.

"It's time to eat," Miriam said. "A nice late supper." Sabbath held his stomach—that late-afternoon turkey leg may have been a mistake.

They entered the restaurant, which was empty save for the screaming of Jennifer and the hostess, both in Russian, and the dead-eyed stares of the wait- and bar staff.

"Reservation!" the hostess demanded when Sabbath and Miriam walked into the vestibule at the front of the restaurant. The place was crowded with tables, like a hall in a castle on a feast day, with huge windows that somehow kept the sound of the streets out.

"We . . . don't have one," said Sabbath.

"The place is empty," said Miriam. "Just seat us. We're with her." She nodded toward Jennifer, who was glaring, red-faced, at the hostess.

"No reservation, no seat!"

"Party of . . . three?" said a man in chef's whites, who had just appeared in the front of the house. His smile was plastered onto his wide face. In his hands he held a cleaver and a white towel with which he was wiping clean the blade.

Jennifer marched up the brief steps to the main dining area, hand out, speaking Russian. The chef juggled his towel and grasped it, kissed it, and said something soothing and lyrical. He nodded to the scowling hostess, then swanned off.

"Come," said the hostess to Sabbath and Miriam, and she led them up. "For you, we have a tie and coat," she said to Sabbath. Then she looked him over more carefully. "A coat, anyway. I can tell that you're not a tie type."

"Chef's menu," said Jennifer once the hostess seated them and returned to her quiet station. "Full *service à la russe.*" She placed her napkin onto her lap.

"Almost every restaurant serves *à la russe,*" Miriam said. "It just means bringing the food out one course at a time." She smiled cattily at Sabbath. "So it's not like a banquet, where everything is brought out at once, and replenished as people eat. Well, except for the removes, of course. That's called *service à la française.*"

"I'm just going by what I was told," Jennifer said. "Shrooms make you chatty, Miriam."

"And coke makes you bitchy, Jennifer," Miriam said. "Cocaine is a drug for climbers," she explained to Sabbath. Abathar's whisper of enlightenment was not forthcoming. Before he could ask, he caught a glimpse of Jennifer's burning eyes. A welcome distraction came in the form of a waiter arriving at the table. He offered Sabbath a red blazer with black piping to wear. Sabbath struggled to put his thick arms into the sleeves without getting out of his seat.

"Your bag, sir?" the waiter asked.

"You definitely don't want your fingerprints on that bag," Miriam told him. The waiter whipped the towel off his shoulder and wrapped his hands in it before hefting the bag up and taking it away. Sabbath peered down at his empty service plate. Something was wrong with his stomach. All his organs seemed to be heating up, as though they were being held over dim embers.

"Miriam is very suspicious of social climbers," said Jennifer, very loudly, as if the virtually empty restaurant were crowded with the noise of conversation and clinking utensils. "You know, the merchant class and all that." She looked at Sabbath meaningfully. That aspersion he understood well, and Abathar's wisdom sought to calm him. Miriam clutched a fork in her hand, nearly ready to jab it in Jennifer's face. This dinner was not going well, and it hadn't even started yet. They all wanted something they couldn't have, and were ready to fight one another for it. He remembered something that Jennifer had been muttering in the yellow cab. *Maintain, maintain . . .* , Sabbath chanted to himself.

"Oysters," said the chef. "Triple triplets." The waiter returned with a colleague, and plates of nine oysters each were placed atop the service plates before the guests. Chablis was served to match. The chef left with the waiters, but not before offering a smile and a nod toward the plates.

"Cocaine makes me so fucking hungry," Jennifer said as

she attacked the shells with her fork. Sabbath reached for a fork, but Miriam put a hand on his wrist. "The small one," she said.

"This is going to be a long supper," Sabbath muttered to himself. The oysters were incredible, reminiscent of the sea but without a fishy taste. Miriam ate hers with gusto, which Sabbath understood to be against the rule of her religion. Perhaps Judaism was as different now as everything else he'd encountered so far, save for the depravity of human nature. The ladies were not maintaining as well as he was.

"Just watch us . . . uh, me, throughout the remainder of the meal so you know which utensil to use," Miriam said, smiling crookedly at Jennifer, who had rushed through her oysters and was now manipulating the shells with her fingers. "Jen, did you *have* to do coke tonight?"

"It's a Midtown asshole drug," Jennifer said. "And we're in Midtown."

"So we have to be assholes?"

"Sometimes," Jennifer said, her gaze drilling a hole through Miriam. "Look, you know what?" she announced to the table. "This is just fucking crazy. The whole week has been. This is what happens when someone goes to church in the current year? If I'm to do anything other than go out to Central Park, dig a hole with my bare hands, and just live in it for the next forty years, I need some kind of edge. Everything in my life is going to hell right now."

"Yes, everything is going to Hell," said Sabbath. He presumed the chef was Gluttony. Would the next course be foul, or poisoned? Would he be strapped to the chair by the waiters and forced to consume until he exploded? And what role would Gluttony have in the plot to destroy the earth with fire, as the Lord God had once done with floods?

"Mushroom solyanka," the chef announced as he returned with the next course, whose trays were covered. Jennifer explained, "Soup!" The oyster plates were removed, and shallow bowls full of a bright pink liquid in which floated cabbage, cucumber, and mushroom replaced them.

Sabbath waited for Miriam to select a spoon from the setting before her, and aped her choice. The soup was excellent: earthy in a way, yet lively. Sweet and sour, without making too much of either sensation. Cookery this good could not be a sin.

"Sir," said Sabbath. "Why have you chosen to serve us tonight?"

"My restaurant is new, and it would suit me to have a more downtown clientele," the chef said. "Your friend here is quite the influencer on social media. I hope she'll take photos of my dishes and post them, to help bring in some of the hip art scene crowd. She made you quite famous, in fact. Your marvelous Enochian tattoo has been the veritable talk of the town." He chuckled, his jowls quaking.

"Did you know this restaurant's name is Russian for 'pig'!" Jennifer said. "Imagine that; all those awful Midtown assholes lining up for an evening of formal dining, but they're really just oinking away at the pig trough. Ha! Hey, where is the wine for this course?"

"Yes," said the chef. "Indeed. The wine." He took the opportunity to turn on his heel and consult with the back of the house.

"Only alcoholics and morons expect a separate wine

course with the soup," Miriam said, leaning over to whisper into Sabbath's ear.

"Miriam has a trust fund, Hexen," said Jennifer. "Did you know that? She used to eat this way all the time." She swallowed three spoonfuls of soup in quick succession. "I have very good hearing, you know."

"Jennifer was hoping that by calling me, I might be persuaded to float her a loan for her art gallery," Miriam said softly.

"That's not true!" Jennifer said.

"I'm glad to hear that, Jennifer."

Sabbath finished his soup.

"At any rate, my money is in trust, which means that I can't actually give it away," Miriam said, turning spoonfuls of soup over in her bowl. The embarrassing silence was ended by the return of the chef and waiters.

"Small dishes, hot and cold," the chef explained as both the soup and service plates were taken away. New, larger plates were set out. They'd been warmed in the kitchen. "Miniature pumpkin stuffed with rice and apples," the chef said as bright pumpkins, their tops tilted jauntily over the casserole within, were plated. "Herring covered in a fur coat of beet." What looked like small bright red footballs of shredded beets were placed next to the pumpkins.

"Seasonal!"

"Madeira," the chef said as new wine was poured. "Are you enjoying yourselves thus far, my friends?"

"I am," said Sabbath. Jennifer had grown agitated and Miriam strangely sullen, but the food was too good for Sabbath to resist. His mood was brightening, even as the drug he had smoked earlier continued to have its way with his internal organs. He could feel his own brain pulsing in his skull. The chef's face was growing rounder, more piglike. Sabbath could smell the sweat on the chef's brow, even hear a drop make its way down his prominent cheek.

"Please, eat the pumpkin before it cools, sir." Sabbath consumed it in two bites and washed it down with the wine. Abathar's wisdom spurred him to say, "Excellent. The dryness of the wine complements the sweetness of the pumpkin . . . Chef Gluttony." *Dry wine,* Sabbath found himself skeptically thinking, even as he said the words.

Gluttony tilted his head in acknowledgment. "Nothing but the best, you see. Nothing but the best."

"The shrooms have definitely kicked in," Miriam said as she closely examined her fur coat of beets. "It's all very intricate."

"Kill him, Hexen," Jennifer said. "Kill him and collect his head."

"You've gotten very bloodthirsty all of a sudden," Miriam said.

"What are we supposed to do? Wait till after dessert?"

"There are police everywhere outside," said Sabbath, "and the front of this restaurant is all windows. I wonder . . . when I kill a sin, does the odd protection against the authorities they grant me during these encounters dissipate?" He swallowed heavily. That was a mouthful, and it wasn't the wine at work, but the drug he'd taken before. "What was in that cigarette again?"

"Angel dust," said Jennifer. "It's supposed to relieve pain and make you better in a fight."

"Jennifer reads the *Daily News,*" said Miriam.

"Angel dust . . . ," Sabbath repeated, thinking of Abathar. He recalled the moment when Abathar revealed his true self in the alleyway and shivered. There was something like that explosion brewing within him. A minor version, a travesty of Abathar's angelic power, but dangerous nonetheless. *Maintain, maintain.* It seemed like good advice for him, even if Jennifer and Miriam weren't maintaining all that well.

Jennifer was about to speak when Gluttony and the waiters appeared again, this time with platters and serving spatulas. "Fish," said Gluttony.

"You have to tell them how much you want," Jennifer said.

"I'm feeling full already," said Miriam. The chef glowered at her.

"Long Island bluefish, baked in mayonnaise and mustard. Liebfraumilch," the chef said. Miriam waved the platter away, murmuring about warm mayo, though she did take the white wine. Sabbath and Jennifer nodded for portions.

"Any fish can have bones," Miriam said to nobody but her empty plate.

"Gluttony," said Sabbath between bites. "All the other sins I've faced, and defeated I should remind you, felt the need to tell me what part of the plan they were to play in their attempt to destroy this world. You've been silent on the subject. I presume this means that I have already won, and that you cannot carry out your plans without the ability of Sloth to lull men to sleep, without the scandal of a politician falling to lust, without the fury of Wrath—"

Gluttony held up a palm. "Please, Sir Hexen, just enjoy the meal. I am pleased to tell you that it will not be your last. I am not here to harm you, nor am I here to play some minor role in the cosmic machinations of the others. Why would I destroy so fertile a world, one with such a burgeoning population of hungry mouths to feed?"

"Why would any of the sins do anything that would kill all of mankind?" asked Sabbath.

"To put everyone in Hell," Jennifer said. Her mouth was full of fish. She spat it into her napkin. "That's it, isn't it? To raise an army of lost souls in Hell and from there to invade Heaven!"

"Theologically dubious," said Miriam. Gluttony nodded toward her. "For one thing, it radically decenters humanity, conceptualizing the human soul as a pawn rather than as the actual subject of universal telos." She sipped her wine. "I am extremely high right now."

"One might say that through laziness, one could see their world fall to ruin, or through rage destroy it mindlessly, or lust for death, and the like"—Gluttony waved away the other sins as he spoke—"but I require life to thrive." He said something in Russian, and two of the waiters cleared everyone's places while the third poured more wine. "Moulin-à-Vent," he said three times, to each diner individually.

"To settle the stomach before the next course," Gluttony explained. He walked off to the kitchen, waving the staff to follow behind him.

"What do you think, Hexen?" Jennifer said.

"About . . . telos? I—"

"No, about what's his name over there!" she hissed, jerking her head toward the kitchen.

"He is an excellent chef," Sabbath said. "I'll kill him after we finish eating."

"Do you trust him to just keep feeding us?" Miriam said thoughtfully. Her gaze was directed at the ceiling. "Ever read the seminal graphic novel *Watchmen*?" Jennifer snorted disdainfully. "I know you read it, Jennifer," Miriam said, "but Hexen, you've not. The climax is that while the heroes are traveling to and then tangling with the villain, his plan is already unfolding. By the time they finish listening to his interminable monologue, it's too late."

"'I did it thirty-five minutes ago,'" Jennifer said.

"See, I knew you read it."

The conversation was interrupted by the entrée: blinchik with beef cheek filling, truffle shavings, caviar, and gold leaf. "Only idiots are impressed with edible gold," Jennifer declared, right in front of Gluttony. "Three molecules thick; gold leaf is cheap, and just gives chefs a reason to add forty percent to the price because climbers and the bridge-and-tunnel crowd from Lawn Guyland fall for it."

Gluttony smiled. "Spoken like a true arriviste," he said. "Médoc du Bordelais," he explained as the latest wine was poured. "They say artists associate with all classes of people, and that makes them dangerous, Ms. Zelanova. And gallery owners also must associate with people of all classes. Does that make you dangerous?"

"Maybe just to the people I associate with," said Jennifer.

"But don't restaurateurs also associate with all classes of

people?" asked Miriam. "Even in fine establishments like this one, who washes the dishes? Who delivers the meat and veg?"

Gluttony just turned his smile her way and responded, "Delightful child."

Sabbath looked up at Gluttony, his cheeks bulging with the delicious meat-filled crêpe he'd just been served. He lifted his right hand, knife still clutched in it, and dragged his thumb against his throat, then pointed to Gluttony with the tip of the knife, then to his own chest with the knife. Then he nodded, and swallowed.

"I presume you'll want to finish your meal first," Gluttony said.

"Oh yes," said Sabbath. "Everything is delicious."

"Everything is delicious," Gluttony agreed.

"I'm feeling pretty full," Miriam said after Gluttony again returned to the kitchen. "And he's been swanning around the table all night. I'm not sure what's happening here—"

"No?" Jennifer said, her voice acid. "Not in touch with the cosmic consciousness after all?"

"You're in touch with the cuntish consciousness," Miriam said.

"Ladies . . ." Sabbath held up his hands. Their voices, their attitudes, were getting on his nerves. The drugs in his system were making him increasingly upset. Supposedly, some Danes, like the ones he'd faced at Assandun, garbed themselves in bearskins and had the ability to whip themselves into some kind of frenzy when they fought. Sabbath hadn't noticed any fighters like that during the battle and, truth be told, always felt that the rumors were the sort of nonsense piss-stained levies spread to explain their own cowardice on the field of battle. But now, he understood. Not the cowardice, but the inspiration of their fears: the men who waited on the front lines, gnawing on the steel bands of their own shields, eyes red, lusting for the horn to sound so they tear the sausage casings out of their opponents and consume them. He didn't know if he could make it to the end of the meal without killing Gluttony, the waiters, that shrieking harpy of a hostess, and if they kept up the mutual sniping, his dining companions. *Maintain, maintain . . .* , he repeated to himself uselessly.

"Your mom's in touch with my cuntish consciousness," Jennifer fired back.

"Very mature," Miriam said. "A 'your mama' joke. Did you workshop that at the creative writing course you took at the New School over the summer?"

"I workshopped your mom at the New School over the summer," Jennifer said.

Miriam snorted. "Okay, that one was funny." Jennifer giggled and they clinked glasses. Sabbath sighed with relief, but his heart wasn't slowing down. Was the rich food killing him, or was it the fire in his lungs from that tainted cigarette? His hands were cold and clammy, and his forehead dripping with sweat. Something had to happen soon.

"My God, sweet Christ, how many more courses are there!" he shouted as the waiters came out with small bowls and port glasses, with Gluttony on their heels.

"Sherbet and rum," he said. "Second service in a few moments."

"Don't worry, guys," Miriam said. "Third service is mostly booze."

Sabbath frowned as the knives were cleared. He had no idea where his sword was or, for that matter, where the heads of the sins had gone. He was going to have to kill Gluttony with his bare hands, and probably also protect the women from the waiters and the kitchen staff if the situation degenerated into a melee.

"Oh God, oh God," Jennifer muttered to herself as she flexed her fingers. "I think I'm gonna lose it. Why are the wine pours so small? And, yes, Miriam, I know the answer: because there's a wine with every course and there are like a million courses. It's rhetorical. Everything's rhetorical!"

"You should have done the shrooms, not the coke, Jennifer," Miriam said. She closed her eyes and exhaled with such finality that Jennifer didn't dare answer back. Sabbath peered at her as well, half hoping that when her eyes opened, she would speak with the voice of Abathar and offer some much-needed guidance. Nothing happened. If not for the fact that her neck stayed erect, Sabbath would have guessed that Miriam had just fallen asleep in her chair.

Gluttony and the waiters returned. "Roasts, hot and cold," he said as small portions were served. "Lamb shashlik," Gluttony announced, gesturing to kebabs on what looked to Sabbath like skewers of pure gold. He'd try to palm one for a weapon, and for some quick cash, if possible. Steam rose from the chunks of juicy meat, and despite what he'd already eaten and drank, Sabbath found himself salivating again. "Buzhenina," Gluttony said as the waiters served thin slices of roast pork with small pools of horseradish and mustard on either side.

"Reminds me of the holidays," Jennifer said. "Christmas in January." She went right for the cold dish, but Sabbath chose the kebab and congratulated himself for eating the roasts in what was clearly the correct order. The cold roast wouldn't get any colder while he ate the hot item.

"What's wrong with your friend?" Gluttony asked, pointing his chin toward Miriam, who had yet to stir.

"Eh . . . she's having a reaction to the mushrooms?" said Sabbath.

"Don't drink the burgundy with the cold roast," Gluttony told Sabbath. Jennifer was doing just that, and cringed. "One never corrects a lady," Gluttony explained to her before turning back to Sabbath and snorting. "But, you! The vodka. Yes, that's it."

"Not bad," said Sabbath after downing the shot.

Next was hot dessert—Guriev kasha prepared the old way, with the porridge poured in layers to create several strata of milk skins between portions of the sweet creamed semolina wheat. Topped with brown sugar and apricot coulis, it was gone in two spoonfuls.

Miriam stirred, and opened her eyes. "I . . . ," she started. "Sabbath, we're in trouble. This room is very dark. Look at the shadows in the corners, by the bar."

"Surely it is near midnight," Sabbath said.

"That doesn't mean anything. We have electricity in this era, you doofus! She's right," Jennifer said. "It was brighter in here before, and the lights are still on just like when we were seated, but it's darker anyway. Active shadows, like they're eating the light. Weird . . ."

"We're in a stomach," Miriam said. "It's obvious now. We're the ones being consumed."

"That's the shrooms talking!" Jennifer said.

"After all you've experienced, how can you say that—?"

"Just because I've seen some impossible supernatural things doesn't mean that anything that comes to your mind while high is a true revelation from the cosmos, Miriam."

"You don't have to believe me," Miriam said. Then she turned to Sabbath, and said, "*You* have to believe me."

"We'll be leaving soon enough," Sabbath said.

"What's the afterlife like?" she asked.

"Uh . . . what?" Sabbath said.

"Did I stutter?" Miriam said. "What is the afterlife like? Is it like this? Are we in Sheol, now, Hexen Sabbath? Is this a foretaste of our Final Judgment?"

"I . . . don't know what it's like," said Sabbath. "I've no memories of the past centuries, and if I did, I couldn't be sure I was even in the afterlife per se."

"'Per se,' he says," Miriam said.

"I thought Jewish people didn't believe in the afterlife," said Jennifer.

"I thought Russian Orthodox girls didn't believe in fucking strangers, or experimenting with lesbianism and then breaking girls' hearts six months ago," said Miriam. "Or rebounding, for that matter."

"What did the angel tell you?" Jennifer asked, swiftly turning to focus on Sabbath, willing Miriam onto some ice floe in the Arctic.

"He told me that God is always love, and that sometimes God's love is fire," said Sabbath. He shrugged.

"Very old school," said Miriam. "I guess you were plucked out of time before contemporary Western visions of Heaven and Hell were formulated. Or, you know, you've read a book."

Sabbath narrowed his eyes. "Why do you seek to taunt me, Miriam? Do you think there's anything you can gain from this mockery, or being an obstacle to the task laid out before me?"

Miriam ran her tongue across her upper lip, contemplative. "I'm sorry, really. I'm just . . . this is a strange trip. I have a sense that something bad is coming. I wanted to be prepared. I'm sorry to you too, Jennifer. I don't mean to be a bitch, I just . . . look, I spend a lot of my time reading books and intellectualizing the big questions of philosophy and theology, but I'm not prepared, really, for any of this to be true. Not even after what we experienced this morning. I'm impressed; how are you holding up, Jennifer?"

"I am extremely fucking high!" Jennifer snapped.

Gluttony returned, the waitstaff behind him. This course, dessert, he carried himself. "Ptichye moloko," he said of the confection in his hands. "Bird's milk cake." As the waiters poured port wine and offered a selection of beers in bottles, Gluttony sliced the chocolate top of the cake with a sharp-looking slicer.

"That's more of a spring dessert," Jennifer said, scowling at it.

"You're correct, madam," Gluttony said, not looking up from plating. "But the four seasons as you know it are soon to end, so why not enjoy what you can, while you can."

Sabbath growled, his appetite forgotten despite the intriguing slice of white fluffy mousse before him, the thin strips of cake that were presaged by the milk skins in the previous dessert, and the black chocolate top so shiny, he swore he could see his reflection in it, even as the dining room continued to darken.

"We've enjoyed your hospitality, Sin," Sabbath said. "But you have no role in the plan your fraternity has hatched, as you've admitted."

"You think sins can't lie?" Miriam asked.

"I think a true glutton would be pleased to show off his role, and not obscure it. Any lie would be more grandiose, more spectacular, not a meek admission that he is superfluous. Isn't Gluttony the weakest of the fatal sins, after all? In my time, most people, even if afflicted with gluttony, had no opportunity to practice it."

"You are right, Sir Hexen," said Gluttony. "On the subject of driving the human species to nuclear war, I have nothing to offer. Have you seen what the men who consider themselves the rulers of this sphere satiate themselves with? Power in the abstract, women and men of the most quotidian shape and taste, foolish displays of bravado better reserved for apes in the jungle. No sophistication, no sense of style. All animals are commanded by their stomachs, but a true glutton is interested in quality as well as quantity."

He raised the cake slicer with a flourish. Sabbath was fast, grabbing a beer bottle, shattering the end against the side of the table, but Gluttony was faster. He opened Miriam's neck with an expert swipe, sending a fountain of blood cascading across the table settings.

"Ah, and with that, I—" Gluttony lost his face to Sabbath's jagged bottle before he could complete the sentence. Sabbath chopped away crudely at the neck, the bottle cracking in his hand, until he saw bone. Then he twisted the head right off. A wave of noise erupted and burst into the dining room as police swarmed in. Jennifer, covered in blood, screamed, then dived under the table. Sabbath threw himself at the police, hacking away with his bottle and the cake slicer he had claimed from Gluttony's dead hand.

Shots were fired, barely audible over the screaming.

A pair of strong hands found Jennifer's ankles and pulled her out from under the table, leaving streaks of blood across the carpeting. She cried out for Sabbath, for Miriam, biting her lip when she remembered what had happened, and then a baton to the back of her head silenced her.

8

A sound heart is the life of the flesh: but envy the rottenness of the bones.

—Proverbs 14:30

Jennifer was almost thankful that her brain had shut down after seeing her friend and lover sliced open in front of her. The fingerprints and mug shots, the casual cruelty of the guards down in the Tombs, the steely gazes of the other women in the cell with her. She would have been upset, terrified even, to suffer through a body cavity search, to be deposited among the sort of women whom she remembered from school as her bullies—they'd owned the hallways, smacked her and yanked on her hair, spat in her face for the traces of Russian accent she used to have.

But after Miriam was slaughtered in front of her, now that she could still smell Miriam's blood in her hair even after the rough scrubbing she got during intake, she didn't feel afraid. She didn't feel a thing. Not even regret that she had announced, "I have a fair amount of cocaine in my system, but I also ate a really big dinner," to the EMS paramedic during the medical questions.

It's good to be insane, Jennifer decided.

Everyone in the cell was pleased to leave her alone,

which was good. Jennifer no longer knew what she was capable of. Her grandmother had been in a prison during the Second World War—she used to tell stories about being transported in a crowded train car full of typhoid patients, and once in prison having to make a shiv out of a bedspring to scar up a couple of other women with it. Only because she was very good at ironing shirts did the prison commanders not lay a hand on her.

A cell in Manhattan Detention Complex wasn't so bad. It wouldn't matter what happened now. Sabbath had failed. He'd spend the next few days in some other cell in some other corner of the building, and then the remaining sins—Envy and Pride—would somehow trigger a nuclear war and destroy the world.

"Don't worry, everyone," Jennifer announced. "We're all going to die very soon!"

"Shut the fuck up," a woman said, not even looking at her. There were seven of them in the cell, and a couple had commandeered the small bed. Another sat on the toilet; she wasn't using it as anything but a chair for the moment. Two others were in the far corner, and the shut-the-fuck-up woman stood in the middle of the cell, glaring at Jennifer. "White bitch," she added, for clarity's sake.

"Oh, shut up," someone else said with a laugh. "You're always saying 'white bitch' when a white girl gets arrested. You think that makes you hard?" A murmur of agreement went up from the others as the cursing woman glared at them all.

"Yeah. Never mind, Sharonda," said the woman on the toilet. She pointed to her forehead. "She's crazy."

Jennifer's skin sprouted gooseflesh. She was doing all the wrong things, but it didn't matter. She had to speak. She looked right at Sharonda, challenging her with a stare.

"When the big one drops, this place won't just be your tomb, it'll be an oven in an empty kitchen in a dead city, you understand me . . . *Sharonda*?" Sharonda walked up to Jennifer, getting in her face. Jennifer smiled. She realized what Sabbath saw when he saw an enemy. Nothing but a pile of weak spots—a nose for chewing on, knees for kicking at, joints for twisting, a neck for teeth or fist. The woman was a bit shorter than Jennifer; she took to the balls of her feet to meet Jennifer's eyes. Jennifer widened her grin, hoping to draw the woman in closer. She'd be easy to push over with her heels off the ground. It was so fun. *Is this what Hexen feels like all the time? Is this what men feel like all the time?* she wondered.

She decided to find out. Jennifer threw her left hand around the back of Sharonda's neck and planted her right fist in her ribs. Then again and again. A roar went up, cries for the guards. Sharonda went for the hair, but Jennifer's arm blocked her right hand. She shoved her forehead against the woman's nose and pushed, then pulled back. Sharonda stumbled and spun, hanging on to Jennifer's hair, boxing Jennifer's ear with her free palm.

What would Sabbath do? Jennifer asked herself, but her nervous system knew the answer even as she formulated the question. She grabbed at an ankle and with all her might straightened up, sending the back of Sharonda's head bouncing off the floor of the cell. Jennifer could hear only the blood running in her ears, not the hoots and cheers of her cellmates, not her own cackling laughter, and definitely not the actions of the correctional officers gathering their shields and helmets and getting in formation to clear the cell. She was still giggling when she found herself being slammed repeatedly against the wall of the cell, still cackling as she was pinned, secured by all four limbs, and physically dragged away. She shouted for her phone call as though it were the punch line for a joke. "Too bad my grandmother is already dead! She'd love it here!"

Jennifer said things and responded to the questions and demands of her keepers for some time after that, but it was nothing that she could recall several hours later, when she woke up from a dream in which she had lost an arm while trying to swim in a frigid black ocean. The cast on her left arm didn't itch; it was one of those modern fiberglass numbers. A familiar-looking man was peering down at her. She couldn't recall his name, but he had been to her gallery. *The gallery!* She tried to sit up, but found that she was restrained with leather straps. Pain stabbed through her left arm. It seemed like an eternity before she remembered everything—Sabbath, Miriam, her arrest. She sniffed the air. The sour funk of hospital air was further tainted by the metallic sizzle on her tongue, in her nose. Still in prison, she figured, in their infirmary or a private room set up as one.

"You have friends in high places," said the man. That triggered a memory.

"Lou?" Jennifer asked, tentative. "No, Mario. He made that mistake."

"You're good," said Mario. He let himself smile. "Aldridge wants to see you."

"Why?"

Mario shrugged. "Theirs not to reason why; theirs but to do and die," he said. "I'll get him."

When Aldridge showed up, his aura filled the room. Jennifer had grown up with him as an occasional figure on television and in the gossip columns, the rhetorical stand-in for a rich New York asshole now that all the Rockefellers were dead. In person, he was very different. His face was less rubbery and more alive than she'd ever imagined. He frowned in a way that dared you to try to make him smile. Even his hair, itself the favorite of editorial cartoonists and late-night talk show host monologues, was better. Instead of looking like a few feet of hair swooped up and combed over a bald spot—did it droop past his shoulders in the shower?—the man's hairdo looked like an amber wave of grain. Like the song. Like America.

Aldridge opened his mouth. "You're a tough lady, you know that. They're all talking about you downstairs. You made a real impression, the way you handled yourself in that fight."

"Oh . . . thanks," Jennifer said. "I'm not proud."

"You should be, though. You should be." He turned to Mario, who nodded. Jennifer spotted Lou through the open door; he was loitering in the hallway along with two other Secret Service agents and talking to someone she could not see. "You taught that bitch a real lesson," he said. His tone had shifted midsentence, and then back again. Jennifer opened her mouth to object, but the words caught in her throat. Aldridge was right. That woman was a bitch. And she had started it. She shouldn't have stepped up if she didn't want to hit the floor.

"Fuck that girl," Jennifer said. She tensed against her restraints. "She'd better be tied up like this too."

"She doesn't need to be tied up," Aldridge said with a smile. "She didn't wake up yet. She'll be fine, though. They've got the best doctors here, real smart guys."

The best doctors here, Jennifer thought, *in Central Booking?* She didn't say anything, though. She deserved the best doctors, didn't she? She'd been through a lot. Maybe he had his personal doctor flown in to treat Sharonda. Maybe that was something Aldridge would do.

"Could you . . . help me?" she asked.

He smiled more widely, like a jack-o'-lantern with slits for eyes. "Yeah, we're getting you out of here." He turned his attention to the hallway and waved his arm. "Let in our new friend. Jennifer, meet Ekaterina."

Jennifer nearly choked when Svinya's hostess walked in. She was still in her black vest and dress pants, and looked worse for the wear, sporting a shiner and a split lip. In her arms, she carried a clear plastic bag, which contained Jennifer's clothes and belongings. Whether it was the police who did it or Sabbath, or even Jennifer herself who punched Ekaterina, she couldn't remember. Ekaterina smiled at Jennifer down in the bed. There was a trace of maliciousness to the grin, but her words were kind. She spoke in Russian, as if she were one of Jennifer's aunts, and explained that Jennifer would soon be free to go.

"See," said Aldridge, gesturing toward Ekaterina. "I found her for you, personally. She told the police you were a victim. That your boyfriend with the tattoo had brought you to the restaurant under duress, and demanded a table.

That after a long meal, he refused to pay the bill and attacked the chef, and killed your friend. Good story, eh?"

"Uh . . . I've watched enough *CSI* to know the police can measure blood splatters and angles and figure out who cut whom pretty easily. Plus, didn't the police see us come in? What about the waiters?"

Mario spoke up. "Ma'am, I was a police officer for a few years, and I'll tell you that, in the end, what the police want is a narrative that explains the crime scene as the first responders witness and report on it. They've got their man. Now you're free to go. You'll probably be called as a witness if the killer doesn't plead out, and given the number of cops your boyfriend put on the injured reserve, he's not going to plead."

"But . . ."

Mario glanced over at Aldridge, hesitant.

"Go on, tell her," he said to Mario. "We got it all worked out. A month from now, you'll be working for me, directly. Personal security. I like you . . . Mario." He smiled, knowing he'd gotten Mario's name right, but Mario did not return the smile.

"Look, Ms. Zelenova," Mario said. "We don't know where your boyfriend came from, but we know a lot about him. He has no ID. His fingerprints aren't on file. He's never been recorded by any facial recognition software before last Saturday, not anywhere on this planet. He doesn't have a filling in his mouth, though he has several cavities." Mario pursed his lips, exhaled roughly through his nose, then began again. "Remember a few years ago, when that nuclear power plant in Japan leaked? There were years of aboveground nuclear tests back in the early days of the

Cold War. Your parents were around for Chernobyl. I lived pretty close to Three Mile Island when I was a kid. We're all slightly radioactive now, every human being on Earth. But not your friend.

"We recovered some of his hair at the scene. As you can imagine, the Secret Service is a bit more prepared to deal with, say, a dirty bomb than the NYPD is. We tested it—he doesn't have a fraction of the uranium in his hair that a man in his thirties should. Even if he'd spent his whole life in a cave in the middle of nowhere . . . I . . ." He shrugged. "I can't explain it. We tested everything twice, and then we tested our equipment."

"The technology the Secret Service has, it's amazing, incredible," said Aldridge. "I have had top-level bodyguards for years, but I never saw anything like what they have before I started my campaign. Mario was telling me about how one time he had to snag this guy in Penn Station—he was headed to the UN with a nuke."

"He triggered our sensors, but he had just come from Brookhaven National Lab on Long Island, and had received an accidental dose. He was a scientist. There was no bomb, but that is a good illustration of how sensitive our tech is, Ms. Zelenova . . . ," Mario said. He had more to say; it was written on his face. He had more to *ask,* Jennifer realized, but he dared not in front of—

"He saved the city, Mario and his team did," said Aldridge. "That bomb could have taken out half the city."

"There was no bomb," Mario assured everyone in the room.

"But if there had been one, it would have been huge,"

Aldridge said. "It would have blown a hole straight through the bedrock, and the island of Manhattan would have sunk like the *Titanic*."

"I, uh . . . don't think . . ." Mario trailed off. Despite the obvious idiocy of Aldridge's claim, there was something compelling to it. Even Jennifer started feeling a little afraid. The radioactive guy hadn't been a terrorist, but what if he had been one? And terrorists had never in history managed to build and detonate a dirty bomb, but there's a first time for everything, isn't there? In a perverse way, Jennifer felt proud. She lived in the greatest city, in the greatest country, in the entire world. Of course everyone was jealous and wanted to destroy what she had.

"Thank you," Jennifer said to Mario. "Thank you for your service." Mario smiled. Aldridge widened his smile even further and said, "Good girl," and it didn't even cause Jennifer's neck to prickle.

"You're a good girl," he repeated. "When the doctor gives us the all clear, we can take you home. It's Wednesday; you've got your opening in a few days. Don't think I've forgotten. I'll still attend, and bring all sorts of photographers and journalists with me. I have a couple campaign stops in Ohio and Pennsylvania, but you know, I like to sleep in my own bed."

"He does," Mario said. "We make a lot of trips back to New York."

"May I go now?" Ekaterina asked. She glared at Jennifer as she spoke, and threw the bag onto the bed by Jennifer's bound ankles.

"Sure you can go, goodbye," said Aldridge. "I'll get you

all set up with a new job in one of my hotel restaurants, just like we agreed."

"But . . . ," said Jennifer, "what am I supposed to do? I mean, shouldn't I say something? Do something? Do I have to sign a form? Will I have an arrest record, or can it be expunged?" She dropped her head against the pillow. "This is going to show up on my credit report, isn't it?"

Aldridge nodded toward Mario and glanced over at the door. Mario nodded back, frowning, and left the room, closing the door behind him. Aldridge snatched up a stool, then glanced around, looking for something. He found a box of Kleenex, grabbed a handful of tissues from it, wiped down the seat, and only then placed it at Jennifer's bedside and sat on it. He crumpled the tissues in his hands and tore at them as he spoke.

"You know what's going on," he said. "You think anyone cares about that stupid cook, or any of the other boys and girls your boyfriend iced these past few days? Two weeks ago, they didn't even exist."

"How do you know—?" Jennifer said. "Oh."

Aldridge nodded once, pleased.

"But, wait, you're famous! You even ran for mayor when I first moved here. I mean, the presidential election started, what, two years ago or something?" Jennifer's blood ran cold. She should have asked Mario to undo her straps before he was dismissed. "Don't kill me. Please, I won't tell anyone. It doesn't matter, right? It's all going to be over in two days, so you may as well keep me alive? Who'd even believe me?" She'd already decided to scream when his petite hand stroked her cheek, then covered her lips.

"Ssshhh," he said. "I'm not going to hurt you. I still need you. You see, your friend managed to slip away somehow." Jennifer blinked twice, trying to ask her question. "I don't know either," Aldridge said, "but if he's still out there, I have a problem, and I don't like having problems. I like solving problems. I didn't spend all this time and money to have my plans defeated. Dark forces are trying to rig things, but you and I are going to make sure everything happens the way it's supposed to." He took his hand from her mouth and started undoing the restraints.

"Dark forces? What are you talking about? You're the dark force!" Jennifer said, pulling her left arm from the loosened belts. "Why do you think I'd help you?"

"A second ago, you were ready to make a deal," Aldridge said, reaching over to undo her right side. He leaned heavily, unnecessarily, on her chest, his belly pressing against her breasts. "Well, smile for me, because I'm in a generous mood. I've got a deal for you." He undid the buckle of the torso strap, then moved over to the legs. He was a big man, a high school jock long gone to seed, but still able to move with some dexterity and confidence.

"Here's my offer," he said when she was entirely free. "Go home. Do whatever you want. Don't worry about the murders or the crimes; you won't be in the news. I'll take care of the news right now." He slipped his cell phone out of the inside pocket of his blazer and started tapping away at the screen. "Alone at last," he muttered to the phone. "And . . . send! There, that tweet will keep those sons of bitches in the news media busy for a couple of days."

"What did you say?" Jennifer said.

"Go home and read it like everyone else, Jennifer," he said. "Just go home and live your life."

"So I'm bait. You think he'll come back to see me," Jennifer said as she clambered off the bed and snatched up her bag with her good right hand. "What's to stop me from warning him about you, and this conversation?" He wasn't going to force her to change in front of him, was he?

"Maybe that's what I want you to do," Aldridge said with an exaggerated shrug. His whole face pinched up, then deflated when he lowered his shoulders. "Maybe it's not. Too bad you can't try it both ways, eh? Now, get out of here before I change my mind and kill you." He shouted for Mario, who opened the door and gestured for Jennifer to follow.

"Is this really part of your job?" Jennifer asked Mario once they were on the stairwell. "He's ordering you around like he owns you. Aren't you supposed to work for the Department of the Treasury?"

"You're right, ma'am, but consider the alternatives," Mario said. "We need a peaceful transfer of power, a status quo election. If what happened here tonight got out, he may or may not lose the election, but the public faith in the American system would be shaken. You might be a cynic and think that powerful people often pull strings to get their friends out of prison, but . . ." He grew quiet. "Well, the news would have a field day."

"Maybe the status quo should be shaken. Don't you think he might start a nuclear war?" Jennifer said.

Mario humphed. "You liberals are all the same, aren't you?"

"So you don't know—?"

Mario trotted a step ahead and turned on his heel, blocking Jennifer's path. The door on the landing was only a few paces away. Why did she even say anything? She'd felt the effect the candidate had on her, that weird sense of both fear and self-regard he'd inspired in her; Mario had been exposed to that persuasive aura for months.

"What? Did he say anything to you I should know about?" Mario asked. "Was it, uhm, untoward? I . . . I could . . ."

"Yeah, who can you possibly report it to?" said Jennifer. "The newspapers? They tried that last week. The current president? Good luck." The cynical front surprised even her. Jennifer needed allies. But Mario was just a stooge, a pawn. "Are you going to let me leave, or no?"

Mario reached into his suit jacket. Jennifer pictured a gun. Her limbs were too heavy, still tingling from the restraints, and her cast wasn't even the heavy plaster type that might do as a bludgeon. She was going to die here. He handed her his business card. It read MARIO HARRIS. "Call me on this second phone number," he said. "When you're ready to talk. You'd better get out of here now. I'll leave you here to change, and you can exit out the fire door on the first level. We've arranged for the alarm to be disabled for the next several minutes only. Goodbye, Ms. Zelenova, and good luck." He took a backward step down to the landing and exited out the steel door to the hall.

Before her clothes or purse, Jennifer went for her phone. There was still a charge, thankfully. She checked the news, social media, for anything about the restaurant and Miriam. Nothing. She wanted to text Miriam's parents, but needed to dress, and that would be difficult enough with a broken arm. And what could she even tell them? It was late; she needed sleep. She needed Sabbath.

Some hours earlier, the police van transporting Sabbath crossed Central Park. Even with all that had happened, he was impressed by it. Abathar's wisdom hadn't much to tell him that he cared about—he had no interest in or need for a summary of the park's origin or what it meant to generations of New Yorkers. He knew two important things: The first was that some of the wealthiest people in this world lived on the borders of this park, and the second was that the police were taking him in the wrong direction. He was supposed to be going downtown, right behind the screaming black-and-white car Jennifer had been stuffed into.

The angel's whisper also told him that the bullet in his shoulder wouldn't be fatal if the injury were treated soon. It was worse than an arrowhead, but he could be fixed. No provision had been made for his treatment, however. He hadn't even been cuffed or strapped to a gurney. Shot, beaten until his eyes crossed, shoved into the van, and allowed to slide across the floor, slamming against the steel walls and bench as the van took its turns roughly through the park.

The van left the park and idled a bit before descending into a parking structure. There was another wait, and some muted conversations as a small crowd gathered around the van. Sabbath felt an unfamiliar pit of dread in his stomach, which started to empty itself. He was injured, exhausted, and the drugs in his system were still wreaking havoc. He swallowed a cheekful of vomit and bellowed, "I surrender! I'll come peacefully!"

The van door opened. Five men, with long batons, cuffs, and other implements unknown even to Abathar's wisdom, surrounded him. One, an obvious leader given his position in the middle of the pack and interesting baseball cap, smiled. "I bet you will," he said. "You have an appointment upstairs."

"I need a doctor," said Sabbath. "A hospital."

"There's a doctor upstairs. Everything is upstairs. Yo surrendered, so don't fucking negotiate," said the head of the squad. Two of the uniformed men took up position on either side of Sabbath and held his arms as the group walked into what Sabbath at first thought was a waiting room or vestibule of some sort until it started to move. Abathar's whisper, and his encounter with Sloth, had already informed him of the existence of a thing called an elevator, but Sabbath was still surprised by the sheer size of the box.

"This is larger than some of the apartments I've been in," he said.

"We hear that a lot," said the leader of the security force.

The doors opened directly into a multistory open-plan apartment with several staircases connecting the floors. The word *maisonette* floated into Sabbath's mind. It was as impressive as the elevator. The far wall was composed purely of windows, with a view of the river and an electric snake of traffic lights on the street below. The furniture was all sleek and neat; the rugs exquisitely detailed in ways Sabbath had never seen before; the far-off kitchen all stainless steel and blinding copper, the couches and soft chairs seemingly untouched, and oriented toward a blank white wall Sabbath instantly understood had to do with projecting movies somehow. For all its size, the maisonette was nearly lifeless, like a castle's great hall three months into a siege. If there was a hint of the organic in the place at all, it was the well-chewed remains of a lamb shank sitting muddily in an otherwise pristine pink doggie bed in one corner.

Two tones sounded. "The doctor's downstairs," the leader announced. "Guys, bring our guest to the rear bedroom. The doc will patch him up in there." Sabbath cooperated, and found himself slightly disappointed by his assigned room, as it was only as large as the elevator, with a king-sized bed and a sleek bureau, a TV just four times the size of Jennifer's taking up much of one wall, and a peculiar set of bookshelves that looked a bit like a tree. There was a door leading to a bathroom with an exceedingly complex-looking cagelike bath with glass doors, a deep tub, a pair of shower hoses, and another television built into it.

One of the men let go of Sabbath's arm and quickly removed some crimson bedclothes from a closet, the door of which receded into the wall when he approached it. He expertly stripped and then remade the bed with the new sheets. "I'm not paid enough to get blood out of satin sheets," he said to Sabbath with a wink. "How you doin'?"

"I . . . all right," Sabbath said. He shrugged with his free arm.

"We'd offer you food, but the doctor may need to knock you out. We'll take care of you later," he said. "Just stretch out on the bed and try not to bleed too much, okay?" The bells in the living room sounded again, and the men in uniform left him alone. Sabbath eased himself onto the bed. He'd felt several mattresses under his back since his journey to the twenty-first century, and all were better than the cloth, hay, and furs he was used to, but this bed represented the same leap in quality from the motels and Jennifer's futon as those beds had from his former life. The foam seemed to ease around, then hold him firmly just when the sense of sinking would have become uncomfortable. It was warm too, as though there were small coals inside, and the heat loosened his muscles. When the doctor walked in, Sabbath could have lifted his neck to take the man in—he just didn't want to.

"Hello," the doctor, an older dark-skinned man, said. "My name is Dr. Beauregard. Best to work quickly and in silence, don't you agree?" He had a bag in one hand, a folding desk in the other, and snapped the latter open with a quick flick of the arm, then placed the bag atop it. He pulled a scalpel from his bag and expertly slashed away at the blazer Sabbath had received in Gluttony's restaurant. One of the security force brought in a bowl of steaming water and left it on the small desk before retreating without a word.

"You've been injured many times," said Beauregard. "I presume you know how not to howl." He tied a thin strap around Sabbath's arm to staunch the bleeding. "I'll have to poke around a bit. You're not supposed to remove a bullet without an X-ray first, so I want to make sure I absolutely have to, and can . . ." His singsong voice trailed off as he peered into the wound. He made a move into the flesh.

"I've never mastered—" Sabbath began. Then he howled.

Beauregard clamped a palm over Sabbath's mouth, and with his free hand pushed something against his wound. Security poured back into the room.

"Hold him!" Beauregard said. "I have to clean the wound and stabilize it." He let go of Sabbath and testily retrieved a small towel from his bag, and twisted it tightly into a bit, which he offered to Sabbath, who gladly accepted it by opening his mouth. The security staff held him by his ankles and wrists, knees and elbows, and Sabbath did his best not to resist. The cleaning stung, as did the stitching and bandaging, but he just focused on the mattress and did his best to float on it as if it were the surface of a salty sea.

"You'll be happy to know that we retrieved your bag from the restaurant," the security chief, who was holding Sabbath's elbow, said conversationally. "We put the whole thing in the Polar, because it was . . . let's say it was interfering with the brand she likes to project."

Again, Abathar's wisdom was largely useless to Sabbath, so he just nodded and attempted to smile with the towel in his mouth.

"Listen," Beauregard said. "That bullet needs to stay in place. I could remove it surgically, but there are risks involved in that too, and it would be challenging even if I had hospital access. Just trying to remove it here, with a house call bag, would be a death sentence. Just try to stay away from metal detectors, and don't move your shoulder very much for the next few days, all right?"

"Will he be able to swing his strong sword arm?" Sabbath heard someone—a woman—say. He tried to look up, but the doctor rested a palm on his forehead, pinning him easily. The woman's perfume cut through the smell of sweat, blood, and men as she strolled into the bedroom to peer down at him.

"You must be my new champion," the woman said, smiling. She was an older woman, but still extremely handsome. Her still-blond hair was well curled, her nose Roman, and chin prominent. She fell just short of beautiful, but attempted to make up for it with careful face paint and sleek lines on her blazer and blouse. She wore a necklace that appeared at first to be silver, but that Sabbath quickly recognized as platinum, with matching earrings and a somewhat misplaced stud over the left nostril.

The security force was entirely enamored with her. They looked at her with expressions that some Irish bard, those arch propagandists, would credit to warriors gazing upon their snow white queen. The doctor was a bit more in control of himself. "He probably has one more fight in him. He looks a little twitchy, though."

She smiled, not at Dr. Beauregard, but at Sabbath. "There will be only one more fight," she said, "so that is good."

There are but two sins left, Sabbath thought. The drugs were still in him, his arm burned with pain, and his stomach was bloated from dinner, despite the flecks of vomit staining his beard. Two sins left, and in hardly the shape to confront either of them.

"You need a good night's sleep, friend," she said, caressing his good arm. Her fingers lingered by his sword arm. "I want this off," she said of the remaining piece blazer, and without waiting for compliance, she took the scalpel from the table and sliced off the sleeve nearly as well as the doctor had the left.

"Aaah, there it is." She traced the broad outlines of Sabbath's tattoo with the tip of her long fingernail. It was painted lavender, an understated shade Sabbath appreciated. "I seem to be all alone in the city tonight. I'm glad you're here to keep me some company, Sir Hexen Sabbath, was it?"

"Mmrph."

"Could we just . . . ?" She looked expectant. The doctor withdrew the cloth from Sabbath's mouth.

"Yes," Sabbath said.

"What an unusual name," the woman said. "Even today, it's more suited to a musical group of some sort. How did your community react when your parents named you such? Your childhood friends?"

"Not well, generally speaking," Sabbath said. His mother, the witch, if only she could see him now. Life had been a parade of war and blood, fire and alcohol, and then he was transported to this mad world of endless wealth and insane behavior—God was dead here, it seemed. So then whom was Sabbath fighting for? "My father died when I was young. My mother had to make certain . . . arrangements with the local priest, and our reeve as well." Maybe things hadn't been so different in the eleventh century, after all, he decided.

The woman nodded. "But still she gave you such a peculiar name. . . . She wanted you to stand out. She wanted something more for you than what she could possibly give through mortal means." That wasn't a question; it was her conclusion. She smiled, tight lipped, waiting only for confirmation.

"Yes . . . ," ventured Sabbath.

"And now, here you are," she said. "Wonderful." She glanced around the room. "Find him a decent change of clothes, wash and shave him, *and* let him rest. I'll entertain him in the morning."

"No, I must . . ." Sabbath stirred, trying to lift himself off the mattress.

"You must sleep," the woman said. "You *want* to."

Sabbath did, and he did.

Sabbath woke up well settled, if not refreshed. His arm throbbed with pain, but that pain he was used to. There was still an ash sizzling in his spine from the drugs, from seeing Miriam's throat sliced open. Jennifer would not forgive him for that, but it hardly mattered, as in a few days he'd be dead. Sabbath's mother, the witch, had been right all along.

Maybe it was Abathar's wisdom, or something he had heard once elsewhere, but there prodded at him a notion—there was an eighth sin, one just as fatal as the famous seven. The craving for the sense of relief that came when abandoning one's responsibilities. You could envy it in others, lust for it, consume it gluttonously, be greedy for it, burn with wrath when it was denied you, take to one's bed in the spirit of sloth once you accepted it.

But you couldn't be proud of it.

"I suppose Miriam got her answers about the afterlife

like she wanted," Sabbath said to himself. His tongue tasted of bile, and he certainly wasn't hungry, but there was the smell of something cooking coming from the kitchen. Sabbath took that as a signal to rise. There was an outfit laid out for him, and it was a much nicer set of clothing than anything Jennifer had managed to provide. He winced as he pulled on the sleeves of the shirt, and struggled with the buttons. The trousers were less perplexing, but the belt was a challenge. A pair of socks that felt as if his feet were being massaged by the lithe fingers of a tiny maiden, and shoes in which he could see his reflection completed the ensemble. There was also a washbasin, a razor, shaving cream, and soap. Abathar's gift played along the nerves of his fingers and led him efficiently through a partial trim of his beard. Finally, Sabbath looked presentable, and found himself feeling strangely pleased that he did, though he had never cared before.

Envy, for that is who she was, was waiting for him at one end of a long table in the dining area. A servant girl was standing over a peculiar charcoal pit built into a countertop, holding a spoon of significant size over the glowing red coals. The girl had none of the dexterity or speed of the waiters in Gluttony's employ, and she avoided eye contact. It smelled like eggs. Not a bad morning spread, but he still wasn't going to eat anything.

"For my sake? I've eaten my fill," Sabbath said.

"If you don't want it, one of the dogs will eat it," Envy said as she cut into her own breakfast. She didn't look up to meet his gaze either. Her eyes were on a flat screen built into her side of the table. "But the egg spoon is hand-forged, and the hearth is fueled by lasers. Even Alice Waters would weep to eat one of my spoon-fried eggs. Sleep well? Feeling any better? Coffee?"

Coffee . . . The angel's whisper urged him on. "Yes! I'd try that," he said. The servant girl quickly and inelegantly brought over a cup full of the stuff, black. Sabbath quaffed half the cup's contents at once. "Ah, thank you, Lord, for the recommendation!"

"Marvelous stuff, isn't it?" Envy finally looked up from her screen and offered Sabbath a practiced smile. "After your time, was it?"

"Yes . . . how did you . . . ?"

"We've been through this before," she said. "On several occasions. It always seems to be a man out of time who does well in the war against us. Few people are ready to give up their lives for the sake of others, so our opponents have selected men who have nothing to lose, men with no families or loved ones, as their champions in the past. I presume now as well."

Envy was intelligent. Smarter than Sabbath. He decided to keep quiet and occupy his mouth with coffee. When he was finished, the servant quickly refilled the cup.

"Perhaps you're wondering why I didn't have you killed in your sleep," she said.

"No."

"Or why I used my many multiple connections, and no small fraction of my immense fortune," she said, gesturing around the apartment, "to liberate you. It's a challenge to bribe that many police officers, especially after you knocked out a few of their teeth. Cops are a wrathful lot, but in the end, everybody wants something. I wanted you, and they wanted money. They also wanted to relieve themselves of the strain of explaining how a chef managed to own and operate a restaurant for nearly a month without any identification, licenses, or financial history. That's how the world works."

"If you say so, ma'am," said Sabbath.

"So why did I want you?" she prodded.

"Sins are garrulous, I've found. Go ahead and tell me," said Sabbath.

She laughed a barking little laugh. From the corners of the apartment, both in the lofted area over Sabbath's head, and in the enormous living room, dogs he hadn't previously noticed stirred. One traipsed down the steps, claws clicking against wood, and presented herself to Envy. It was a peculiar creature, with fur cut and arranged seemingly just to make Sabbath laugh. Its snout and head were surrounded by a giant globe of tight curls, and its flanks and tail shaved close. Its ankles and the tip of its tail also sported puffs.

"Ah, Jean-Luc, how are you today?" She fed him from her palm a bit of white from her spoon-fried eggs. "Poodles after your time as well?"

"Poodles." Sabbath tried the word out. Abathar's whisper brought him up to speed on the dog—its reputation for intelligence and role as a symbol of a certain level of social status. He giggled despite himself.

Envy raised an eyebrow that lowered the temperature of the room by ten degrees. "When was your time, Hexen Sabbath?"

"Why does it matter?"

"It doesn't matter," Envy said. "I just want to know."

"How do you know my name?"

"It was the name you signed in with when entering the massage parlor owned by my sister."

"Ah," he said. "Yes."

"I want our time together to be positive, Sir Hexen."

"You want a lot of things, I'm sure. Those who have a lot of things often want more," Sabbath said.

"Don't confuse me with Greed or Gluttony," she said, wiping her hands with a napkin before running her fingers like a comb through her curls. "I'm not a mindless grasper or a foolish sensualist."

"What are you, then?" Sabbath took up his fork and knife finally. It felt good to have steel in his hands again, even if his shoulder twinged with pain.

"I'm a winner, Sir Hexen," Envy said. "I plan on winning this game, and by that, I mean I expect to be the last sin standing. I'll need somewhere to stand, and this world, this time, has enough to satisfy me. I'll stand here, and you'll bring me the head of Pride, and I'll place it with the others in my freezer chest." She gestured toward the open kitchen, where the servant was quietly polishing some glasses.

Sabbath snorted.

"For now," Envy added.

"I see," said Sabbath. "So, why are we breakfasting together, ma'am? Most of your comrades are dead, and the plan for your war must be hanging by a thread. Simply refuse to play your role, and all will be well, no?"

"No," she said.

"No? Why not?"

"You're a prideful man, aren't you?" she said. "Of course you are. That's why they—" Her gaze drifted up to the ceiling a story above her head, and then back to Sabbath. "—sent you, after all. When did you ever allow yourself to lose? What stupid fights, self-destructive conflicts, have you ever avoided, if the alternative was losing face, or experiencing that burning sense of shame that all men hate?"

"Truly, ma'am, I cannot think of a single stupid fight I've managed to avoid."

"And that's pride," said Envy. "What you may not know about this world is that nuclear proliferation is something of a thorny problem, to say the least. The earth may end in fire whether or not we have anything to do about it. It could happen by accident. Small nations see the big nations with their missiles, and want some of their own."

"Ah!" said Sabbath. "Envy."

"Yes, very clever, Sir Sabbath," Envy said quickly. She dabbed at the corner of her lip with her napkin, then threw a bit of English muffin across the apartment. The poodle ran after it, leapt, and snapped the crumb out of the air. "But, yes, envy. They want what their superiors already have, and why not? The United States is the only nation ever to use a nuclear weapon in war. There are other nations that have fought repeatedly—India and Pakistan—but once both joined the nuclear club, they went back to diplomacy, preening over the results of cricket matches, and minor border conflicts."

"Ah, so envy is not a sin at all, is that your plea?" asked Sabbath.

"Of course it's a sin," said Envy. "I have no need to lie to you, or manipulate you. I have something you want, is all.

We'll get to that. But what I am *attempting* to explain here is that, yes, envy is a sin. It's not immediately destructive, but one day, the wrong dictator may get his hands—and it will be a he, I assure you—on a nuke and use it. Or fail to maintain it for the sake of his own leisure. He'll plunder the public treasury, the weapon will degrade for lack of upkeep, and then it will go off. And once one nuclear weapon goes off, I guarantee you the other nuclear powers will perceive an attack and launch their missiles in every direction."

"Why would they do that?"

"Fear," she said with a shrug. "Or perhaps even"—now she smiled again—"envy. Why should they be left out of the carnage? What fun is a toy that one is forbidden to play with, especially when the neighbor boy flaunts his? Malignant narcissists rule the world. I'm sure that truth is not after your time."

"Indeed no," Sabbath said, remembering Duke Richard's airs, and his cowering as well. *Whatever happened to him? . . . Oh, dead.*

"The point is that even with our machinations in disarray, Pride will win so long as he lives. He'll find a way to launch a single missile or detonate a single bomb, and the world will follow suit. If his head is connected to his neck, the world is in danger. So I propose an alliance," Envy said.

"Between you and me?" Sabbath said.

"Between you and me," Envy said. "I'll help you. I have resources you need. Pride is a powerful man, and primed to rule the planet. I hope I don't cause offense by pointing out that you're multiply injured, wanted by the authorities, and absolutely friendless. Also, you smell. You're a disgusting derelict."

Sabbath stabbed his eggs with his fork, lifted it to his mouth, and swallowed without chewing.

"That's the spirit," said Envy. "I have something you want as well, or I can get it for you, anyway. The other woman who was arrested—" She glanced at the tablet built into her end of the table. "—Evgenia Zelenova. Ah, a Russian. He likes those."

Envy turned back to Sabbath, folded her hands in front of her. "He had an idea similar to my own, I think. He pulled strings, had her released from custody. But she is not free. Your woman belongs to Pride now. How does that make you feel?"

Jennifer wasn't his woman. Nor was she even fond of Hexen Sabbath, not anymore, though he could not blame her for that. He'd entered her life suddenly and violently, with an incredible story and bottomless demands for her assistance. In return . . . he managed to get her friend killed. Jennifer weighed heavily on his mind. He did want to see her again. No, he wanted to see her *before,* to somehow meet and get to know her in the days before this bloody week, on equal footing. . . .

The rational move, and this understanding came to him in a moment, would be to dive across the table, plant the utensils in Envy's bronze-green eyes, twist her head from her shoulders, and then relax in her fine apartment until such time as his tattoo revealed the location of Pride again. But something deeper than that flash of logic, a thing more primal, kept him in his seat. When he thought of Jennifer, Sabbath ached.

"I don't like it," said Sabbath. "I want her. I don't want him to have her."

"So it sounds like we can come to some sort of agreement, at least in principle," Envy said.

"Why do you need me?" Sabbath asked.

"Surely you know that any ordinary man would simply fall under Pride's sway," Envy said.

"Why don't you do it yourself? Summon him here and dispatch him."

"Would you come had I summoned you?" Envy asked. "There's no honor among thieves, and he knows that. He's also on an extremely tight schedule and under enormous public scrutiny. He's running for president, you know."

The knowledge of Abathar flooded Sabbath's mind again. The mass media, the Secret Service, the political balance of not only the country called the United States but the entire world. And he learned something else about Pride as well. Unlike the other entities Sabbath had confronted, this one had a history that predated the manifestation of the seven deadly sins upon the earth.

"You'd just be gunned down without me," she said. "And I have no way to get him in a private place, but you do, because he wants you dead. You and he are a lot alike. As long as you are alive, you'll keep trying to stop him. So long as he is alive, he'll keep trying to bring about the end of the world."

"And you think I'll fail?" asked Sabbath. "Are there not five heads in your freezer that can attest to my mettle?"

"Pride's . . . different," said Envy. "As I said, he's running for president. Maybe you don't entirely comprehend what that means, but you must realize that it's an important office, and that he didn't appear, emerging from the dark fantasies of humanity, just a few weeks ago to take up a position and tilt the world into the abyss. He's a person, in ways I and my siblings are not. A true person, with all the powers his office as the personification of Pride grants him as well."

Sabbath shrugged. "So? It's not like I've never killed a person before. I've killed peasants and nobles all the same. Unless his neck doesn't cut, he'll fall like all the rest."

"You're not at your best," Envy said plainly. She was at her best, even in loungewear, the morning still in her eyes, crumbs decorating her cheeks.

Sabbath had nothing to say to that. He could feel himself dying, from his injuries, the exhaustion. Abathar would be weighing his soul one way or another come Sunday. Or sooner. "Why trust you? Perhaps this is just a plan to kill me, to deliver me unto Pride. For that matter, why do you trust me to cooperate with you?" He had to keep from biting his lip in anticipation as Envy contemplated her answer. He wanted to believe her. He needed allies, he was ashamed to admit to himself. Envy's body was that of a woman just easing into her senior years without ever having strained herself physically, but she sat too confidently to be an easy opponent. There were guards about, assuredly.

And there were dogs. Sabbath saw them now, out of the corner of his eye. A pair of poodles on the staircase, another by the door. One panted lightly behind him. They looked ridiculous—all poufs and bows, like something a madman would wear to prove himself a queen—but their postures betrayed intellect, cunning, and an eagerness to serve their mistress.

"There's no need for you to trust me," Envy said. "You just have to comply. Plot and plan all you like to come back here after you dispatch Pride; I'll be gone, as will this maisonette. My true home is here." She pointed to her chest, letting her robe fall open slightly to show Sabbath the curve of her small left breast. "You'll rid the world of *most* sin, Sir Hexen. Not bad for a mortal, really."

"And envy will predominate, then?" he asked.

"Envy *does* predominate," said Envy, her tone suddenly acid. In the distance, a poodle growled. "But Pride is the sin from which all others spring, or so they say."

"Is that in Scripture?" Sabbath asked.

"It's probably somewhere." Envy waved her hand dismissively.

And if I kill you now? is what Sabbath wanted to say. Envy was a peculiar sin. She didn't lull him into sleep, like Sloth, or fire his loins, as had Lust, or goad him into battle like Wrath. . . . She just existed, and whatever she said made sense. He could perceive the deceit behind her words, but he *wanted* them to be true. She was successful, powerful, and he wanted to be a part of what she was. It would be so much easier to ally with Envy, if only to forestall the confrontation he was too weak to win. . . .

"All right," Sabbath said. "What is the plan?"

"You stay here, you rest," she said. "I'll have the doctor return and do what he can, and a massage therapist. I have access to certain drugs—" He grimaced, and she flashed a mocking grin. "Not street drugs, authentic prescription pharmaceuticals. We can get you back into fighting shape."

"We don't have much time," Sabbath said. His own inventory of his limbs told him that he would be no better tomorrow. Between Wrath's beating and the bullet wound, he was at a fraction of his strength and skill. The angel dust, the sleepless nights in strange places, the shock of all the cars and pollution and flesh and shouting. What he really wanted to do was curl up in bed and leave Envy to do it all.

"We won't need much time," Envy said. "Pride doesn't suspect me of betraying him. He's a narcissist. He cannot imagine not being loved by someone who swore loyalty to him. But my plan is simple. He told us all of his forthcoming visit to the—" She looked back down at the tablet. "—Above Below Arts."

Envy smiled at Sabbath yet again. She was good at twisting her face into a smile as though discovering someone for the first time, no matter how long she'd been with them. It was a glimpse behind the veil—what sat before Sabbath wasn't a woman, but a machine designed to act like one in a certain narrow range. A doll with moving parts.

"I want those blank canvas paintings," Envy said. "I'm going to buy them. No exhibit, no photo opportunity for Pride or for little Jennifer Zelenova, and then Pride will confront me, and with your assistance I shall defeat him, and you will get to save the world."

Jennifer walked. It took near an hour, and it was cold, but she needed the October air in her lungs, the wind on her face, anything to help wipe off the stench of the lockup, the hospital bed, and that man pressing against her. The subway was too much like prison—a steel cage full of angry, unbalanced people. No ride-shares or cabs either; Jennifer didn't want to be alone with a man. On the streets, at least she could run, scream for help.

Jennifer daydreamed of a shower, a hot one with better pressure than the pipes in her building had ever managed, but when she finally got home, she ran right to her phone charger, plugged in her cell, and perched over it like a vulture as the battery icon slowly filled. Jennifer's fingers were awkward, trembling, as she turned it on. A few months prior, Jennifer had briefly met Miriam's mother, and her number was still in the phone. She'd have to text, but didn't know what to say. Maybe she should check the online news first. Maybe call her own parents, just to let them know that everything was all right, though she knew nothing would ever be all right again.

All Jennifer's maybes vanished when the phone came to life and the screen immediately filled with notifications. Dozens upon dozens of incoming messages sent the phone vibrating and tumbling off the arm of her futon, to the floor. She scrambled after it, folding her legs under her to kneel.

Tons of stuff on Insta—her image of Sabbath's tattoo had sparked a debate, and even a set of conspiracy theories. ARMAGEDDON caught her eye. There were dozens of comments to scroll through and her hands were shaking, but it was nothing real, just some idiot who had decided that "Islamicist terrorists" had seven suicide bombers on the island of Manhattan and that the tattoo was some GPS gadget embedded under the skin of "a Jason Bourne type."

"If only!" Jennifer shouted at her phone. "If fucking only!"

There were other notifications awaiting. Four voice mail messages from her previous landlord, which she deleted without listening to. A number of emails about *Ylem,* a couple of which she probably should have answered instead of archived. A hysterical Facebook Messenger chat request from an artist who went from ingratiating herself with Jennifer to denouncing her as a "bridge-and-tunnel wannabe" over the course of fourteen unread and unanswered chats. 'K, Jennifer responded perversely. It was typing practice for what she'd have to do soon enough.

There was nothing from her parents, nothing from Miriam's. She went to Google and checked the news, typing in her own name, and Miriam's, and that of Svinya. There was no reportage at all, not even on the police blotter or on social media. Did not one person with Twitter see something, did not a single tourist get prodded by their Google phone to take a picture of the famous restaurant for Google Maps? A couple halfhearted searches about the restaurant turned up nothing about the chef whose form Gluttony had assumed, nor even the peculiarity of an elite restaurant opening in Manhattan without a celebrity chef at the helm.

None of it was real, she thought. *Oh God, oh God, maybe Miriam is alive after all.* She called Miriam, got voice mail, hung up without leaving a message. She texted her as well, and the message was quickly marked SENT but not DELIVERED. Miriam's own social media feeds hadn't been updated for a couple of days. There wasn't even a single obscure reference to crossing the Hudson to hang out with Jennifer a few days earlier.

Jennifer could call Miriam's mother, or go to the water closet, consume every pill in the medicine cabinet, then walk back out to the living room and plop herself in the tub to die. Maybe someone could use her futon after the janitor dragged it out to the street, so best not stain it after her final, fatal loosening of her bowels. Or if it was all a dream, then she was still dreaming, and the pills wouldn't matter.

If the pills did work, it would be better than calling her friend's mother and telling her that Miriam had been murdered by a man with a knife. It *was* real. Jennifer wept. There had been so much blood. Something about it had poisoned her. It's why she had been able to handle the woman accosting her in the holding cell. It was Hexen Sabbath. He had brought blood with him into her life.

Maybe the best thing to do would be to feed him to the presidential candidate, after all. Let the whole fallen world end in fire, as it had once ended in water.

Him, Jennifer thought. It didn't make any sense. Greed had barely been human, Gluttony some strange nonbeing who had appeared out of nowhere, but this man—and which sin was he supposed to be, anyway?—had been alive, and rich, and famous, since Jennifer was a kid.

Jennifer hadn't spent much time in church, but the year her grandmother died, her father got on a bit of a religious kick, and sent Jennifer off to after-school religious instruction at Saint Sophia's, in Kissimmee, Florida. It wasn't like the Catholic schools in the movies. There were no nuns, no uniforms, no underlit crucifixes casting shadows over the innocent faces of the students. It was just the priest, Father Valery, his beard and belly reminiscent of Santa Claus, leading a dozen kids through prayers in phonetic Russian, handing out chocolates, and when one of the kids would ask a thorny theological question about dinosaurs or Harry Potter, he'd answer with a shrug and a single sentence.

"That, my child, is one of God's mysteries." Father Valery was from the Old Country. *God* ended in a *t,* and *mysteries* had an *r* that rolled for a quarter of a second. That was probably the answer—the man who would likely destroy the world one way or another was just one of God's mysteries. For a mad moment, Jennifer thought she should just call her philosophically minded friend and occasional lover Miriam and ask her thoughts on the topic.

Oh.

No Miriam. No shower. No more phone. She let it drop from her hands, then climbed onto the futon without even bothering to pull the frame out, grabbed the crocheted blanket she kept rolled up atop the back cushions, and hid under it. Sleep did not come, but neither did conscious thought. She was like an insect, peering dumbly with a million eyes through the holes in the crochet pattern. She heard her phone buzz, but it was better just to pretend to be an insect, and that the buzzing was coming from inside her.

Hexen Sabbath rested fitfully for an entire day. Envy was nearly as good as her word. The bed was comfortable, and the massage therapist both careful and helpful. Another of

Envy's hired people pushed needles just under Sabbath's skin, making the flesh beneath bubble and twitch in ways that made Sabbath gasp, then relax. The sword was sharpened and polished, then brought in on a pillow for Sabbath to inspect. He opened an eye, grunted his approval, and dismissed the sword-bearer. Dr. Beauregard returned and gave Sabbath a full examination, cleaned his wounds again, gave him a series of injections, and shrugged as he spoke to Envy as though Sabbath were not even in the room.

"Look, he's not a horse," he told her. "You can't just shove some ginger up his butt and call it a day."

"Have you even tried?" Envy asked, her arms folded in front of her. She laughed at her own joke, but neither of the men in the room did.

"I've fought greater opponents while sporting greater injuries," Sabbath said as he pushed himself up to a seated position. "Is this man a warrior? A trained soldier? Has he ever even been in a fight? I've dealt with half a score of men at a time, on the battlefield and in the tavern, when I've had to."

"He's definitely been through the wringer over the years," said Beauregard, "which is precisely the problem. Someone with this many wounds should have died years ago."

"He did," said Envy. The doctor raised an eyebrow.

"Don't ask," said Envy. "Don't think. Just do what you can. He's not a racehorse; he's a show dog. He doesn't have to be the fastest; he just needs to look and act the part for conformation."

"Conformation? He's not one of your prize poodles either," said Beauregard.

"I am a man," Sabbath said. He stood up, inserted himself between Envy and the physician. "And I will fight like a man. I will not be treated like a beast in a stable. We need to find Pride immediately. You said that you could arrange a confrontation, and provide support that would grant me an open field on which I could take his head. So then, I've done all that you have asked, O Sin. I have betrayed the angel who brought me hence, and my Lord and Savior as well, because I want to win. I want victory more than I want Heaven. There is no more time to waste." He turned to the doctor. "You may go." The doctor wavered a bit and glanced at Envy, who dismissed him with a curt nod.

"You're afraid," Envy told Sabbath when they were alone. She slid close to him, tilted her head as a lover might, her lips close to the edge of his jaw. "I know bluster when I hear it. Envious people, desperate ones, so often betray not God but themselves, when the object of their desires is just out of their grasp. What is it, Sir Hexen?" She placed her palms on his shoulders and ran her hands down his back, lingering over and tracing the lines of old scar tissue as she spoke. "Do you miss your girl?"

The words stuck in his throat for a moment. "I . . . do." It was complicated, which women had never been for Sabbath before. In this modern world, it seemed that every woman could lie with whom they liked. *Whom they liked,* not *whom they had to.* That was the complication.

"Do you miss your girl?" Envy asked again, punctuating the question with a brief kiss on Sabbath's scraggly chin, "or do you just miss girls?" That was less complicated. His entire body was aching, but there was something about willing an erection that eased the pain for a moment.

"I believe that I'll not live past the day after tomorrow," said Sabbath, "so I may as well get what pleasure I may while I still can."

With surprising force, Envy planted her hands on Sabbath's chest and pushed him backwards onto the bed, then clambered atop him, tearing at his belt as she slithered out of her robe. "You want this!" she declared, slapping him across the face, then slapping him again when he jerked his head back and glared up at her.

Sabbath didn't want it, he realized. But he laughed, smacked her on the thigh a quick half dozen times, then grabbed the back of her neck and pulled her down to him for a heavy tongue-sucking kiss. He grabbed her hips hard enough that Envy would have prints on her flesh after Sabbath died.

Sabbath knew he was safe from the hand of death six days a week, but the seventh was coming, and with it his end. When he wanted to prolong a fuck, Sabbath used to think of seemingly endless rituals in the church his foster father would make him kneel through twice daily. Hexen Sabbath's very name was a sin. The slit from whence he'd been born by his witch of a mother had been the cradle of sin, and surely the act of his parents coming together was a sin too. *Thou shalt not suffer a witch to live,* and yet his father planted life in the witch's womb. Even believing his mother's prophecy, though it had held him in good stead across a lifetime of war, was a sin.

He may as well go out a sinner. Envy's small body rocked atop him as he thrust upward, sending her small breasts quaking. "Fuck," she said. "It's like you're on top of me!"

Maybe Envy does predominate, Sabbath thought, the sweaty sin writhing atop him. *Desirous like greed, passionate like lust, hungry like gluttony . . .*

Rageful like wrath.

They were sticky with sweat and other fluids, happy to just lie together for a long moment. Sabbath found himself uncharacteristically contemplative—usually after sex all he wanted was some ale, or a joint of meat. Now he wanted to think the next thirty-six hours or so through. Envy's sexual overture had clearly a trap of some sort, even if it was one Sabbath had been happy to fall into for a moment.

He could kill her now. Snap her neck as she nuzzled his chest. But Envy may have her uses still, and her security force may be on site. He wouldn't die this day, but Sabbath could imagine another bullet going through him, severing his spine. Maybe they'd just drag him to the bathtub, let his life swirl down the remarkable modern drain for a night and a day, then chop his carcass to pieces for quick disposal on Monday morning.

He glanced down at Envy. Her eyes were fluttering, growing heavy. Almost like a real woman's eyes might after being well fucked. What had she said? *Or do you just miss girls?* Sabbath smiled to himself. *Ah, just like a woman.* Envy was envious of Jennifer, who was a real woman, born of real parents, who had lived a life of joys and sorrows. She wanted to be her. That's why she wanted the paintings; it's why she wanted Sabbath.

Envy had *collected* him.

But what was it that drove Envy to do such a thing? *Ah yes.*

"You know," he told her. "You're an attractive creature, but you lack the sensuality of your sister. Ah, Lust—now, there was a woman!"

Envy drew herself up, face twisted in rage. "You dare!" She raised a hand, the nails suddenly talons.

"Kill me," said Sabbath. "Perhaps in Hell it will be my punishment to lie with you forever . . . once your brother Pride destroys this planet and sends you back to the underworld for all eternity." He smiled, remembering that he would not die this day. That he *could* not die, not until Sunday.

Then Envy slid off him. "I see how it is, Sir Hexen. You're all business. Indeed, you're all murder." She drew her robe around herself and walked to the door. "I'm glad you are a killer, not a lover," she said as she loitered by the entrance. "I didn't really want you as a play toy, anyway. But you'll be my personal killer, won't you? You have no clue of how to be anything else. You have no choice. Rest well, little man." She closed the door quietly, as if having just put Baby Hexen down for a nap.

No, not had to. Sabbath had always had a choice. Yes, the Vikings had brought with them their women when they founded the Danelagh between the Rivers Tees and Thames; and, yes, when Æthelred ordered the death of all Danes in England on Saint Brice's Day, young Sir Sabbath had done his part by meeting with one of his lovers, the comely Ragnfrith, lying with her one more time, then sending her fleeing into the wood before he burned the settlement in which she lived to the ground. The king's whim was Sabbath's command, unless Sabbath had a better offer that day.

Sabbath's old sense for danger, honed from years in the battlefield and in strange beds, told him that clearly, it was time to go. He would have to talk his way past the security force rather than brandish his sword, but he felt confident. No civilization ever reserved the jobs of armed thug and factotum for the best and brightest. He would tell them he needed some fresh air or that he wanted to go down to the tavern for a drink, and that they could come along with him if they wanted. That trick was an ancient one even in the eleventh century, but Sabbath had never known it to fail.

He slid off the bed and into his pants, which in Envy's mad rush for him had been wadded up around his ankles. Sabbath's left arm burned with pain as he dressed himself, and he took a moment to plan ahead. What did the apartment look like, exactly? How many paces to the door? Where had his sword been stashed? He'd have to take some time to look around. He turned his hip to better walk on the edges of his feet, from the border of his heel to his pinkie toe, and silently stepped out of the bedroom and into the main living area of the apartment.

Nobody seemed to be about, which was good, and his sword and its display pillow had been left casually on the kitchen island where the servant had prepared food earlier. Sabbath's stomach growled, and he gathered a mouthful of saliva and sent it down his throat to quiet down the offending organ.

It occurred to him, for the first time, that he could try to explicitly appeal to the wisdom of Abathar. *What do I have to be concerned about?* he thought, asking the still smaller voice that had whispered in his ear so many times this past week. No answer. Abathar would not intervene again.

What might a modern man worry about in this situation? he asked, and that triggered an answer. Hidden cameras. His method of silent walking didn't matter if there were cameras embedded in the ceiling. The security force need not be stationed in the masionette; they could be gathering in the elevator or the building's lobby. Perhaps they were in the building's garage, waiting to follow Sabbath wherever he might go. It could all be some stratagem of Envy's as well. Sabbath desired his sword and his freedom; did that rate as envy somehow? Was the Sin being fueled by his wants?

Too many possibilities; the best thing to do was to assume that there were cameras and that security was observing him, but waiting to see what he would do. Then he heard a low canine growl.

In general, one need not be concerned about trained guard dogs when one is already in the house, but Sabbath's was not the general case. "Fucking angels," he said aloud. The dogs answered. One was resting on its belly on the other side of the kitchen island. Another stood at alert by the elevator door. A third was posted on the steps leading to the second floor of the maisonette. It occurred to Sabbath that Envy had tried to seduce him in the servants' quarters, rather than inviting him up to her boudoir. So that's what she had truly thought of him. Perhaps she was just sleeping off the pretty good fuck he'd given her.

Sabbath reached an arm out toward his sword, and the dog by the kitchen island clambered to its feet, its fangs already bared. The other two snapped to attention. Sabbath sighed deeply, no longer bothering to be quiet. He could kill three dogs, but it would be difficult. Dogs were low to the ground and worked together well; he'd have to swing low and short, jab with the point of the sword, and keep rotating. The one good thing about fighting dogs was that they were smarter than men; when they were injured, they surrendered, instead of trying to fight to the last breath like fools.

Of course, these dogs might be different. They might be envious of men and their ability to blindly murder themselves. The one guarding the sword had a certain intelligence in its eyes that Sabbath hadn't known in the canines of his era. Abathar's wisdom—*Now, it speaks!* thought Sabbath—hinted that a thousand years of selective breeding made poodles exceptionally clever, in general.

"In general" again. Sabbath spat on the tile before the poodle, half in disgust, half as a test. The dog didn't flinch, and didn't move to sniff or lick up the spittle. If anything, it gazed at Sabbath with an expression that he could only read as mild contempt.

Sabbath entered the kitchen area, the dog's gaze following him. He tried his best to stand straight and tall, to radiate no fear or anxiety, and to find some meat. There were several refrigerators to choose from, including a low cube he remembered held the heads of the five sins he'd already eliminated. Free of the influence of this quintet, maybe the world beyond the masionette was becoming more industrious and less piggish with each breath, increasingly peaceful and less horny by the second—he contemplated that possibility with a laugh. *Ah, the poor human race, to be sentenced to life in a nunnery!*

Ah no, but there was plenty of sin in my time, and in the centuries since the last time the sins ran wild on the earth.

He opened one of the doors of the other refrigerators, looking for some meat to offer the poodle. Many things had changed in ten centuries, but food was generally all the same. Generally. He had hoped for a fine roast chicken only somewhat picked over, or some congealed stew with cubes of meat ready for salvaging, but the fridge contained nothing but plastic bottles. Sabbath opened one and sniffed at the contents—the smell was sickly sweet, but like no fruit he recognized. Abathar's knowledge gave him the answer: a meal replacement fluid, designed to taste somewhat like chocolate, which he had taken a bite of at Gluttony's restaurant. Chocolate was good, but his stomach still twisted at the thought of guzzling down three bottles of this muddy brew a day.

"How about you, dog?" he asked, shaking the bottle at the poodle nearest him. "Care for a swig?" The poodle remained impassive. "No, I don't blame you one bit."

There weren't even any eggs. Perhaps they were stored elsewhere, or maybe Envy arranged the servant girl and the meal solely for his sake, to impress him. Sabbath kept an eye on the dogs as he went through the other refrigerators and freezers. There was some ice-covered meat in plastic wrap, but Sabbath had no clue how to defrost it, and no time either.

"What do you eat?" he asked the poodle, and the poodle bared its teeth again and licked its chops. "Shank of Sabbath, is it? Let's just be friends." He squatted down and held out his left hand. The poodle didn't approach for a sniff, but didn't growl either, so Sabbath waddled a step closer.

The dog tensed, then retreated, circling around the kitchen island and into the dining area, closer to the other two dogs. Sabbath kept his position, glanced at the sword, hesitated.

Sweet Lord, am I really concerned about the strategy of a trio of dogs?

Then Sabbath's gaze alighted on the hand-forged iron spoon. It would do as a club. He snatched it up and swung it in a wide arc as a warning. The bowl came flying off the handle, bounced off a wall, then bounced off the hardwood floors.

"Piece of shit!" Sabbath shouted, throwing the spoon's stem to the ground. The dogs sprang into action. Patience and technique no longer mattered.

Sabbath flew like a shot and grabbed the hilt of his sword. Before he could raise it from its pillow, the poodle on the stairs had leapt from them and hit Sabbath hard, pinning him to the tiles. Sabbath sacrificed a forearm to its mouth to keep its fangs from his throat. The other poodles approached, flanking him. Sabbath's right hand was occupied, his left useless thanks to the bullet and the impact.

The truly unnerving thing—they were silent. Even the poodle whose jaw was clamped on his right forearm was just holding him, not sinking its teeth any deeper than need be to keep Sabbath in place, not growling or shaking its neck to tear at his flesh. When the other poodles, identical in dark gray, surrounded Sabbath, they just stood in place like statues, watching.

"Do you understand?" Sabbath said. He could barely believe himself. "Your mistress is not a human being. You're animals, you're a part of this world, a part of God's creation in a way that men are not. You should . . . fight on my side to save this world . . . you should . . .

"You're fucking dogs, fuck this." Sabbath sighed, placed the tip of his tongue behind his top incisors, so he wouldn't accidentally bite down on it when he made his move. Then he leg-scissored the poodle atop him and swallowed a scream as he swept the dog and tore its teeth from the flesh of his forearm. Sabbath got to his feet and leapt out of the way of a second poodle nipping at his heels. They flanked him expertly, cutting off the route to the elevator, the steps leading to the second floor, the guest room in which Envy still slept, and the en suite bathroom beyond.

Sabbath kept them at the edge of their lunging reach with low kicks as he cast about for a weapon. What was a kitchen without a butcher's block or knives? No rolling pin, iron frying pans, or cauldrons to swing, a lit fire from which to retrieve some smoldering kindling? Where had all the crockery and utensils he'd sworn he saw the night he was brought here gone? He scuttled backwards and rammed the small of his back against the cube freezer.

In a flash, Sabbath had three ideas.

Open the door and climb in. No, insane. He'd trap himself.

Hop atop the cube and fight from there. Not insane, but futile. The dogs had demonstrated their ability to leap very well. He'd just have a smaller platform from which to fight.

Open the door and . . . the heads! Gluttony might still be fresh. Sabbath's fingers found the edge of the door. He braced himself, kicked at the dogs, and with a grunt pulled the door open one-handed. The unsealing sounded like nothing he'd ever heard. Even the poodles hesitated for a moment. He found the duffel and swung it like a fishing net laden with bountiful catch, a ribbon of blood from his arm flying across the polished surfaces of the kitchen. The dogs scattered, but regrouped quickly, nipping and tearing at the bag.

It was hard to unzip the bag one-handed, but one of the dogs inadvertently helped by clamping down and tugging in the opposite direction. The heads were in a sorry state, but none more so than Gluttony, which was still half-full of blood despite the flesh of the face hanging loose. Sabbath grabbed the head by the hair, dropped the bag, presented it to the poodles, and hoped beyond hope that dogs were sinners too.

They were. They dived at the head, yanked it from his grip, and ran after it as it fell to the floor and rolled over the tiles, red streaks and paw prints on the gleaming white.

Sabbath went for the sword. His arm was bleeding badly, but he didn't feel anything other than the familiar pain of torn and punctured flesh. The muscles and nerves were probably fine. He sliced the velvet pillow on which the sword had rested in half, dropped the sword back onto the marble counter, and wrapped the fabric around his forearm to staunch the bleeding. He teared up from the strain of using his left arm. In a moment, the dogs would tire of consuming Gluttony's head. He'd hoped, prayed, that they would turn on one another and fight for the lion's share of the feast once they had a taste of a deadly sin's body and blood, but the dogs were damned disciplined. One lifted its face to peer at Sabbath, its muzzle slick with gore, before dipping back down to lick at Gluttony's ruined neck stump.

He'd have to leave barefoot. Abathar's knowledge consoled him; Envy lived in a nice part of town, with little rubbish or broken glass on the pavement below. Sabbath decided he'd waylay the first convenient man he encountered and grab a pair of shoes at sword point regardless. He moved swiftly, but without running, across the extensive living room to the elevator doors. He understood, in a flash, that elevator cars were generally summoned with the press of a button, but there were no buttons to be seen.

"My kitchen," said Envy, her voice hollow thunder. "My kitchen, a disaster, and my precious poodles rolling in filth." She stood in the doorway of the small bedroom off the kitchen, her robe on yet untied. She put her hands on her hips and turned toward Sabbath. "And you! Where do you think you're going? What do you think you're doing?"

"I'm taking my leave of you, Envy."

"We have plans."

"We both had plans. My first plan was to slay you where you stood, as I have your brothers and sisters in sin."

"Your sword is in hand, and you've been bloodied," said Envy. "Is it still your plan to kill me? From the other end of the apartment?" Her gaze followed the trail of blood from the kitchen to the elevators. "Oh, my Oriental rugs! It's hard enough keeping them clean with the poodles about. I'll need to replace them now."

"I want to see Jennifer," Sabbath said.

"So do I. She isn't answering her phone. The gallery is closed despite the posted hours. The emails we've sent are unread."

"Then let me go, so that I might see what is the matter," said Sabbath. "Open the elevator door."

"No."

Abathar's knowledge whispered something. "There must be a fire exit; staircases," he said.

"No, there must be nothing here at all, except for what I want there to be, when I want it to be, and how I want it to be." She snapped her fingers. The dogs stopped gnawing on Gluttony's skull and heeled at her feet. "We had an agreement, Sir Hexen. A plan. You flying off half-cocked—" She paused to give him the once-over and snicker at her own joke. "—will serve no purpose but that of your ultimate enemy. You're being prideful, do you understand?"

Sabbath smirked. "You're just jealous that I'd rather spend time with Jennifer than with you. I sampled your wares and then prepared to take my leave while you slept."

"You're not leaving, Sir Hexen," said Envy. She gestured

toward the door to the small bedroom off the kitchen. "Go rest up. I've sent some people down to the gallery to rouse your woman. The plan will continue as I've described it. You could barely handle my dogs in the state you're in, and you're bleeding. I'm not going to allow you to call the elevator. You'll do what I want."

The poodles took up new positions, one settling by Envy's feet, another in front of the kitchen island, facing the living room, a direct route to Sabbath, and the third stationed itself by the stairs.

Sabbath lifted his sword, inhaling sharply as he did. He wanted to hide the pain he was in, but the wonderful acoustics of the large room made it clear that he was suffering. Envy grinned. Then Sabbath understood.

This is what she wants. She needed me to defy her, needed me to seek out Jennifer, so she would have something to destroy. Cain envied Abel as the Lord God favored Abel, but instead of seeking to win God's favor, Cain slew his brother despite the ruin that God would bring unto him.

"You sent your men away?" Sabbath asked.

Envy shrugged grandly, then stopped to adjust her robe back onto her shoulders. "Some of them." She tied her belt tight. The dogs grew more attentive. The one with the bloody muzzle licked its chops.

"Tell me, Sir Hexen," Envy said. "Are you the sort of man who'd kill a dog? They're innocents, you know. Humans bred them, humans domesticated them, humans trained them to be hunters, guardians, companions. Killers. They carry the burden of men's sins."

"As a matter of fact, Madam Envy, I am exactly the sort of man who'll kill a dog, and I'll kill their bitch too."

Envy rolled her eyes. "You're just another idiot thug. It takes literal divine intervention to get you to see the inside of a maisonette as nice as this one, and you all but destroy it. I'm going to chew your tongue out of your mouth after my dogs kill you." Then she said something in French, and the dogs ran for Sabbath.

For a moment, it seemed easy. One poodle charged and simply threw itself on Sabbath's blade, squealing as the sword pierced its belly. With its last breath, the poodle raised its hind limbs from the floor, yanking the sword from Sabbath's grip and sending him sprawling to the floor.

College had been a time of social and political awakening for Jennifer. She was a conservative in high school, thanks partially to parents who had "made it" despite the obstacles of childhood immigration and lingering accent, and largely to the raunchy sex scenes in the works of Ayn Rand. The bit in *The Fountainhead* where Dominique goes to the bathroom and sees all the purple bruises left on her skin by Roark was a shaky foundation for free-market values and a distaste for altruism, but fifteen-year-old Evgenia Zelenova, whose parents had grown up in the USSR, had given it the old college try.

Halfway through her first semester, thanks to being taken under the wing of a gay poet with whom she coincidentally shared all her classes, she shed her politics if not her interest in sudden, rough sex, and adopted instead a mix of feminism and existentialism. What interested Jennifer was the idea of freedom, no matter how it was phrased politically. A yellowed paperback of *Being and Nothingness*—its previous owner having scratched out *Man* and replaced it with *Woman* throughout—spoke to young . . . Evie. (The name Jennifer would come later, when she landed in New York.) *Woman is condemned to freedom.* That sounded true.

Miriam had believed it too. Jennifer had tried the *Woman is condemned to freedom* anecdote on Miriam back when they first met, and it had worked like a charm.

She thought of it now as the banging on the door to her apartment increased in both volume and intensity. Whoever was in her hallway had abandoned the idea of knocking, but hadn't quite reached the limit of their patience and started trying to batter the door down. Jennifer was entirely free to act. She could get up and push the futon in front of the door, or call 911 without moving, flip open the dead bolt and greet whoever was in the hallway with a charming hello, a confused query, or bared teeth and sharp nails. That fight in the Tombs had made her feel free, if just for a moment. Maybe another random brawl would be therapeutic.

Or she could just continue to lie in bed. Let them bust down the door and kill her or just pick up the futon and leave it, and her, on the curb. There was an infinity of choices, of potential futures, awaiting her. It was almost paralyzing.

Then door shook on its hinges. Whoever was outside was also condemned to freedom. They had decided to enter the apartment, no matter the consequence. Jennifer toyed with the idea of running to the stove, turning on all the burners and the oven as well, and then lighting a match when the door finally flew open, but the terror of her hair and flesh going up in flames stopped her. It got her out of bed, though. The whole apartment shook this time. She braced herself, counted to two, and timed a kick at her side of the door. A muffled grunt came from the hallway.

Jennifer peered through the peephole. "What do you want?" The man outside, rubbing his shoulder, had the look of a cop about him, but was a fake in a navy blue shirt. He had two other men with him, dressed identically. Private security of some sort, or criminal scammers.

"We just want to talk," said the man.

"Bullshit! You're trying to break in."

"You won't answer your phone," he said. "Nor email. Nor messages on social media. Your gallery's been closed all day. We have an offer."

"An offer for what, and from who?" Obviously, Thomas Aldridge had infinite resources. Jennifer wouldn't have come back home, except that she had almost no resources of her own. She couldn't . . . No, that wasn't right. She was free. She could have picked up a stranger and exchanged intimacy for shelter till the missiles came over the horizon or gotten on the PATH train and secured a room at a cheaper hotel and drank her way through the honor bar. Hell, she could have gone straight to JFK and booked a flight to Orlando, borrowed her father's assault rifle—Russian immigrants in Florida loved their Second Amendment rights—then spent a day on Amtrak to bring it back to the city, just in time to see the entire world explode. Would she gun down some assholes just to put them out of their misery, and then have the necessary seconds to put the last bullet in her own brain, or would she just burn and leave a shadow forever scorched on the side of a building instead?

"An anonymous art buyer. We want the whole show. The whole—" He pulled a notepad from the breast pocket of his shirt. "—*Why-lem*?"

"Ee-lem," Jennifer corrected him. "Some art buyer you are."

"Are you going to come downstairs and open the gallery?" His tone was somewhere between testy and threatening.

"Who is the buyer?" Art whales tended to be aggressive. Sending down some mall cops to negotiate a buy was unheard of, but it wasn't all that different from trying to corner the market on Warhol Marilyns, stealing paintings off museum walls to buy machine guns for the Irish Republican Army, or selling diamond-encrusted skulls back to the artist through shadowy consortiums in order to keep market prices in the eight digits. Ayn Rand championed the entrepreneur who would stop at nothing to be satisfied. That was a kind of freedom too, wasn't it?

"She wishes to remain anonymous for now," the man said, "but we're ready to take you to meet her. It's a Yorkville address. A very nice building on a very nice block."

Jennifer couldn't trust them, but it didn't matter. Ten minutes ago, she'd been waiting for a flash of white light, a nanosecond of burning pain, then an eternity as vapor around a cinder floating in the inky blackness of space. What else bad could possibly happen? *Besides,* Jennifer thought, *I survived a jailhouse fight. I'll kill these motherfuckers if they pull any shit on me.* Three men, all bigger and stronger, but they were just some assholes collecting a check to put their kids through Catholic school on Staten Island or some lame shit like that. Dad Cops. They were condemned to freedom, but they'd always freely choose their kids, their teeth, their eyes. With the end of the world at her back, Jennifer had nothing to lose.

"All right," said Jennifer. "Give me a second, and meet me down at the storefront."

She checked herself in the mirror after the men trooped away. It would take more than a second, but they'd wait. She needed a comb through her hair, a good flossing eyeliner and lipstick at least, struggled one-armed into her second-best suit jacket, the pepper spray—her eyes still stung from the memory of it, and then she thought of Miriam and lost her vision to her tears—the box cutter, the emergency burner phone, and the derringer. Two .22-caliber bullets that she didn't even trust to shoot herself with, and she hadn't shot or cleaned it in months; plus it was legal to own only because it was an antique, but she was free to act. Free to carry a gun, to shoot a man in the chest at point-blank range, to go back to Central Booking for another body cavity search, and then she'd smile when she told her cellmates about the end of the world. Jennifer Zelenova didn't have to cower anymore.

"Ma'am," the man said when she walked out onto the street, keys in her hand.

"So, your buyer's a woman," Jennifer said. "Anyone I know?"

"She's not just the wealthy dilettante wife of some rich man, if that's what you're getting at," the man said. The two others behind him made noises of agreement.

"Did she tell you about the exhibit? Did you get our catalog?" Jennifer asked. The man said nothing at all to that. Their uniforms didn't have name tags. One of them was even wearing sneakers instead of sensible cop shoes. "Are you art handlers? Does she expect a delivery today?"

"We'd rather talk about it inside," the man said. "It's chilly," said the one in the sneakers. The third didn't even look at Jennifer. She thought of the tiny pistol in her pocket, how it held only two bullets. She didn't want to get blood on the canvases.

"Fine, then," she said, jingling the keys in her hand. As she suspected, they were Joe Six-Pack types, entirely flummoxed by the exhibit. Sneakers gaped, and the leader asked, in as politic a way as he could, "Is this your entire space, Ms. Zelenova? Ma'am?"

"Listen, fellas"—she was pleased that these men were bemused—"this is what the exhibit is. Seven blank canvases from seven different artists. This isn't a museum, and I am not a docent here to explain things to you. You can read the little wall cards if you want. You can Skype your boss on your iPhones and show her what's on the walls. This is all highly unusual. I normally wouldn't put up with this at all, but I didn't want you waking my neighbors."

"Waking the neighbors? It's one o'clock in the afternoon!" *The third man speaks!* A Staten Island accent strong enough that Jennifer almost whipped out her own phone to record the voice. Jennifer guessed he got the gig because he knew how to drive a big truck or something.

"This is an artists' neighborhood still," said Jennifer. "Everyone works from home."

The leader of the trio looked around, nodding distractedly, as if he were checking out a selection of used cars. "Well, she just wants one to start. The best one."

"The best one," Jennifer repeated. "To start."

"That's what she said."

"Well, what's the best one?"

"You tell us."

"Doesn't your client know?" Jennifer asked. "Did she send you down here with the instructions to say 'One art, please' and doff your caps?" She didn't care that the men's postures had changed as she spoke, the heads tilted like those of confused yet angry dogs. The leader took one step forward, pushing into her personal space, and loomed over her. The gun felt satisfyingly heavy in the pocket of her jacket.

"Look, you know what rich people are like," he said, and it was true, she did. "Our boss isn't looking for something to put on display; she's looking for a hedge. The best painting is the one that she can hang on to for a decade or more and then, if she needs to, sell for more than she paid for it. Why do you think she sent us down here? Do you know how many galleries we passed on the way to this place, only to find it locked up like you'd gone out of business? We want something that's cheap now and that will be expensive later. That's the best art."

Jennifer hoped her poker face stayed intact. "All right, come in." She unlocked the gallery door and flipped on the lights. As she guessed they would be, the trio were nonplussed by the exhibit.

"I see why you were confused when we asked for your best painting," said the man in sneakers.

"These are all the same," said the leader.

"How about you?" Jennifer pointed her chin at the silent third man in the group. "Got any witty comments?"

He took in the exhibit thoughtfully. "These aren't blank," he said finally. He walked up to the smallest canvas, one just a little larger than a movie poster, and scrutinized it. "They're painted white. White paint on a white canvas. Maybe ivory."

"That one is painted ivory," Jennifer said. "There's blank canvases, and then there's monochromatic painting. Minimalist blank canvases and Dada blank canvases."

Sneakers snorted. Jennifer smirked. "Robert Ryman's white monochromatic paintings, with visible brushstrokes, sold for fourteen million dollars at auction ten years ago." Money always stunned unbelievers for a second, even if they didn't shut up entirely.

"What was the painting called?" he asked after a long moment of rolling the number *fourteen million* around in his head.

"Untitled," Jennifer said. "He didn't even name it. It's a square too—not even an unusual shape, just about four by four, so not even an enormous canvas that would be hard to stretch and mount."

"Well, what are these worth?" the lead guy spoke again.

"Whatever anyone wants to pay. I'm loath to break up the set, honestly."

"We're not carting all seven . . . uh, paintings uptown," the lead man said. Jennifer looked closely at his face for the first time. He was a nondescript sort, which was odd. Most New Yorkers had some trace of ethnic sensibility about them. This guy wasn't even a white-bread WASP, but something else. Same with the silent character on his left. The man in sneakers, though, he contained some distinctive look about him. His eyebrows were shaggy, he had a bit of a belly, a crooked nose. And he looked as confused now as he had when the trio first followed her into the gallery. The other pair had regained their former impatient composure.

Jennifer decided to try something. "There's an eighth painting." Sneakers stirred, making the floor squeak under him. The other two didn't even blink. "It's in the back."

She gestured at them to wait where they stood and walked to the kitchenette, then unlocked and stepped through a door at the very end of the gallery. In the closet, she took several deep breaths and hoped that none of them had gotten a glimpse of the size of the room she had stepped into. It was a walk-in closet, and amongst the lost coats and old catalogs was a small stretched canvas in a floater frame. She could carry it easily with her one good arm. Once, Jennifer had entertained the possibility of painting her own work, but the gallery, and New York itself, had consumed all her time.

Jennifer wasn't even quite sure what her plan was. She had hoped that the men would talk amongst themselves and say something worth overhearing, but only Sneakers spoke. The other two didn't answer when he asked questions about their client—he was a temp, and nervous. "Yo, guys, I have to tell you. I faked it; I'm not a professional art handler. I don't know if I should cart a million-dollar painting uptown. And, well, it's white; what if I get fingerprints on it—?"

"It's small," Jennifer said as she stepped out of the closet, expertly blocking the interior with her body and the overflowing contents of her arms—the canvas, Bubble Wrap, a roll of acid-free paper—and slamming the door shut with a hip-check. Sneakers appreciated the show. The others didn't even check her out. "Let's go."

"I'm glad you're coming with us," said the leader of the trio. He didn't sound glad—it was more like he had learned the sentence phonetically. Jennifer walked to her desk and prepared the canvas for moving. "I'll handle the art. Call ahead. I want a cashier's check or a wire transfer," Jennifer said. How much did she owe? Three months on the gallery, two on the apartment upstairs, two of her credit cards were maxed out and one over the limit. That was about twenty-five grand . . . and she had about seventy thousand in student loans and other small debts to friends and her family. Of course, she needed to eat, and really wanted to get back to Venice, which she had fallen in love with. Maybe a trip to Moscow to bring over some art. "Quarter of a million," she said. "Cashier's check for a quarter of a million. Made out to Above Below, of course."

"Or a wire transfer?" the leader said, withdrawing his phone from his pants pocket, thumb at the ready.

Forty-eight hours and a fifty-dollar fee? Fuck the wire transfer, Jennifer thought. "Cashier's check. And a limo to the nearest Chase branch after."

"We can drive you—" Sneaker started to offer.

"Limo," said Jennifer.

Envy sighed as she picked her away across the room, over the puddles of dog blood, the pebbles of broken glass, and the shattered sticks of furniture. Slumped by the elevator door, Hexen Sabbath was breathing heavily. Her poodles were not.

A few feet from him, she stopped, raised the hem of her robe, and presented a slippered foot. "Forgive me," Envy said, "for wearing my old beater slippers. You've made a mess of things and it's hard to get a same-day appointment for a decent pedicure." They were the most beautiful slippers Sabbath had ever seen. Pure white except for the red and black stains along the edges of the soles just now collected by Envy's journey across the battlefield, with golden trim and a depiction of an angel's timeless face surrounded by a golden laurel wreath, on the instep. Sabbath noted that the angel's eyes had no pupils, and shuddered.

"Versace. The best one can do for prêt-à-porter bath slippers. I have a half-dozen pairs, for when I have a bunion, for when I need some sunshine and decide to walk the dogs myself. You know, chores," she said. "Do you understand?"

Sabbath didn't, and Abathar's knowledge was silent, but he nodded anyway. These slippers were both dreadfully important to her, and yet inadequate.

"My real slippers are bespoke. Fur lined, a bit of golden horse bit—though, of course, one mustn't wear slippers on horseback, but you know that, don't you? Though *chivalry*"—she slushed the word over her tongue, as the Franks did—"was not formalized in your time, was it? But you've done your time on horseback, yes?"

"Yes."

"They took wax forms of my feet. They were overnighted to Hong Kong and the slippers made in a single day, then overnighted back to me. I love those slippers. Had things turned out better, I would have worn them for you, Sir Hexen."

"Uh . . ."

"But look what you have done to my home. You've ruined it. I'll have to manifest another. A better one. Better dogs too . . ." She pursed her lips as she looked down at the torn-open poodle she'd need to step over to get to Sabbath. One of the others had a broken neck, its snout twisted nearly all the way around. The third dog's jaw and snout were destroyed by the corner of the coffee table Sabbath had rammed down its throat.

"You don't deserve to be killed by me while I'm wearing my good slippers, you understand?" Envy said.

"I understand. . . ." Sabbath did an inventory. Three more open wounds. A deep scratch over one eye. Dislocated shoulder, but that he could pop back in once he had a moment, he thought. Calf tendons that were all but severed. He'd walk with a limp for weeks, had he weeks to walk. Two more teeth gone. Abathar's wisdom taunted him with a vision of dental implants. . . . No, it wasn't Abathar. He'd remembered a television commercial he saw in the cheap Chinatown hotel room that had been his hideout. What if Envy had visited him there? The thought of her in that flimsy cube of a room made him chuckle.

"What's so fucking funny?" she snapped. "You don't deserve any of what I was going to share with you, but I'll let you see one thing." She removed a small knife from the pocket of her robe, her fingers pinching the blade. It was weird, more like a shining spike, flattened at one end, than any dagger Sabbath had ever seen. She wiggled it, smiling, before gripping the hilt. "My exquisite left-handed letter opener. It was a gift. From me. For me. I've never even received a piece of correspondence worthy of it. If you went to purchase something like this, they'd sell it to you. They'd tell you that the blade was platinum, but it wouldn't be. It would be brass, coated in platinum a couple of molecules deep."

"Yours is . . . pure platinum . . . ," Sabbath said. He almost smiled again.

"No," she said. "Titanium core."

"Of course. Nothing but the second-best for you, eh, Envy?"

Envy's face flushed. She clutched at the letter opener, waved the tip in Sabbath's face. "But for you, I would have been the best! You didn't even have to do anything but stay in bed and nap. Your girl would have come here, Pride would have followed, and you could have dealt with him."

"And you with her . . . ," Sabbath said.

"But now, I have to deal with you instead," Envy said. She knelt down before him, stroked his cheek. "I'm going to take back all that I've given you. We'll start with the stitches." Her hand found his throat and squeezed it; she slammed his head against the elevator door with surprising strength. With her free left hand, she buried the point of her letter opener under the first stitch in Sabbath's shoulder and severed it. Sabbath winced, but couldn't move; her right hand was a vise.

She took out the second stitch, and the third. "Oh, but I also gifted you with some antiseptic medication. You wouldn't know much about that, would you, man of the past?" She withdrew the letter opener, admired its edge for a moment, then punctured the side of the poodle that had taken Sabbath's sword in its gut, worked it through the flesh, and withdrew it dripping with grue. She showed off the blade to Sabbath, who tried to reach for it with his right hand, but Envy tightened her grip on his throat.

"I can kill you quick . . . ," she said. "But I want to do it slow. I get what I want. I'll just choke you unconscious, and you might wake up without a nose, without your toes, without your cock. I'll feed and water you till the end comes, so you can see it. So don't *fucking* try, and I'll leave you intact." Sabbath gurgled out an unintelligible answer, his face red going on purple. Envy jabbed the stained letter opener into his wound, working loose the rest of the threads, feeding the filth into his blood. Sabbath gurgled in pain.

Envy laughed, and kissed him on the cheek. "Yes, you keep that heart pumping. Send the poison through your veins, like rats scurrying through sewers. Oh, but you don't know much about sewers, do you? Even the most beautiful and glamorous of queens and princesses of your era had to relieve themselves in a dark corner of their rooms, and walked around smelling of shit." She finally let go of his neck. Sabbath inhaled wheezily.

"I do love the modern world! Ah, and speaking of." She reached into the other robe pocket and pulled out her smartphone. "Let's take a selfie together! You're already a social media star. . . ." Envy trailed off as her phone lit up. "Texts. I receive so many texts. Everyone wants to hear from me."

Envy muttered to herself as she typed an answer. "Quarter mil . . . goddamn. Already on her way . . ." She looked up at Sabbath and smiled. "This will be exciting. Pardon me, I have to call my bank and make some financial arrangements. At least some of my plan will be coming together, and as it turns out, I may not even need you to lure Pride here and deal with him." She turned her back on Sabbath and thumbed the screen on her phone.

Confident bitch, Sabbath thought. He was regaining some of his wind, but not his strength. He'd survived worse than a few dog bites before, but nearly a week of wounds and scars and excess was encumbering him like a mule's heavy pack. It was obvious. After she completed her call, she was going to turn around and drive that unusual blade into his throat. Her stance—right leg behind, the weight on it, left foot balancing lightly on the big toe—betrayed her. She'd pivot and lunge. Even the choking had been nothing but a way to mark her target, to get a sense of from how far and with what force she'd need to strike to get a clean kill . . . or an imperfect one that would leave him gurgling and drowning in his blood for her viewing pleasure.

"No, my staff isn't available. You can send someone. No, yes, well, you can download some kind of valet app and hire a messenger that way or use an old-fashioned messenger service. Yes, fine, fine. I'll hire the messenger service. Wait, just, yes, I know your address, I know your name already, you told it to me, hang on, I'm getting a text." She took her phone from her ear and peered at the screen. Sabbath felt a twinge of impatience. *Kill me already!*

"Oh Christ," Envy said to herself as something new happened on her screen. Sabbath chortled at that, but she either didn't hear or didn't care. Her posture shifted, she was about to turn and perform the killing blow, but then her phone buzzed in her hand. "Yes, no. No, I need time . . . no, it's not the check. Well, maybe a Starbucks—there are three on this block! No, don't, I want you to—"

Envy threw the phone onto a couch cushion that had fallen to the floor during the melee. She exhaled deeply, blowing air out her nose. "You try to do something in an artful and interesting way, and incompetents always ruin it." She sounded as though she were about to burst into tears.

"I'm sorry, Envy," Sabbath said. She seized up, and he grinned at her. The remark wasn't a shit-encrusted dagger to a bleeding wound, but it stung her sufficiently well.

Sabbath hoped Envy would be flustered enough to make

a mistake, but she wasn't. She swung her arm back and closed the distance, then drove the letter opener toward his throat.

Abathar, help!

Nothing.

The blade.

God, forgive me!

Sabbath fell backwards as the wall behind him gave way, the blade passing right over his head. A flash of the elevator ceiling, then Jennifer looking down at him. She glanced up and out through the open elevator doors, said "Oh shit!" and jammed the edge of the large square object she was carrying into Envy's throat. Two men grabbed Jennifer—she cried out when one slapped his hands on her cast—and the third intervened to stop them. "Yo, yo!"

"Sabbath!" Jennifer shouted. He could lift his head, move one arm slightly. He grabbed the nearest man's leg, yanked it toward him, and sank his teeth past the fabric of a plain black dress sock and into an Achilles tendon. The man howled, and Sabbath chuckled through his full mouth, thinking of how he must have sounded when the dogs were on him.

"Fuck! This! Shit!" Jennifer said. She shook off her other attacker, hopped over Sabbath, pulled out a tiny pistol, and shot Envy twice in the chest. Both women screamed, but Jennifer was louder when Envy rushed her and dragged her to the floor. Sabbath crawled up the man he was attacking, wrapped his arms around his torso, and took him down, landed atop him, reared back, and slammed the man's nose flat with a headbutt. The two men were tussling in the corner of the large elevator. Sabbath saw an opening and took it, kicking up and inverting the knee of the other plain-looking man, who crumpled easily.

"Help Jennifer," Sabbath said, his mouth full of someone else's blood. The man who had turned against his fellows nodded and rushed out of the elevator. Envy rose to meet him, grabbed him by the neck, and threw him across the room. His sneakers went flying off his feet as he hit the wall.

"Fucking humans," Envy said. "You don't get it, do you? If anyone could just show up and shoot us, we never would have made it this far. This world is a zoo its keeper has abandoned."

Jennifer, on the floor at Envy's feet, turned her head and said, "Help." Sabbath moved. He got up on one foot, then the other, hissed, and hop-walked toward the poodle with the sword sticking from its guts. It slid out easily.

"You like this bitch, don't you?" said Envy, pointing down, with a smirk. Her robe had fallen open again.

"What the fuck is this?" Sneakers asked. "What happened here? . . . Is that a dead dog!"

"Three dead breeding bitches," said Envy, her gaze still on Sabbath. "The female is more intelligent, more trainable. Watch." She stepped on Jennifer's hand and ground her heel against her fingers. "Tell him to drop the sword."

"No—ow! God, Sabbath!"

Envy lifted her foot and placed it on Jennifer's face. "How about your pretty eyes, Ms. Zelenova. Will you be a good girl?" Her big toe teased Jennifer's eyelid, her heel pressed against her lips and teeth.

"Mmmrf," she said. "Drrf uum."

"That could have been 'Drop it,' eh, Sir Hexen," Envy said. Sabbath hesitated. "Or it could have been 'Stop her.' Hard to say. What do you think she wants?" Envy shifted her weight onto one hip, and beneath her, Jennifer screeched.

"Why are you doing this?" asked Sneakers. "I don't understand."

"Envy is an extremely destructive emotion," said Sabbath. "It consumes that which it covets, it poisons all it touches, but not least of all itself. All I had to do was wait," he said, an eye on the man. Then he turned to Envy. "You've destroyed yourself. Look around you."

"Stupid pig," Envy said. "I'm winning. I've got what you want right here." She ground her heel into Jennifer's face. "Put the sword down."

"If that's what you want," Sabbath said. He stepped forward, lurched, threw himself onto his bad leg, and spun. The sword flew out of his hand, twirling.

"Fu—" The rest of the word was sliced clean out of Envy's throat as the blade ripped through it. A geyser went up, and Jennifer's scream filled the room.

"Oh God oh God oh God," said Sneakers. He crawled to the elevator, just in time to see the two men he'd been working with all day collapse into puddles of black blood, uniforms and all. "Oh shit oh shit oh shit," he mumbled, crawling backwards.

"My face, my face, my fucking face." Jennifer ran her fingers over her nose, checked her teeth. "Oh God, a body . . ." She squirmed away from Envy's headless corpse, kicking herself free of the sin's long limbs, planting her heel in the groin and shoving hard.

"This apartment has an excellent shower," Sabbath said. "We should all avail ourselves of it." Then he fell.

9

For the day of the LORD of hosts shall be upon every one that is proud and lofty, and upon every one that is lifted up; and he shall be brought low.

—ISAIAH 2:12

"I don't understand," said Jennifer.

"Whatever you don't understand is one of God's mysteries," said Sabbath. He groaned, and turned on his side, away from Jennifer.

"So Joachim was real, but nothing else was." Jennifer had finally exchanged names with the sneaker-wearing temp while they patched up Sabbath as best they could with the small first aid kit they found in the maisonette. Joachim stabilized Sabbath while Jennifer collected the heads, including scooping up the remains of Gluttony's. Joachim then stumbled over and freaked out about the blank canvas, now torn and spattered with blood, until Jennifer explained that it was worthless; then he had laughed and inexplicably offered her a high five. In the building lobby, Joachim met the bicycle messenger that was to deliver the cashier's check to Jennifer, and finagled it out of him with some fast-talking. He called a cousin with a car and rode with them back downtown, and even helped Sabbath climb the steps. When the cashier's check faded to nothingness in Jennifer's hands while they all watched, Joachim finally begged off and promised not to tell anyone what he had seen or heard, or even to leave his favorite barstool till Monday.

"Yes," said Sabbath. "The others were demons."

"But why?"

"Does it matter?" asked Sabbath.

"Well, why didn't Envy just create three helpers, instead of two?" she said.

"I think it is the nature of Envy to always fall short of what she wants, so perhaps she needed three but could only conjure two," Sabbath said. "Good thing that the envious never get exactly what they want."

"Do you think he was . . . sent?" Jennifer asked.

"By whom?"

"God," Jennifer said. "I mean, it was lucky he was here. Three of those phantom clones or whatever, and we never would have made it out of the elevator."

"That's us, Sir Lucky and Lady Fortuna, the lucky couple . . . ," Sabbath grumbled.

"Tell me about Abathar," Jennifer said.

"Abathar told me he would not intervene in my behalf again," Sabbath said. "When we last spoke directly, I saw him fold a person up as one might a napkin and consume him utterly. Angels are God's messengers; their presence terrifies and humbles not just the men they appear before, but the world itself. They shake the firmament, control the elements, ride wheels of flame across the sky, can murder with a glance if God wills it. Joachim was not sent by God.

He was just a factotum in the employ of a cruel—" He almost said *goddess,* but that would be blasphemy. *Woman* wasn't quite correct either, despite the skin Envy had worn for him. "—thing."

Jennifer opened her mouth, then closed it again. Sabbath broke the momentary silence: "Many of us are in the employ of cruel things. You were not meant for war, Jennifer. I am sorry about your friend."

Jennifer didn't have anything to say to that either. She sobbed quietly, her limbs at her sides, keeping herself from touching Sabbath. She wanted to hold him, but an embrace would just aggravate his wounds.

The phone would have to be Jennifer's comfort, despite the old texts from Miriam, the endless voice mails. She never did get around to texting Miriam's parents. For a moment, she entertained feeding Sabbath enough sleeping pills to make him miss the deadline. The world would blow up, but at least she wouldn't have to face telling strangers that their daughter was killed. That too was a kind of freedom, she supposed.

There were texts from a 202 number that she didn't know, but that somehow rang a bell. The Secret Service agent, Mario, making arrangements for the exhibit, and the Aldridge appearance at it. He wanted to move the opening up to late Saturday night.

"Hexen, I think Pride is coming here," Jennifer said. "Sooner than I thought. I don't know how it works, but he's different from the others. He's like a real person, not someone who just appeared with a restaurant or a massage parlor a couple of weeks ago."

"Pride is the foremost of sins, I've heard . . . ," Sabbath murmured.

"But . . . how could it—?"

"One of God's mysteries," Sabbath said.

"Why would the sin of Pride be God's mystery, Hexen?"

"Also God's mystery," Sabbath said.

"But why—?"

"I need to sleep, Jennifer," Sabbath said. "I need to rest."

"What are we going to do?" Jennifer asked, her voice hollow. She could just tell Mario to cancel the event or at least stick to the Sunday plan, but she had a feeling it wouldn't work. Pride wasn't the sort of person who ever took no for an answer. She could leave now, with Hexen or not, but that wouldn't help either. She was powerless; shooting Envy to no effect had taught her that much.

Trying to supercharge Hexen Sabbath with street drugs had been a pretty severe miscalculation. Maybe had she and Miriam both been sober, they would have escaped, or at least been smart enough to stay the fuck home while he went uptown to deal with Gluttony. An art history degree, a fiery temper, and Boxercise twice a week weren't enough to save the world.

The only thing she could think to do now was pray. As she closed her eyes and tried to remember the Russian words she'd learned as a girl, Sabbath started snoring, loudly. Jennifer's eyes popped back open, and she decided to search for meaning in the water stains marking her ceiling instead.

———

It was like a dream, but Hexen Sabbath was sure it was not one. It was more of a memory, though not of any moment he had lived on Earth. The place was much like a desert, but the sky was low somehow, as if Sabbath were walking in a cave made of air. The sun was huge in the sky, and it burned.

Someone was with him. Abathar. Sabbath's fingers twitched, eager for the hilt of a sword, but he had no sword, no scabbard, nor any clothes at all. He was naked, and he was ashamed. Abathar was dressed in something impossible to describe. It changed as they walked, like a fast-moving cloud with a shape at first reminiscent of a robe, then a gown, then a modern suit.

"Abathar," Sabbath said. "What has happened? You said you would not intervene again."

Abathar smiled, tight lipped. He was much taller than Sabbath, taller than Sabbath recalled him being, and looked down at Sabbath as an amused father might scrutinize a slow child.

"It's funny, what happens when we pluck a man out of time. You get a sense of eternity, albeit a primitive one," Abathar said. "That's not happened yet, in linear time. This is our first meeting. This is your foretaste of the afterlife."

"I've died . . . in New York?"

"Not yet, Sir Hexen. You died on the field of Assandun."

"That was a Friday. I can only die on a Sunday."

"So you say, Sir Hexen," Abathar said.

"The afterlife . . . is uncomfortable, but not so bad. What is this place?"

"The blinding sun above is God's love. Here it will burn

you. For now, this moment, you're under the shade of an angel's wing," Abathar said. "My wing. A moment within a moment that hints at your eternity."

Sabbath glanced up at the sky. "Is this encounter meant to inspire me? Is it a dream?"

"More a memory than a dream, though like many memories, it emerges from the fog of a fevered mind only at an inconvenient moment," Abathar said.

"What brings . . . or rather brought you here?" Sabbath asked.

"I wanted to thank you in advance," Abathar said. "And posthumously. No matter what happens or has happened, you do, will, and have earned these seconds of relief. Savor them."

"Will I even remember this?"

Abathar shrugged, his broad shoulders somehow pushing up the whole low sky. "You already have."

Sabbath awoke with a start, and groaned as he pulled at several of his wounds, which Joachim had fixed with medical glue.

Jennifer turned over to face him, her eyes wet and bleary. "I tried to pray and I don't think it worked," she said. "We're still here. I'm still in pain. You still look like death chewed you up and spit you out."

"I dreamt of Abathar," Sabbath said. It clearly had been more than a dream, but was confusing enough to experience that he didn't think he could explain it to Jennifer.

"Abathar!" Jennifer whispered. "Hexen, are you a Christian?"

"Of course I am," Sabbath said. For a moment, he contemplated the details of Christianity as he knew it. He was no scholar, nor even one to pay attention during Mass or to the prayers on feast days, but he had the sense that being a Christian was either an extremely difficult thing or a very easy one indeed. "Look, an archbishop gave me the cross you sold, anyway. It was a valuable item, as you know. They wouldn't have given it to me were I some heathen, no?"

Jennifer waved her hands. "I don't know. But, listen—Abathar. He's not a Christian angel."

"How do you know?"

"Miriam told me," she said. "She looked it up on her phone."

"Ah, those wondrous devices," Sabbath said, imagining crushing one in his hands.

Jennifer turned on her side and struggled to reach her own smartphone. "Look, I'll show you . . . ow. I can't believe it; twenty-eight years without a broken bone, and now I've got a cast after a fucking prison brawl. *Chained Heat*!

"Ugh, look," Jennifer said, brandishing her phone. "Just type in 'Abathar' and you get . . . you get one line on Wikipedia, but click here and see? The Mandaean ethno-religious group. Ever hear of them?"

"I have not."

"Isn't it weird that Abathar is their angel, and not once mentioned in the Bible or something?"

"Jennifer, are you suggesting that Christianity is a false religion, or that Abathar is an agent of Satan, or something else?" Sabbath asked, his voice tired. "At any rate, it hardly matters. Six sins are dead, and they all made it clear that they are eager to destroy the world."

"Maybe it's a trap," Jennifer said.

"You have never been to war," Sabbath said. He turned from her, rolling onto his own back, and sighed deeply. "There are tricks and stratagems; ways of luring the enemy out to fight, subterfuges to disguise your forces, but one uses them when one is at a disadvantage. Only the weak scheme, Jennifer. Abathar, if he be a foreign angel or an unknown devil, could just have kept me dead and awaiting judgment, or destroyed me in my sleep. There's no need for such complexity."

"If that's the case, why are so many things just God's mysteries? God would have all the advantages—why does he need 'tricks and stratagems'?" Jennifer asked.

"I am not a theologian," Sabbath said. "But perhaps caretaking the universe is rather more like a government or family than war, and the sins are wayward children, sticking out their tongues and throwing horseshit at passing nobles."

Jennifer screwed up her face. "Did people really just pick up horseshit with their bare hands and throw it at each other back in the one-thousands?"

"Yes," said Sabbath. "Now, let me sleep, or I'll tell you more about daily life in my time." Jennifer had something to say, but Sabbath fell back to sleep almost immediately. She wondered if he were dreaming of Abathar again or even somehow reporting to him.

It was difficult to prepare the gallery for the official opening of the *Ylem* exhibit single-handedly, and Jennifer was single-handed in more ways than one. Normally, her intern or a friend would help her. Miriam had been good at parties. Jennifer dared not endanger anyone else, though, even if she was hungry for some company. Plus, she needed assistance because her left arm was in a cast. It could have been worse. . . . *No, it couldn't be worse,* Jennifer decided. She had to unfold the folding tables by herself, and set up the tablecloths to hide how cheap the folding tables were. The closet wine supply was looking skimpy enough that she went back upstairs to raid her own fridge—and down a couple of glasses herself. She could have had more delivered, but whenever anyone passed by the windows and peered into the gallery, her heart would thump in her chest. Everyone was a potential spy, a possible assassin. Sabbath thought the final conflict with Pride would be straightforward, but Jennifer couldn't believe it. There had to be more to saving the world than lopping off seven heads, and more to destroying it than nuclear war.

Only the weak scheme. But Jennifer was weak. It was time to scheme.

Sabbath's body awoke before he did. The impulse to rise, take a fighting stance, brandish a weapon, was engraved on the surface of every nerve in his body. He was half out of bed and reaching for the floor lamp before he was even conscious. His eyes opened to see Jennifer struggling to carry a pile of suit jackets and trousers through the door without them spilling out of her arms.

"Get naked, Hexen," Jennifer said. "And you're going to be the first man to get one of my patented haircuts since my college boyfriend. All the girls called him Friar Tuck after I was done with him, but I'm sure I've improved in the interim."

A cascade of images and associations led to Sabbath's understanding that Jennifer had just threatened him with a tonsure.

"Beard's going too," she said, dumping the clothing on the futon Sabbath had just vacated. "I'm a pretty good judge of size, I think. You're stocky, like a couple of my uncles, but I couldn't be sure, so I bought half a dozen suits. Try them all on. I have some neckties already; we'll match them up."

"Why do you own neckties?"

"Sexual purposes," Jennifer said briskly. "Bondage and such. Maybe if we ever have a real date, I'll tie you to the futon for fun. Maybe . . . Look, it doesn't matter. Let's just get through this. I raided a Goodwill. I literally sold three bottles of wine to a wino to get the cash for this."

Jennifer explained the plan as she started to cut Sabbath's hair—she didn't do too badly, really—and shave off his beard. Pride would be attending with the Secret Service in tow, and the agents were sworn to protect the candidate's life with their own. They'd have guns and could kill Sabbath easily. "Not so easily," Sabbath said, and Jennifer responded by snipping at his earlobe.

"You're going to have one shot at this, and showing up like a ragged hobo isn't going to help. You have to blend in with everyone else," Jennifer said. "A lot of people are going to attend the opening."

"Why?" Sabbath said. "To look at blank paintings?"

"If I'm being honest, for the free booze and the chance to have their picture on some art gossip's blog," Jennifer said. "Plus, art makes a good hedge. If Aldridge becomes president, the economy is going to go crazy. Up, then straight down. Cornering the market on contemporary blank canvases is safer than gold. Art prices are largely divorced from other financial markets."

"Why don't you keep the paintings, then?"

"A hedge only works if you have money to start with, Hexen. Hold still. These hipster straight razors can be blunt."

"Like you."

Jennifer smiled at that.

"What if someone tries to speak with me? What should I say? Should I pretend to be a mute?"

"Nah," said Jennifer, a trace of the South suddenly in her voice. "All ya need do is say one of two things. Look at the paintin' and say"—her voice returned to the tone Sabbath had grown used to—"'It's an attempt at a gesture' or 'It is creating a space.'" She wiped stray hairs from his cheeks. "Babeh-face," she said in that peculiar voice again, before reverting to the practiced New York norm. "But if you really just want to nap standing up for a bit, shrug and ask, 'Well, what do you think?' That's the only reason anyone would want to speak with you—to hear themselves talk."

"In my time, public gatherings of society with free alcohol were the premier opportunity for meeting new lovers," Sabbath said.

"Same now. Did you spend a lot of time listening to your lovers, or did you pick girls who were happy to squeeze your biceps and hear all about your knightly adventures?" Jennifer asked.

"Uhm, well," Sabbath said. "How am I supposed to secure my sword in this outfit?"

"I'll hide it, along with the heads, on a low wheeled cart, and bring it out. You act as surprised and appalled as everyone else, then grab the sword and get to cutting. I'm sure the Secret Service will see six rotting heads as some kind of threat and go for me, and that might be enough to give you a chance."

"Dramatic," said Sabbath, "but they'll surely see the sword as the threat and rush to seize it. We should hide the sword somewhere else, and use the heads as the startling distraction."

"You're scheming, Hexen," said Jennifer. "Does that mean you're feeling weak?"

Sabbath didn't answer, but he did take up the hand mirror and consider his half-shaved face.

"You can say that you're feeling weak, if you are. I am."

"I'm not," said Sabbath. "But I am enjoying the vision of the heads of my vanquished enemies being set out on display before the ultimate prize."

"It's a performance piece, and an installation, all at once," Jennifer said. Abathar's wisdom told Sabbath about such categories of art, but he was still unsure.

"You do not need to be present tonight, Jennifer. I could open the door and greet the guests. Keys have gotten smaller in a thousand years, but I'm sure I could handle it."

"I'm sure you couldn't," Jennifer said.

"It's making a gesture, and creating a space," Sabbath said.

She snipped around his lips, removing the last wayward hairs of his former beard.

"People expect me to be there. I invited them. Aldridge owns the building now. He bought it, just like that," Jennifer said. "He expects me too."

"I see," said Sabbath slowly. Jennifer presented him with the hand mirror again, and with it he peered up at her. *This woman, she is truly remarkable. Could* she *have been sent? Pfah, what are you thinking, Sabbath. You need to vanquish the greatest of all sins by yourself.*

"You look good," Jennifer said. "I'm going to look up how much ibuprofen someone can take before their kidneys shut down. We'll split the bottle." Sabbath opened his mouth to say something, but Jennifer quickly added, "It's real medication. Not a street drug."

Sabbath demurred politely when she offered him a handful of rust-brick pills, and raised an eyebrow when she shrugged and slapped them into her mouth as if they were a batch of seeds.

For a moment, Sabbath felt better. But then he remembered what day it was. *This may be it,* Sabbath thought. *Pride may tear me apart, or perhaps he'll keep me alive to see his final victory—and I'll be incinerated along with Jennifer and every other man and woman on Earth. A performance piece and an installation all at once.*

Sabbath decided not to share much with Jennifer. She boiled some pasta and poured sauce from a jar onto it. They folded the futon into a couch and ate off a low table Jennifer usually stored under the futon. Sabbath found the skill of twirling the noodles up with a fork to be beyond him, so ate with a spoon and knife—the latter pinning the contents of the former down while bringing the stuff to his mouth. He was glad not to have a beard anymore; it would have taken hours to comb the food out of it.

"You're dexterous," said Sabbath.

"I wasn't the first time I ate it," said Jennifer. "Nobody's good with spaghetti at first. Like most little kids, I picked up the bowl and dumped it on my head." She laughed at that, and Sabbath smiled, showing off the teeth he had left.

"I've often prepared for a battle with a meal, Jennifer, and have even eaten with women—"

Jennifer gulped her mouthful quickly. "Look, I don't want to—"

"I was going to say that I've never had a dinner so intimate before unsheathing my sword," Sabbath said. He had the sudden urge to adjust his necktie, loosen his collar. "This is a unique experience in my varied life and extraordinary week. There is a sense of an ending to it all."

"Oh . . ." Confidence leaked out of the crack in Jennifer's voice. "Ending of the world?"

Sabbath shrugged. "Of me. It was prophesied that I would die on a Sunday. As you might imagine, I've behaved with a certain recklessness the other six days of the week, every week. For many years. But I'm not being reckless now. I imagine that this humble dinner is what other men of war might wish for in the hours before battle."

He looked at the clock. "I suppose I could choke on my food now or slip and break my head open anytime between now and tomorrow evening. If that happens, Jennifer, do your best to kill Pride, and save the world."

"Uh . . . oh God." Jennifer inhaled, then exhaled deeply. Her voice got small. "I tried. I shot Envy, I—"

"You'll need to remove the head."

"C-can I do that?" Jennifer said. "I mean, not physically, no, yes, physically. But will it work if I do it?"

"Why wouldn't it?" Sabbath said with a shrug. "It's a head. People need them."

"Maybe you're the chosen one . . . ?"

"'Chosen one'?"

"Like, the only person who can kill a sin," Jennifer said.

"Abathar mentioned nothing of this. He said I was immune from the corrupting influence of the sins, having been fairly well corrupt myself in life."

"Fairly well?"

"I believe he said something along the lines of: 'an absolutely loathsome and degenerate sinner. You can sink no further,'" Sabbath said. "But I've noticed over the course of this adventure that I have succumbed, here and there—"

"Here and *there,*" Jennifer said, her normal sassy tone reasserting itself. "Feeling a bit lustful or envious, you mean?"

"Yes," Sabbath ventured. "But, you see, do you understand what it might mean?"

"That you're becoming a good person now, so the sins

can influence you to be a bad person?" Jennifer said. "Give me a break, dude."

"Dude!"

"Dude!" Jennifer said. "Look, Hexen, I . . . I like you a lot. I care about you. It's been an intense few days. I've . . . seen things, done things, I'd never imagine doing. I can't even watch scary movies! My parents wouldn't let me as a kid, and when I grew up, I'd watch with my boyfriends and they'd literally tell me when to turn away from the screen. Some things they didn't even let me watch. God, I'm babbling now. Just tell me what you're getting at."

"I like this, Jennifer," Sabbath said. "That is all. Even for all the blood and grue, I like this. It's not a sinful feeling—I don't want to ruin this by seducing you; I don't want to drink till my stomach feels sour, I'm not so fearful of tomorrow that I wish to hide under the covers. I am in a good place. Thank you." He was tearing up.

Jennifer opened her mouth. She did drink some wine, a huge gulp of it. The tears came anyway. "This whole week has been a nightmare. I've tried everything—avoiding you, helping you, fighting, just trying to be existentialist about it, cowering in fear—nothing's worked. The week isn't over yet. It's like the subway under the East River. I can't get off; I just have to deal with it until the end. But . . . this is nice. This is a nice moment." She put an arm over his shoulders and kissed his eye, his cheek, his neck, wherever there was salt water.

The cheap suit came off easily.

When Mario Harris was a young child, his parents were excited that PBS was going to air a special television miniseries, *I, Claudius.* They not only let young Mario stay up and watch it but insisted that he do so, to "get some culture." The show was a nightmare of corpses and curses, incest and blood, and even the occasional raw, naked tit, all on the same channel that showed *Sesame Street* and *Mister Rogers' Neighborhood.*

Mario's father was silently livid for the entire hour, every week. His mother would coo at the things she found pleasant—"Ooh, they lay on couches while eating. That must be nice." "Exercise is important!"—and occasionally make a sort of low growl sound at the sex and violence. Mario spent the evening sweating through his clothes, afraid to smile or gasp, or even roll his eyes at the bombastic British stage acting. He had his opinions, but his parents would find them all wrong. One awkward comment, and his folks might swallow their pride, admit their mistake, and not let him watch anymore.

The episodes detailing Caligula's rise and reign were nerve-racking. His madness was compelling, the weird dance confusing, and actor John Hurt's bloody mouth after he tore the fetus from his sister-lover's womb and ate it was just unforgettable.

Mario thought of it now, as he often did. Lou had just returned from a food run. Protectee Aldridge, code-named PENNYBAGS, ate the same thing every night: two Whoppers from Burger King, Mello Yello, three orders of onion rings, and extra ketchup for everything. A dozen ketchup packets, every night. The Secret Service wasn't allowed to secure a bottle of ketchup. "Ketchup from packets tastes better than ketchup from the bottle, and I know exactly how many to use on each burger and every onion ring. Do it my way!" he'd said the one time Lou had forgotten the packets and grabbed a squeeze bottle from a 7-Eleven. "Packets!"

Tonight, like every night since then, Lou had remembered.

Aldridge's ketchup-packet consumption was so obsessively organized that he ended every dinner with the same exact amount on his chin, like a crimson beard.

Like the face of Caligula whispering, "Don't go in there," to young Mario from the television.

It had been a huge relief, like a sweet breeze coming in through a previously blocked window, when after nine long weeks, the Praetorian Guard murdered Caligula. Hurt was such a good actor that for a second Mario teared up. His father sighed and said, "Oh, wow. That's a real twist ending!" to which Mario's mother responded, "It's ancient history, dear," and chuckled to herself.

The Praetorian Guard. It would be too easy to say that Mario was a Secret Service agent now thanks to his youthful exposure to wooden swords and toga, but *I, Claudius* did spark Mario's interest in history, political science, and the very idea of a government treasury. Even now, Mario imagined wooden crates bursting with gold coins and jeweled necklaces when he thought of the word. From there, a career in public service seemed inevitable. The Secret Service had long since transitioned to the Department of Homeland Security, which suited Mario fine. He wanted to keep his homeland secure, from all threats, foreign or domestic.

Aldridge looked up from his meal and smiled at Mario, his mouth looking bloody. "Satisfying!"

"I'm glad, sir," Mario said. They were both New Yorkers, Mario and Aldridge. Mario had grown up watching Aldridge transform himself from young playboy and gossip column regular to influential billionaire and *Meet the Press,* and now he was . . . this. Mario never would have guessed that Aldridge ate nothing but fast food, barely spoke to his stunning wife, and was always on the hunt for "lady friends." There were times the old man seemed almost senile, and then there were moments where he was a proud lion, strutting and posing, and in those moments, even Mario believed that Aldridge could win the White House, despite all the pollsters and prognosticators. He could rule, the way an emperor might, by turns cunning and capricious.

He could pluck a wayward onion ring off the floor and shove it into his mouth like a toddler experimenting with eating worms.

"Put on the television, Lou," Aldridge said to Mario. "I want to see if the late-night hosts are talking about me." They were, of course, and they had nothing good to say. Aldridge smiled and laughed, flashing those big teeth and licking them till they were white again. "You know, when I lost the mayor's race years ago, I thought I'd never be mentioned on *The Tonight Show* again. Now nobody can stop talking about me. It's like everyone will die with my name on their lips."

"I can't lift it," Jennifer said. "This is a two-handed sword, isn't it?"

"If you're a girl, it is, I suppose." Sabbath smiled at his own joke. Jennifer did not.

"It hurts my wrist, and I can't even get my thumb around the hilt."

Sabbath was naked, and feeling strangely serene. There was a small Buddha figurine, sitting in the lotus position, atop the toilet tank in Jennifer's bathroom. The whisper of Abathar had warned him away from idolatry, but Sabbath didn't think such a tiny figurine could do his soul any harm. Sabbath was tickled by it, and adopted the pose now while he sat on the futon. It was evening. Sabbath had slept well, with minimal pain, and now the artificial lights of the streetlamps and passing traffic came streaming through the sole window in Jennifer's apartment. She looked good, just as naked as Sabbath except for her cast, holding the sword. Jennifer was better at it than she probably realized.

"Get your hips and pelvis under it when you raise the sword point, Jennifer," he said. "Don't wield a heavy blade with your arm, but with your body and bones."

Jennifer adjusted her stance, tucked in her tailbone, and hefted the sword again. "Huh, okay. Still awkward . . ."

"Don't start depending on arm strength now," Sabbath said. "You're very used to using your arms to lift weights, but experience is a liar. Imagine your spine is a screw, twisting into the ground. Now, move it, swing the sword that way—a small movement of the spine will move the blade in a much larger arc."

"Ugh!" Jennifer swung the sword, grunting, then smiled.

"And now a slash is a bit more difficult. Use the large

muscles in your back; draw an *X* in the air with the point of the sword. Bring the sword up diagonally, but don't put the point behind your shoulder. Let its weight do most of the work; your body the rest."

Jennifer swung the sword; it flew out of her hand and bounced off the floor with a clang. She yelped, covered her face with her hands, and the moment before the spinning blade found her, was yanked by Sabbath onto his lap. The sword was still again.

"All right," he said. "Happens to everyone. Back to it."

"Don't die, Hexen," Jennifer said.

"Well, I guess I can try to slice away at Pride's limbs first, and if I fall to him, you'd have a better chance of lopping off his head."

"We've been at this for an hour. I've pulled like fourteen muscles," Jennifer said.

"Imagine if you had to do it every day, for three hours, and then spar with rivals who'd be pleased to add your teeth to their collection?"

"Life in the Middle Ages, eh?" Jennifer extricated herself from Sabbath's lap and rubbed at her right arm with the cast on her left.

"Beats shoveling shit and poking at the ground with a stick, like ninety percent of the population had to do," Sabbath said. "I even learned to read, Latin and English." Jennifer nodded. "English has changed a lot," he said.

"Yeah," she said. "Just don't die. You can write a book about your experiences if you don't die."

Sabbath smiled, like the toilet Buddha. But he knew that one way or another, he was going to die.

"You might even have the chance to live your life like a good person," Jennifer said. With that, Sabbath frowned. *No, I won't.*

Somehow, setting up for the opening took hours, despite the hours already spent on preparing the venue. Jennifer had Sabbath move the tables, and the wine, and then move them all again. He had to clear out the closet and install the heads and his sword there, on the two-shelf steel wheelie cart normally used for hors d'oeuvres.

She left him to wait in the empty gallery while she went to get ice—"for those fucking heads!"—at the corner store, after he had become momentarily confused by the difference between a debit card and a credit card. "I can't expect you to go on mere errands, eh?" she said. Abathar's wisdom had filled him in just as Jennifer stomped out the door.

Then there were the phone calls. Jennifer, seated behind her desk, all smiles to begin with, was like the four seasons—cheerful and sunny, like the spring. "I'm just calling to tell you how much I'm looking forward to you coming. . . ." Then blazing hot like the summer: "Yes," she said, practically purring, licking her lips audibly. "Absolutely. Everyone will be here. You won't believe what we have planned." Then the chill of autumn set in. "Well, swing by and swan through, maybe? You know Above Below; it's a small space. Yes, blank canvases." Then winter. "What do you mean you can look at a blank canvas in your studio? Fine. Minimalism is dead? Fine! Oh, is that the dead thing now? Fine." That last *fine* was like a glacial fog settling in over a long night.

"Perhaps," Sabbath ventured, "it is best that we don't have a large audience for tonight's showing."

"I still need to make money, Hex—"

"We are going to kill a very famous man, a presidential candidate, here, tonight," Sabbath said. "What usually happens to assassins and their accomplices in this land?"

"Jesus," Jennifer said. "Prison. Mental hospitals. Sometimes they're shot down by the Secret Service. Well, I think so." She clutched at her smartphone nervously, as though she was desperate to look something up. *Abathar should just have given me one of those things,* Sabbath thought. "But that won't happen tonight, right?"

"Why wouldn't it?"

"Because you're from the eleventh century, and you're deceased. You came here to change history or something, so it'll all, you know, reset afterwards," Jennifer said.

"Reset, to a week ago?" Sabbath asked.

"Or to two weeks ago, or however long it's been since the sins have manifested," Jennifer said. "Maybe even the man that Pride is, I don't know, inhabiting, will go back to being almost normal, the way he was before."

"How can you be so sure that is what will happen, and if the world does experience a 'reset,' then why does it matter if people come tonight and buy these paintings?"

"I'm just saying, it's how it works: if you kill the head vampire or the alien queen, all the other ones die and everything goes back to normal. In movies. Haven't you—?" Jennifer stopped. "Fuck," she said. "Honestly, I guess I just wasn't thinking about anything past this evening. Fuck . . ." Her eyes, already red from the tears of days past, welled up again. "I can't go back to prison! I can't die! Oh God, Miriam . . ."

"Look, you were there for no more than a few hours—" Sabbath started to say.

"And this is what happened," Jennifer said, raising her left arm in its cast. "They'll kill me in there. I'm not a hardened criminal. *You* look, you have to go, Sabbath. This was a dumb idea. Go wait for his motorcade on the corner and kill him there. Jesus, what if people have seen you hanging out in here all afternoon? Oh God, what if they saw me buying that suit yesterday? I could be on tape! I'm going to die! I'm going to be arrested!" Jennifer had more to say, but no air to say it with. She raised her hand to her throat and wheezed, gulped, stared up at Sabbath.

"Just try to relax," Sabbath said. She made a gesture he didn't understand, then through Abathar's wisdom he did. There was a paper bag one of the old wine bottles had come in for some prior party, and he dug it out of the trash. She snatched it away from him, put it to her mouth, and tried to breathe, contracting it, then expanding it as she exhaled. It took nearly two minutes, but finally Jennifer stopped hyperventilating.

"You're a changeable woman," Sabbath said darkly.

"Jesus," she muttered. "I'm not prepared for any of this. Nobody could possibly be. . . ." She looked down at her desk. "It's easy for you," she said. "You don't have a life to live after this. That makes sense, right? There are plenty of sinful badasses on Earth right now, but which of them would throw their lives away? None, because they *have* lives. I have a life too, Hexen. I did, until this week, anyway."

"Jennifer, I . . . ," Sabbath said. "Maybe you're right. I had a dream about Abathar, but it wasn't a dream, more of a memory. But in that memory, I had awareness of that which had yet to occur. Maybe Abathar can alter time, separate you from events—"

"Abathar, who I've never seen, and who won't intervene again?" said Jennifer, her voice hardening.

"He won't intervene in my behalf," Sabbath said. "He still might in yours. You're an innocent, after all."

"Innocent." Jennifer blew a wayward red curl off her forehead. "I've had sex outside of marriage, with *you*! You've been dead for a thousand years, that has to be a double sin! I beat someone up, used the Lord's name in vain a million times, had sex with women and married men, and I don't regret any of it. Why should I?"

"Well, it's complex," Sabbath said. "If I'm honest, I must say it never made much sense to me either."

"I'm not repentant. I see no reason why God would care about any of this stuff. So how worthy of heaven, or whatever comes next, could I be?"

"Abathar would weigh your soul and decide," Sabbath said.

"Why is it up to me to save the world with you? You should have just let the mugger or rapist or whatever he was beat my head in. Hell, maybe I'm in Bellevue, with a serious contusion, and dreaming all this."

"Ah, that's a possibility as well!" Sabbath said, suddenly

unsure of what that would mean for his own existence. The thought seemed to mollify Jennifer for the moment, though, so he went with it. “Dreaming? Abathar? Perhaps history will reset itself, or perhaps we’ll simply score a clean win and be allowed to go free.”

Jennifer had something else to say, but she didn’t have time. The door to the Above Below gallery swung open. The Secret Service had arrived.

10

> But the fearful, and unbelieving, and the abominable, and murderers, and whoremongers, and sorcerers, and idolaters, and all liars, shall have their part in the lake which burneth with fire and brimstone: which is the second death.
>
> —Revelation 21:8

Above Below's opening was not exactly bustling, and Jennifer was upset. Her smile felt drawn on, her stomach was constantly gurgling; she was sure everyone could hear it over the murmur of the small crowd inside, and the news crew out on the street. A presidential candidate had this small, obscure art gallery on his agenda for the evening, and it was a bizarre move. Despite being a lifelong New Yorker and a self-proclaimed "cosmopolitan sophisticate"—which had drawn laughs from cosmopolitan sophisticates—his campaign so far had appealed to the forgotten men and women of the heartland.

Jennifer refused interviews, and barked at a camera crew for setting up lights right by the gallery windows. The glare could damage the canvases, or at least make the subtle details difficult to see. Receiving only sullen looks in reply, she sent Hexen Sabbath out to speak with them. He whispered something in the camera operator's ear, and the lights were turned off immediately.

When Sabbath returned, Jennifer grabbed his elbow and led him to the back of the gallery. "This is going horribly," she hissed. "Look at these people!"

Sabbath glanced over his shoulder. "What about them?"

"Keep your voice down!" she whispered. "They're not art people! They're not even Manhattanites. One of them asked me for a beer. I gave him a Stella Artois, and he asked if I had anything 'more American.' Another one wanted to know if I liked the Yankees or the Mets. That's how he decided to flirt with me, and right in front of his girlfriend. And she's wearing yoga pants! At night! I think they're all from *Staten Island* or something."

"Do you think they are servants of Pride?" asked Sabbath. He looked around the room again over Jennifer's objection. For once, he was the best-dressed man in a room, Secret Service excepted. Whatever was going on here, it wasn't because of Pride.

Except that it was. "Nobody in five miles of where we're standing is planning on voting for Pride. . . . Well, except for some Wall Street assholes, I'm sure. But nobody else. He drove away my normal crowd, and now these grubbers are here, drinking my booze. They couldn't buy one of my paintings even if they pooled all their money. Fuck, even if everything goes right, I'm bankrupt and homeless by Christmas. Fucking great."

Sabbath leaned over and whispered into Jennifer's ear, as quietly and calmly as he could. "In my time, all art was church art, and everyone from the lowest peasant to the king could gaze upon it. Appreciating the figures of Christ and the saints was the one moment of equality in a viciously unequal society. You should feel blessed—"

"Hexen, what the hell has gotten into you?" Jennifer was so close, she was menacing Sabbath's ear with her teeth. "The human skull wasn't designed to take as many concussions as you have this week. Just try to stay focused. Just—"

She stopped as Mario approached. "Ms. Zelenova, a pleasure to see you again. Healing well?" He ran his gaze up and down Sabbath, taking in the missing teeth, the crooked nose, the scarred cheek, and the bruised neck. "And who is this? One of the artists?"

"Yes, but for my next show. *Seven Heads in a Duffel Bag,* we're calling it."

"Wasn't there a movie of the same name? . . . No, that was eight heads," Mario said, his eyes still on Sabbath.

"The eighth head is . . . a space," Sabbath said. "I'm making a gesture." He made a gesture with his hands, as though he were rolling a large ball, or head, between them.

"Fascinating! I'm afraid my art appreciation ends with J. M. W. Turner. Do you like his work, Mr. . . ."

"Henry," Jennifer said, quickly taking Sabbath's wrist and forcing his hand into Mario's. "Henry Savot."

"Is that French?"

"No!" said Sabbath.

"Yes," said Jennifer.

"I'm mostly British," said Sabbath.

"Ah, so you must know Turner's work," Mario said, flashing a wide smile. "What do you think of it?"

Sabbath practically pulled Abathar's knowledge from the ether, gritting his teeth from the effort. "Uungh, uh, I find Turner to be refreshingly modern," he said. "His use of smog and smoke, the way he uses realism to obscure his subjects and objects in a way prefigures tonight's *Ylem* exhibit. Turner paints a train, or some ships, and all but wipes them away with atmospheric effects. These canvases, which appear blank but are actually covered in white and ivory brushstrokes, are *all* atmospheric effects. Uhm . . . Ryman calls himself a realist, does he not, Jennifer?"

"He does!" said Jennifer. "And one of his monochromatics sold for fourteen million dollars a few years ago. I hope we do one-fourteenth as well tonight. Heh-heh. Did you want some wine, Agent Harris?"

"I'm on duty," Mario said. "Speaking of, I wanted to tell you, he'll be here very soon. The motorcade is coming down Mercer Street now. He'll want to shake hands and such. We usually do our best to form a wall between our protectees and the public, but we're bodyguards, not jailers. He can do what he wants, and go where he wants."

"So I've heard," said Sabbath. Jennifer nudged him with her elbow. "I've . . . uh, also done some similar work in the past, Mr. Harris."

"Yeah," Mario said, looking at Sabbath's well-marked face. "Maybe recently."

"Art doesn't always pay the bills."

"No shit," said Jennifer.

Mario laughed. "Good luck tonight." His eyes flicked toward the Bluetooth in his ear. "Okay, he's coming."

Jennifer looked at Sabbath, whose attention was focused

on the entrance, and the street beyond. Whatever was supposed to happen now was actually going to happen. The sword and the heads. Pride and whatever he was going to bring to bear. The plan . . .

It was Pride's plan all along, wasn't it? Have an event here, a final conflict between Pride and Sabbath. She should have done anything but this—given the paintings to Envy, taken Sabbath to anywhere else in the world, and made Pride change his campaign schedule and follow—anything, anything at all.

But Jennifer had been too proud. Nobody was going to push Evgenia Zelenova around. She wasn't going to blink at a bluff and go running. But Pride would see right through Sabbath's disguise, wave a little finger, and have the Secret Service take him away to prison or Guantanamo Bay or some killing floor in the basement of the Pentagon or Area 51.

Condemned to freedom, she reminded herself. *It's time to wheel out the heads.*

Then, as if on cue, he was there. Pride filled the room in a way that felt literal. Whatever else people had been talking about, contemplating, or considering, vanished from their minds. No more minimalist monochromatic paintings, no more Vienna sausages on plastic sabers, there was only him and his smile, and his hands in the hands of others, stroking shoulders, touching the small of women's backs, surging from the entrance to the end of the Above Below Arts like sand poured into an oddly shaped jug.

Pride stopped in the middle of the gallery, opened his arms, and gave a two-handed wave. Secret Service agents fell into positions around him. The gallery was small and the crowd thin, but to Pride it was as though he had just ascended a stage at Madison Square Garden.

"Art lovers!" he said. "Culture lovers! Greatest city in the world! So glad you all could make it. I'm very pleased to have just purchased this building; it's my newest acquisition. And I didn't do it for the money, either. I did it for her." He gestured, and all eyes turned to Jennifer, who had just wheeled a cart full of ruined, rotting heads out of the large supply closet.

People should have gasped, or retched, or at least reached for their smartphones. Pride didn't even raise an eyebrow. He waved her over. "Come here, come here." She left the cart, edged past Mario and another agent, and let Pride slide his arm over her shoulders. Jennifer felt strangely at ease, carrying a bit of his weight on her. This was *her* gallery, not his, even if the deed to the building was in his possession. She had lured him here, the room was full, and almost everyone had their eyes on her. People would remember Jennifer Zelenova, the Above Below, and the *Ylem* exhibit after this. She'd be in *The Village Voice,* and *Artforum,* and maybe even *Paper,* and then even art history textbooks. 2016 would be her year after all. Only then did she remember that she had told Mario that the next exhibit was going to be called *Seven Heads in a Duffel Bag,* but there were only six on the cart. He was staring at the heads from across the room, but then turned his gaze toward Pride, as did everyone else.

"They say that modern art is impossible to understand," Pride declared to the attendees. The news cameras were inside now, crowding him. "But let me tell you something about art: a lot of my best friends—the best, smartest, most discerning people in the world—love modern art. When I'm on a friend's yacht or their private jet, they all have art on the walls. Go uptown, go to any of my buildings, I have all sorts of interesting pieces on the walls, weird twisty sculptures in my lobbies. . . . You should see my house. It's beautiful. Everything's gold. My toilet? Gold."

He was applauded by a room full of people who'd never even dream of eating with a golden fork, much less sitting on a golden commode. Jennifer had to stop herself from clapping her hands together.

"And I like this stuff too." He gestured at a wall of canvases. "Look, these can be anything! Maybe you want a nice painting of a stream with a lighthouse on the corner and some little guy fishing. Just look at one of these and use your imagination. Or that smaller one, that could be a picture of a knight in armor, hacking the head off some peasant boy." There were murmurs from the crowd, but of approval. Jennifer cast about, looking for Sabbath. But he was gone. So too was the sword.

"And then we have this!" Pride stepped forward, his grip on Jennifer strong, leading her to the cart of heads. The Secret Service agents formed a wedge through the crowd. "Amazing, really! What a . . . What do you call it when there are two things side by side and it means something?"

"Juxtaposition," said Mario.

"No, that's not it," Pride said. Over Mario's objection, he continued. "We have the pure blank canvases, and then these gory heads—diverse bunch too. People like that diversity, eh? See, I brought you all here to get a load of this show, and you like it. I say blank canvases are good, and now you all want to buy a knockoff blank canvas for your own homes. I say decapitated heads are good, and, well . . ."

Pride smiled. "You're going to like that too. What was it I said at one of my rallies—it was all over the news, like everything I say. Oh, that reminds me . . ." He slid his arm from Jennifer and dug into his suit jacket pocket for his phone, then sent a quick text.

"I got a little something to show off too. But to get back to my story, remember when I said at one of my rallies that I was going to do something that no other presidential candidate would dream of even promising? Hey, here's the delivery boy!"

Joachim pushed open the door to the Above Below with his ass and lower back, then fed a long wooden pole through his hands before turning around to enter the gallery. It was a spear, well over six feet long. Jennifer knew it. "A pilum," Jennifer said. "From Rome. Or a facsimile thereof."

"Pilum," Pride repeated. "You paid attention in college. Good for you."

Joachim presented the spear to Pride casually, as if handing over a pizza box.

"Joachim, hi," Jennifer said.

"Hey," Joachim said. "What is all this?"

"Don't you know?" Jennifer said. "What are you even doing here? You said you were going to lay low!"

"All right, so who's first!" Pride announced, and he didn't wait for volunteers. The spear tip whistled through the air; then there was a scream and buried under it a wet squelching noise. The partygoer on the end of Pride's spear clutched at the shaft, agog at the mess of his belly. But then he smiled. He looked up and croaked out, "Wow. Thank you. Wow." Pride braced himself, yanked hard, and spilled the man's guts on the floor.

The disemboweled man collapsed as if entirely hollow, but the wet-sounding impact proved that he was not. The man had been real.

"Don't worry, everyone—I own the place, floor included," Pride said. "So, who wants to go next?"

"Me," said Mario. Then he drew his sidearm and shot Pride in the head. The spell was broken, and finally the gallery-goers responded as humans would. With shouting, chaos, and a stampede out the door.

Jennifer grabbed Joachim and pressed him against a far wall. "What the fuck!"

"I didn't know!" he yelped. "It was just a job! Do you know who that—auugh!" Jennifer's knee found his testicles pretty handily.

The other agents had tackled Mario, and the one called Lou had his gun drawn. Over the shouting, Jennifer could hear one of the local broadcast journalists screaming, "What do you mean the feed is dead!" to her camera operator. "We need to get this!"

Then Pride stood up and brushed his long hair over the steaming red-and-black hole in his temple. "I said, 'So, who wants to go next?'"

"Kill him . . . ," said Mario, his voice grinding against his ribs and the crush of bodies on top of him. Then the spear split his head open. The other Secret Service agents retreated, hands up, unsure of what to do. Lou leveled his pistol at Pride, but then meekly lowered it.

"Holy shit, holy shit," said Joachim from the floor, hands over his crotch.

"You need a real job, Citizen," Pride told him. "So do the rest of you. Chase away the cameras, fellas," he told the Secret Service, and they obediently formed a wedge and led everyone out of the Above Below at a trot, then shut down the lights from the vans outside.

Pride stepped over Mario's body and gave it a kick. "Not so strong-minded now with your skull crushed, eh?" Then he turned and hefted the spear at Jennifer. "So, is this a facsimile or the genuine article?"

"I think *everything* about you is fake," she said.

Pride guffawed. "Wrong again, Inaccurate Jen. The genuine article. A thousand years older than that cross you sold to my girlfriend uptown last week. She really wanted it, but she wants a lot of things, so she sold it again. I think some weird cult in a warehouse in Ohio has it on display now." He turned and blew a kiss to Envy's decapitated head. "Hey, baby, still love ya."

"You can't win," Jennifer said. "You can't destroy the world."

Pride shrugged. "I don't want to destroy the world. Maybe I just want to kill you."

Joachim lurched forward, rising from his knees. Pride expertly swung the pole and knocked the blunt end against Joachim's head, putting him down.

"Where's tattoo guy?" Pride asked. "You know, the savior of the world?"

"I . . . don't know," Jennifer said.

"Too bad. I wanted to warn him," Pride said. He smiled widely.

"Warn him about what?" Jennifer asked. *Keep him talking,* she thought. *Where the fuck is Sabbath? Where are the cops? Didn't anyone see anything?* Mario had resisted. Jennifer's mind felt mostly like her own—she'd been influenced before, but now she was free again. *Condemned to freedom.* Was there nobody else on the whole fucking block who could resist temptation?

With a flick of the wrist, Pride swung the spear so it was horizontal in his hands. "Heads up!" He lightly tossed it to Jennifer, who surprised herself by catching it. "You'd better know how to handle antiquities."

"Pride," Sabbath said. His sword was in his right hand; he appeared to be a little out of breath atop everything else—his slow gait, the bruises on his face, the exhaustion obvious in his bearing. "Step away from Jennifer, and from Joachim. Your time is come."

Pride smiled. Jennifer gripped the pole of the spear tightly. *Do it, Sabbath!* she screamed in her mind. *Do it now!*

"Excellent. I'm glad you're back, Friend," Pride said. "That sword has seen better days, hasn't it?" Indeed, the blade did seem scuffed and scored, its sharp edged pitted. "And so have you. And I know you want to say something like 'Pride, this shall be the last day you see,' but I want to get my piece in first, okay?"

Sabbath grinned. "Yes, all right. Take your time, Lord Pride."

"Now, like I was saying to you, Zelenova," he told

Jennifer as he slid off his suit jacket and let it drop to the floor, "I want to warn your man. You think we seven sins want to destroy the world? What would be the point of that? Give it a good shaking, yah? Maybe even give the world a good fucking—well, depends on which of them you asked." He nodded toward the cart. "Sins lie, you know, but here's the truth."

Pride undid the cuff links of his left sleeve and casually let them fall to the floor atop his jacket. Then he rolled up his sleeve and held up his arm. On it was a tattoo of a broadly familiar design, but where Hexen Sabbath's depicted the borders and byways of the island of Manhattan, Pride's ink was a map of the greater portion of Eurasia.

"Let me tell you a story," Pride said.

Jerusalem was already ancient when Longinus was sent there from glorious Rome. He had run afoul of his commanding officer, thanks to a misunderstanding regarding the age of the officer's daughter, and the functional equivalent of exile was better than the alternative. Jerusalem was a town of twenty-five thousand bumpkin shepherds and tenders of olive trees far from the million-strong center of the Empire, but there was plenty for a man with a strong arm and a commission to do, and Longinus did it.

The Temple was being rebuilt in those days, and even in that time of fervent devotion and true wonders, the joint was a real estate boondoggle. Herod got to levy great taxes, and appealed to the nationalist sentiment of the Jewish population of Syria and Judea both to spend 10 percent of their money within the walls of the city—a "second tithe." Hundreds of hands were kept busy through the endless construction projects of which the new Temple was the greatest. Herod's Temple was important enough that even mad Caligula, who had made himself a god and would see his own statues in every house of worship across the suzerainty, allowed himself to be talked into leaving it sacrosanct. Had he defiled the place with his graven image, the whole of the Eastern Mediterranean would have risen up to swim across the sea and pull Rome down, pillar by pillar, around his immortal ears.

You might say that Herod's intricate web of kickbacks and payoffs, no-show jobs and subpar construction materials had defiled the Temple enough already. But it kept the tax monies pouring in, and the lower social orders well fed and docile. Best of all, the Temple kept that omnipresent but unseen, omnipotent but imperceptibly subtle, omniscient yet silent One True God on everyone's minds. The infinitely corrupt Herod had conceived a way of inculcating the entire population of Jerusalem with a loathing for sin. Crime was down, the number of whores in the city sadly reduced, and the sons of Judea were pleased to risk their necks keeping the vagabond tribes outside the city walls, where they belonged.

Idealism fueled by corruption, in a small, hot, stinking town with a surging population and a single natural spring. Everything was for sale in Jerusalem. Even water, the stuff of life itself, was bought and sold in the city. Poverty meant being baked to death under the desert sun. Poverty was a mortal sin. Poverty was hell, in Jerusalem.

No surprise that rabble-rousers of various sorts—prophets and revolutionaries, poets and lunatics—found eager audiences. Longinus and his contubernium were kept very busy indeed, breaking up political meetings and throwing heat-addled Messiahs out beyond the city walls, where they could meet their Maker without offending the eyes of the moneyed elite.

Immanuel wasn't even the worst of the lot. Nor was he the most popular. He had no more than a dozen cadre, and a layer of fellow travelers mostly composed of his mother's childhood friends and some fishermen he met once. It was supposed to be just another job. Lead the longhair out beyond the gates and let him fend for himself among the bones of his erstwhile competitors.

But Immanuel came back. Somehow he survived in that desert. It had happened before once or twice. One man named Ibu had found his way back into the city, though his skin was scorched practically black from the sun, and his ribs could be counted by Longinus, who was half-blind, from five paces away. He said that God had given him the ability to eat rocks as though they were bread, and when he spoke, he showed off a mouth full of jagged, shattered teeth.

But Immanuel wasn't like Ibu. He had been untouched by his time in the wilderness, and told a story about how he was offered the ability to eat stones as though they were bread, but refused it. Immanuel was some kind of Communist, demanding that his followers leave their families, give away their possessions, and walk in his footsteps. His kingdom was in Heaven, and the easy money of Temple work offended him, though he was a carpenter by trade.

He refused to work for Herod's contractors. He appeared in the Temple one day and kicked over a table after an argument with a money changer. Immanuel was becoming the gossip of the town, a veritable folk hero. The water carriers and well keepers were telling stories about him. Immanuel had to go.

A show trial was held, he was convicted, and crucified. All in a day's work for the civil government and the Roman legion. But Longinus thought there was something special about Immanuel. His return from the wilderness without even a scratch or a burn to betray his time beyond the walls of Jerusalem had unnerved the legionnaire. So while Immanuel hung from the cross, Longinus gutted him. That was supposed to be the end of Immanuel, but instead it was the end of Longinus.

Followers of Immanuel pooled their money and hired a *magush* of another sect, the occult Mandeans, to summon a spirit of judgment. That fiery entity, who filled the sky like a sandstorm, caught Longinus up and secreted him in a lion's den, where the soldier was consumed by a hungry beast, only to have his flesh grow back onto his bones every morning, only to die screaming every night.

Generations of lions feasted on and consumed the ever-regenerating Longinus, though the cats were careful never to chew his head free from his neck. He saw everything that ever happened to his body. Longinus lost count after a thousand and one of his lives were consumed by bloodied fang, but many, many more came after that.

"A thousand and one lives in a thousand and one nights?" Abathar asked when he returned to the cave. "A thousand

and two hundred years of nights, more like it. But even that is a blink of God's eye given the infinity of Hell. Come with me and do my bidding, and you shall be free. There are seven men that need killing. Take up your god-killing spear once again, O man who cannot die save his head be split from his body." He handed it to the soldier, as if it had been snatched away.

"And that's why I'm here now," said Pride. "I saved the world, as Abathar asked me to, from the seven deadly sins, but he didn't free me. He didn't thank me. None of you mortals have. I've gotten better at counting the long years. Two hundred eighty-three thousand, seven hundred ninety days of ingratitude, of billions of people living life free and easy, without one breath of gratitude spared for me. I had a long time to read the ancient lore, learn the secret languages, know when and where the sins were going to manifest. I've lived two hundred lives, learned to carve my ever-living face to resemble anyone I need to be. I can be anyone I want. This time, I would lead the sins, as Pride, and gain my due, my rest, my heavenly reward."

"But you . . . are free," said Sabbath.

"Yes," said Jennifer. "Everyone is free. Even in the cave, you were free. Even Christ on the cross was free, and he chose to die to fulfill his cosmic plan. We are condemned to freedom."

"Uh . . . I meant free in the sense that he wasn't in the cave anymore," said Sabbath. Both Pride and Jennifer glared at him.

"I want Abathar!" Pride bellowed, his eyes cast heavenward. He snatched the spear from Jennifer's hands, sending her tumbling to her knees. "With this spear, I killed the Lord God; with it, I can kill a mere angel!"

"Wait, isn't Longinus a saint?" Jennifer asked. "He is! My *dedushka* had an icon. He was a soldier during the Great War, and said the icon of the centurion protected him in Stalingrad. He killed so many Nazis that the commissars let him keep it. I loved his stories of the war, and he told me about Longinus. Longinus was healed of his blindness by the blood of Christ that spilled from his wound, and then Longinus—*you*—converted to Christianity and performed miracles."

Pride sneered. "That's just Christian propaganda to explain my continued existence in this world in the centuries before I learned to slice and mold my face. I'm no saint, Evgenia Zelenova. I'm a killer, but I have only one more thing to kill, and that is Abathar." He turned from Jennifer and shouted again at the ceiling, "Abathar!"

"Does this mean you don't want to become president and destroy the world?" Sabbath asked.

Pride rolled his eyes. "Mortal worm, I've *been* president. William Henry Harrison. I was nearly found out, and had to leave office early, the hard way. I don't want to be president again. I don't want to destroy the world. But if Abathar doesn't show soon and free me from the curse of life eternal, I'll free myself by turning this whole planet to a handful of ash floating in space."

Sabbath raised his sword, gesturing at Pride's neck. "If you simply want to be free, I am sure I can arrange it. I'll free your head from your shoulders."

"You can barely stand under your own power," Pride said. "I've died half a million times, swordsman. I can smell the stench of it on you. Even if Abathar, or the Lord God himself, granted you the power to end me through your little sword, you'd never beat me. This body wants to live. No matter what I do to kill it, it defends itself. I would have committed suicide in the cave—" He glanced at Jennifer. "—had I been *free* to. You mortals may be condemned to freedom, but I am not."

Pride's arms moved to heft his spear, his knees bent into a fighting stance. "It wants to live. It won't let you kill me. Run, Hexen Sabbath. My weapon has the reach advantage, I have two thousand years of martial practice etched on my nerves and muscles. You'll just be one more fool I kill. I want Abathar, not you. I want a bloody pool of broken wings at my feet. I don't care if I live until the sun goes nova, if I just get the one thing I want."

"Jennifer, come here, please," said Sabbath. "Get behind me."

Jennifer lifted herself and turned to face Sabbath. Her eyes were traced with red veins like grasping fingers; her lips trembled. She tottered over to him, squeezed his shoulder, and took up next to him.

"Let's do it," she said. "Let's do this together."

"Please . . . ," said Pride. His hands shook, sending the point of his long spear quivering. "I've killed so—"

"I imagine you have," said Sabbath. "I imagine that over the course of two thousand years, many people have tried to kill you, and in all sorts of ingenious if ultimately futile ways."

"Yes . . ."

Sabbath glanced up at the ceiling. "Hmm." He lunged, parried the spear point with his blade, and drove Pride back a step.

"Don't!" Pride said. "I want Abathar! Abathar! I've crushed enough ants in my time. Don't—!"

Sabbath swung again, and this time Pride parried, and with a grunt pulled the spear back before the tip found Sabbath's throat.

"Abathar has told me he will not intervene in my behalf again," Sabbath said. "He doesn't care if I die. Taunting him by murdering me will do you no good."

"Put down the spear," Jennifer said. "Give it to me. You did that before, of your own free will. Give it to me, and let Sabbath try."

"Abathar! Come to me, or I'll kill these mortal servants of yours! How much blood do you want on your hands, Angel of Judgment? I judge you!" He turned his gaze back to Heaven, to the ceiling. "Abathar, come, or I'll drown these people in their own blood, then set the world afire. Come to me, or . . . hmm." Something about the ceiling above him stole his focus for a moment.

"You've seen many things, Longinus," Sabbath said. "But have you ever seen—?"

The ceiling bulged, trembled, then split wide open as Jennifer's clawfoot tub slammed onto Pride, followed by a massive torrent of water, the futon couch, the refrigerator, and everything else Sabbath could shove into or place atop the bath. Pride's scream stopped suddenly as his lungs flattened and mouth filled with water. The spear snapped into two, and the pieces went flying. Sabbath threw himself against the wall, bounced off, and swung his sword wildly, separating Pride's head from his shoulders.

"A flying bathtub?! Ha ha! Hexen Sabbath is victorious again, even over the immortal Longinus!" he bellowed. "I've done it! The heads of the seven sins are mine to grant unto the Lord God. Abathar, come give me my heavenly reward!"

"First things first," Abathar said, though his words came from the temporary worker Joachim, conscious again. He stepped carefully over the wreckage and walked past Sabbath to attend to Jennifer, who was lying in a pool of wreckage and blood.

"Jennifer, are you all right?" Sabbath called out as he hurried to her as best he could, stepping over puddles and shattered bits of furniture. "I had to hack away at your floor with my sword, pull up the board, and load the tub with everything I could find to lay my trap, but your insurance payout should make you whole. As Pride was an immortal and had simply disguised himself as the presidential candidate, perhaps you'll be able to escape the law—"

Then he saw the shard of the broken spear in her side, and Abathar, now back to his more familiar human seeming, kneeling next to her and stroking her hair.

"Abathar, you must save her!" Sabbath shouted. He put the pitted edge of his sword to the angel's neck. "Save her or I'll do what Longinus could not, and kill you here."

"That won't work. Neither your threat nor your entreaty. Your sword could kill Longinus as the Lord allowed it; it could not kill me. Nor am I the angel of saving the wounded from death. There is no such angel."

Abathar appeared standing before Sabbath now, while he still knelt at Jennifer's side. "I am the Angel of Judgment."

"And the Mandeans? The wizard that Longinus spoke of?"

"The Mandeans know of me. All seekers know something of the Truth, but only the few may know it All," Abathar said.

"And what do you know of Jennifer?" Sabbath pleaded. "What will become of her. Is she dying?"

"She is dying," said Abathar, kneeling by her side. "She speaks."

Jennifer's eyes were wide, and she looked fearfully at Sabbath. "Am I . . . going to be free now . . . ?" she asked in a whisper.

"Yes," said Sabbath. "Yes, you are."

Jennifer's eyes closed. She shuddered once, coughed up a mouthful of red human blood, and was still.

"No, she will not," said Abathar. "I judge her worthy of the fire of God's love. Hell, as you call it."

"I told her that she would be free," Sabbath said. The sword was still at Abathar's throat.

"I judge you worthy of the light of God's love, Sir Hexen," said Abathar. "You, a living man, are free to choose, however. What will you choose?"

"Am I really free, Abathar, and destined for Heaven?" said Sabbath. "Or is my destiny somewhere else?"

Abathar didn't smile, but Sabbath saw some trace of

amusement pass over his face. “You’re clever, Sir Hexen. It is your cleverness, not your rage, that saw you through to defeating Longinus and saving the world.”

“Saving you, you mean. The spear could have killed you,” Sabbath said, to which Abathar said nothing.

“It is possible that Jennifer may still yet find a place in God’s holy light, in Heaven. This whole week has been rather exceptional. Your place there is almost entirely undeserved, despite your late reconsiderations of the life you led in the eleventh century. And you are due to die tonight. The hour has passed; it is midnight. It is Sunday, the Sabbath. Were you to fall upon your sword, Sir Hexen, the sin of suicide would not be forgiven. You would not have the moment to repent it on your dying breath. You would be in Hell, where you belong, and there would be an empty seat at the right hand of God, which Jennifer’s immortal soul could occupy after the Last Judgment. Would you sacrifice yourself for the one you love, as the Savior did for you?”

“I could commit one more sin,” said Sabbath, considering the sword in his hand, “and defy the Lord one more time in this most base of ways.” He let the sword drop from his grip and hit the floor. “But I will not.”

“Yes,” said Abathar, standing before him again, even as he remained at Jennifer’s side. “That is the right thing to do. Do not be a slave to your earthly passions. Only through letting your passions, the world itself, die within you, can you see the Lord’s light.”

“Oh no,” Sabbath said. “I meant only that I am not the type to commit suicide. Not when there are other, more satisfying sins I could commit.” With that, he threw himself to the floor, pulled the point of Longinus's spear from Jennifer's body, and sank it into Abathar's neck.

"Killing an angel might do the trick," Sabbath said.

And then Abathar exploded in a ball of white-hot light.

11

But I will forewarn you whom ye shall fear: Fear him, which after he hath killed hath power to cast into hell; yea, I say unto you, Fear him.

—Luke 12:5

"The blinding sun above is God's love. Here it will burn you. For now, this moment, you're under the shade of an angel's wing," Abathar said. "My wing. A moment within a moment that hints at your eternity."

Sabbath glanced up at the sky. "Is this encounter meant to inspire me? Is it a dream?"

"I believe you know the answer to your own question now, Sir Hexen. You no longer require my whispers in your ear," said Abathar.

"No, I suppose I do not," said Sabbath. "Is the world safe? Has time reset? Is everyone all right?"

"The world is safe, for another seven hundred seventy-seven years. And, no, time did not reset. Everyone is not all right. The United States is roiling in political chaos, given your spectacular assassination of the presidential candidate. War is coming and there shall be plenty of souls to weigh and be found wanting. You have reinvigorated my office, as was ever my design. Virtually every single person you encountered in your time has been killed or soon will be, and dead they shall stay until the time of Final Judgment."

"Ah yes . . . does that include you?" Sabbath asked, but Abathar did not answer.

"And Jennifer, then?" Sabbath ventured.

"Sabbath," said Abathar, "you try my patience."

"I am already dead, Abathar," said Sabbath. "An eternity of the fire of God's love, minus the moments you shelter me in the shade of your wings, is still an eternity. By which I mean to say, I can piss you off all I want; you cannot do any worse to me now. Humor me, Angel, and speak straightforwardly."

"Evgenia Olga Zelenova is experiencing the beatific vision and shall forevermore. She sees God face-to-face, and God's face is love, Sir Hexen."

"Good," said Sabbath. "That is very good."

"You will also see the face of God now, Sabbath, but his love will be the love that burns, and it will burn forever. It will not be very good. It will not be good at all."

"No exceptions?" Sabbath said.

"You *were* the exception in life, Sir Hexen. You ended your life when you murdered a messenger of God."

"Yeah . . . ," Sabbath said. "I'm pretty fucking cool. I don't give a fuck about anything. That's what Jennifer told me when we met. She knew my soul at a glance."

"I take my leave now, Sir Hexen," said Abathar. "I will not say farewell."

"Farewell, Abathar. Thank you for what you did for Jennifer," said Sabbath.

"Yes," said Abathar, and with that, he was gone. The

blazing sun overhead began to burn, and cook, the flesh from Sabbath's bones.

And he looked up into the fire, and thought of Jennifer, and in Hell, in the blasting fire of God's all-punishing love, his lips melting from his skull, Hexen Sabbath smiled.